COUP DE TETE

A Bonapartist Thriller

Paul Bristow

Published by YouWriteOn.com, 2011

Copyright © Paul Bristow

First Edition

The author has asserted their moral right under the Copyright, Designs and Patents Act, 1988, to be identified as the author of this work.

All Rights reserved. No part of this publication may be reproduced, copied, stored in a retrieval system, or transmitted, in any form or by any means, without the prior written consent of the copyright holder, nor be otherwise circulated in any form of binding or cover other than that in which it is published and without a similar condition being imposed on the subsequent purchaser.

A CIP catalogue record for this title is available from the British Library.

To my family

Coup de Tête

A Bonapartist Thriller

by

Paul Bristow

Chapter One

Tuesday 4 November 1851 - afternoon

Montfaucon, above Paris

Down there was the city. It bled north and south out of the gash made by the river. At the centre was the cathedral, the palaces of president, parliament and the police, the courts of justice, and the prisons. Further out were the villas of the rich, the lodging-houses of the labourers, and the hospitals where the poor came to die. And at the outer edge was a confusion of old farm-buildings and abattoirs and porcelain works and fabric manufactories.

The ridge of Montfaucon stood still further to the north. For the pampered classes of Paris, it could have been on the far side of the moon. The gibbet stood there in the old days, but the guillotine took that sport away and moved public executions into the city. Now the hill was the cesspool of Paris. Hour after hour the waggons crawled up the slope, hauling barrels filled with human waste. Lagoons of filth covered the hill-top. Mounds of dried excremental powder spiked the landscape, waiting to be taken away and worked back into the earth.

And there were other cargoes too. Here was also the knacker's yard of Paris, the slaughter-ground lying alongside the lagoons. Here the knivesmen slit the throats of horses that had barely enough strength left to climb the ridge, or butchered the carcasses that were dumped from the waggons. The flesh, left to rot, was devoured by the rats that colonised the place. The bones went to enrich the soil of France.

The people of Paris turned their eyes away from Montfaucon. But on days when the sun shone and the wind blew from the north, the stench entered their noses, and their heads filled with a dizziness and a sense of filth and putrefaction.

Jacques Meulnier wiped clean the blades and saws he had used for his butcher's work. He had been hard pressed to finish today. For the last week, the Seine had been breathing out a chill fog that filled the lungs like glue, and the old nags were dropping like flies. He'd had half a dozen dead ones to sort out, and two brutes to despatch. They may have been at their last gasp, but they knew what he would do with his knife. Their struggles had been almost too much for young Joseph and him. He put the tools back in the store, and straightened his aching back.

The sun was low in the western sky. It broke across the surface of the lagoons. And against the brightness of its reflection Meulnier saw a dark unmoving silhouette. The weariness that he felt gave way to a sudden recognition.

Joseph was resting against the wall of the store with his eyes closed. Meulnier shook him by the shoulder. "Come with me," he said, and went to the side of the lagoon.

The sewage workers had already finished for the day. But there was a pole by the side of the lake which was used for fishing in the slurry for clothes or anything else of value. Meulnier used it to guide the object to the wall of the lagoon.

"What is it?" Joseph called. "Have you found yourself a new jacket --" He stopped in mid-sentence. "Jesus, Mary, and all the saints," he breathed. "Jesus, Mary, and all the saints."

Meulnier looked at the youth. "Help me get it out of this shit. Then we'll drink something." Joseph did not move. Meulnier turned back to the flotsam. Working with a brusqueness that helped him press down the surge he could fell in his throat, he hauled it out and dropped it on the ground.

It was a man. Naked, except for the slime which now dribbled off him. Dead, and swollen by immersion in the lagoon. And headless.

Meulnier stared at the torso. "That was no guillotine blade. Looks like a butcher's cleaver. My God." And he spun away unable to hold back the nausea any longer.

***

Tuesday 4 November - evening

The Elysée Palace

The tall, narrow windows of the study faced eastwards. Even in the morning the sun made little impact in the room, which receded deep into shadow. Now the darkness around the edge of the study was profound.

At the centre stood a great desk, carved from ebony and inlaid with the golden insignia of the old imperial family. And in the heavy chair behind it, three-quarters turned away so that his eyes were towards the windows, sat the nephew of the Emperor. Louis-Napoléon, now in the forty-fourth year of his life, and his third as the elected President of the French Republic.

The other two men in the room waited for him to speak. One - Jean Gilbert Victor Fialin, son of a customs official and self-styled Vicomte de Persigny - sat on the edge of his chair and leaned anxiously towards the desk. Persigny had served Louis-Napoléon faithfully for fifteen years. He had no purpose than to be the guard-dog of the dynasty.

Where the light and shadows played around the fire stood Charles Comte de Morny. He leaned languorously against the ornate marble fire-surround, but his gaze never relaxed. Morny had been the associate of the Prince-President only since the start of the year, but he was linked in a way that Persigny could never emulate. Three years younger than Louis-Napoléon, he was the result of a liaison between Louis' mother and a cavalry general in the Emperor's army. It had taken four decades, and the collapse of the Bourbon and Orleans monarchies, to reunite the half-brothers.

At last Louis-Napoléon spoke in his accustomed drawl. "So what do you propose, Persigny? Am I to send the army into the streets, to blast the barricades in the Faubourg Saint-Antoine and raise up a mountain of the dead, over which I must climb to reach an imperial throne?" There was no anger in his voice, and his words were spoken almost like an invalid who reproached his doctor for prescribing a bitter medicine.

"But what is the alternative? The fools in the Assembly refuse to change the constitution, to allow you to serve a second term as President. They will reject your message of today, to restore universal suffrage. So be it. We must impose the changes which they will not grant."

"And when the barricades go up? And when the army shoots down the working-men of Paris? Am I to be the new Prince of Blood, the new Cavaignac?"

"Cavaignac? The simpleton who won only a quarter of the number of votes that gave you the Presidency?" Persigny snorted with contempt. "Cavaignac is a political corpse."

Louis-Napoléon shook his head wearily. "I want

no more political corpses, Persigny, and your policy would create them in their thousands."

"Your Excellency is right. An Empire may be created by breaking our enemies, but not by crushing our countrymen. The Emperor must be the protector of the people, not their oppressor."

Persigny twisted on his chair and saw the glint of Morny's eyes. "Fine words indeed, but how would you save France from the red terror?"

The other man stepped forward, fully into the light thrown by the candelabrum on the desk. The face had the same features as those of the President, the same long nose, soft mouth, finely trimmed moustache and beard, but also a vitality that was Morny's own.

"Let us be clear. I agree with you fully about the need to protect our country from the enemy within. We must be vigilant, but we must also be prudent. We may have lost the support of the Assembly, but we must not sacrifice the support of the people."

"So we delay again," protested Persigny. "The hour of destiny will not strike twice."

The other seated figure rose to his feet and laid an affectionate hand on Persigny's shoulder. "My dear friend, I know how long you have been straining to hear that sound. It has been fifteen years. I sense that we shall not need to wait much longer. And when the hour finally comes, you, and I, and my dear brother here, shall see a new Empire, and a new France." He shut his eyes momentarily, and pinched the bridge of his nose. "Come, we can take this forward tomorrow. There is someone that I must see tonight --" he paused, and gave the others a knowing look, "and you too should seek out better company than mine for the remainder of this evening."

He led Persigny out of the study, his arm resting lightly around his shoulder. Morny smiled in response to Louis-Napoléon's mood but, as he followed the others, there was no softening in the cast of his eyes.

Chapter Two

Wednesday 5 November - midday

Ile de la Cité

Splitting the river Seine at the centre of Paris lay the Ile de la Cité.

The island bore more of the effluvium of history than any other part of the capital. At one end stood the cathedral of Notre-Dame, where France's kings had come over the centuries to celebrate their triumphs: now they were gone. At the other were the Palais de Justice and the Conciergerie, where the lowest criminals were tried and imprisoned.

It was no coincidence that the Prefect of Police had his establishment on the island as well. Sitting on the Quai des Orfèvres, his officers were only a few paces away from the courts and cells of the Palais de Justice.

And in the summer of 1851, still a decade before Baron Haussman transformed Paris with his clearances, the square mile between the monuments to religion and justice were a morass of tumbledown streets and houses where much of the city's crime was planned. Police and underworld were close neighbours; at times, they were indistinguishable.

The Rue aux Fèves twisted from one side of the

island to the other. Mud-dark hovels ran its length, their upper storeys leaning out over the street to shut out sight of the sky. There were few windows above street-level; those that existed seemed simply to have been punched out of the earthen walls, and lacked glazing or shutters. Some of the houses sold meat, or coal, or old clothes from ground-floor stalls, and all had iron grills to protect even the shoddiest offerings from being stolen.

The street itself looked as though it had just been flooded by the river. Cobble-stones switchbacked between the houses, but they were clogged and covered by earth and by filth that had been thrown from doors and windows. No soil-waggons served this part of the population. Only rain cleaned the choked passageways.

But there was money on the island. Some was stashed away. Much of it went on liquor. There were taverns here as well, dens with low, smoky ceilings, lime-covered walls, and floors of beaten earth disguised with straw.

The *Chien Fou* was one such. It stood at the corner of Rue aux Fèves and Rue de la Calandre, an even more treacherous gulley which ran back in the direction of the Prefecture of Police. A flickering light in a lantern above the entrance showed the name, and the claim: "Here you can eat well, and drink better." Inside was a room big enough to hold two rows of six tables, fixed to the walls, with a counter at the back where the drinks were served. The air was thick with smoke, from pipes but also from the kitchen behind the counter; and an oil-lamp on the bar provided a fitful illumination.

It was noon. Most of the tables were filled, and had been since the start of the day. On each table was either a pitcher of wine, or glasses of eau-de-vie, or both. Few of the patrons were eating; the regulars knew that Ma Friche was better at boasting about her meals than at preparing them.

But one man was eating well. Sitting at a table near the door, he looked to be in his natural milieu. He wore the same battered clothes, and well-worn shoes, as the other drinkers; and his face showed the same imprint of a life of hardship and deprivation, in its weathered colour and network of deep lines that furrowed the brow and the chin. One of these lines stood out - a scar that ran down his forehead into his left eyebrow, and pointed to a false eye below. This was why he sat with his back to the wall, and regularly turned his head from side to side, using his right eye to scan for danger.

Daniel Delourcq was with his fellows in the criminal world, but he was a watcher. However long he spent during the day in the Rue aux Fèves, he returned in the evening to report to his superior officers in the police. As old as the century, and as rooted in Paris as the trees in the Tuileries Gardens, he had run away from home at the age of thirteen to join the Imperial Army, and had been with Bonaparte until his final defeat at Waterloo. A piece of shrapnel from the British canon had put his eye out then, and he had been lucky to survive.

For the next twenty years, back in Paris again, he had made a questionable living travelling faster between the coast and the city, with tobacco, fabrics and occasionally weapons, than the customs officials could manage. Then, in the early years of the bourgeois king, Louis-Philippe, he was offered the chance to join the poachers-turned-gamekeepers of the Paris *Sûreté* - a flying squad of former law-breakers who could wipe their slates clean by using their knowledge against their partners-in-crime. "Dé-Dé" had had enough of the cat-and-mouse game with the *douaniers*; he wanted to settle down with Françoise; and he took the king's silver.

He had no regrets. Paris was his patch; instead of being slammed in prison or sent off to Brest or Toulon, he had the freedom of the city; he knew the world he was dealing with, and they knew him - and both sides worked on a basis of mutual respect.

The street door half-opened. "Dé-Dé" hissed a sour-faced old tramp, who took messages for the Prefecture. "You're wanted back at the shop, now!"

Delourcq scoured his plate with a crust of bread and emptied his glass of red wine. He took a handful of coins from his pocket and dropped them on the table. "See you soon, Ma" he shouted to Mère Friche.

Pigeon, the tramp, had already disappeared when Delourcq stepped out into the Rue aux Fèves. He spat into the mud, out of contempt for Pigeon, and for good luck. Then he turned into the gloom of the Rue de la Calandre and walked briskly to the Prefecture.

It was a large building on four floors, with corridors that extended a long way back from the frontage on the Quai des Orfèvres. The Prefect himself was installed on the first floor. But the office which the Head of the *Sûreté* occupied was at the back of the building, in a well of darkness formed by the overarching walls of the Palais de Justice.

Delourcq exchanged a nod of greeting with the clerk who sat at the high desk in the corridor outside, and went in. A gas lamp burned on the wall, above the short, bald figure of Louis Canler. He looked up from the papers which he was reading. "Delourcq? Have you made any progress on those golden candle-sticks that were taken from the Church of Saint Sulpice?"

"No, sir. I reckon they've been smuggled out of Paris to be melted down."

Canler looked him in the eyes for several seconds, then said: "That's certainly what I would do if I had taken them. And your other cases? Trimblaux, the unfortunate pawn-broker? I recall that you strongly suspected who the murderer was - some water-carrier, I think."

"Yes, sir. Ferrand, Jean-Baptiste Ferrand. I have spoken to his woman, and she said that he was desperate for money and told her that he was going to rob Trimblaux."

"But Ferrand has not been arrested?"

Delourcq shook his head. "He vanished before Trimblaux was found. His woman swears she doesn't know where he is. I've watched the lodging-house for a week, and Ferrand hasn't returned. He will eventually, and then I'll get him."

"You've done well, Delourcq," said Canler, "but I've asked Leroux to watch out for Ferrand instead of you. I'm giving you another case. I want you to go to Montfaucon now, once you leave this office. We've been notified that a corpse has been found out there. It's outside the city limits, of course, but the local police agents think that the murder - and this was a murder: the victim had been beheaded - must have taken place in Paris. And frankly," and here Canler looked away from Delourcq, "passing the case to us makes life easier for them, and increases the probability that the murderer will be found."

"Montfaucon? That huge shit-heap?"

"The very same. It's just as well you're not dressed for a ball. Get out there as quickly as you can. The corpse has been sweating overnight. Here." He opened a drawer in the desk where he sat and took some money out of a chest. "Hire a cab."

"No need for that, sir. I can get through Paris quicker on foot."

"Take the money, Delourcq. You may need it." He obeyed, and made for the door. "Oh, one other thing. You'll be working with a senior officer, Captain Boizillac."

"I don't recognise the name. He's not with the *Sûreté?*"

Canler looked at the papers on his desk. "No, he has just been assigned to us. A youngish man, who's been with the municipal police for the last two years. An army type." He shot Delourcq a warning glance. "He's clever, but he's not used to this sort of work. And he's also not the type of man who drinks at the *Chien Fou* - so tread carefully."

Delourcq paused a moment, then headed out into the streets.

***

Wednesday 5 November - afternoon

Montfaucon

It was five miles from the offices of the *Sûreté* on the Ile de la Cité to the cess-pits on the hill. A little more than an hour on foot, or thirty minutes if he chose to be tossed around in the back of a cart driven by a drunkard. He would walk.

Delourcq crossed the Seine over the Pont au Change, then followed the Quai de Pelletier to the great square in front of the Hôtel de Ville. This had been where the guillotine was set up for public executions, until twenty years before. Delourcq remembered the years of the restored Bourbon kings, when the crowds had gathered here to see the blade fall and the severed heads drop. Then the Government had relocated the execution site to the Barrière Saint-Jacques, out in the wasteland at the city's southern edge. Few bothered to make their way out there. Like others, he regretted the change. It was a barbaric spectacle, but it put the fear of God into the masses that saw it.

From here the route ran to the north and west, most of the way along the Rue du Temple. After only half a mile, the splendid halls and mansions were replaced first by lodging-houses for clerks and seamstresses, and then further on by a raggle-taggle of questionable hotels and dilapidated boarding establishments; and at last came the doss-houses and hovels. In their midst stood the Temple church, next to the old clothes market, where a mass of stalls offered the chance to buy cast-off garments, bedding and furniture to the not-so-poor of Paris. (The poor could not afford even these low prices.) Delourcq had reluctantly accompanied Françoise here, and carried home several coats, dresses and pairs of shoes.

The road crossed the boulevard that had been driven along the line of the old ramparts and bridged the Canal St Martin; and it reached the city limits in the fields that stretched to Belleville. This was no man's land for Delourcq. He had sometimes traversed it by night during the time when he had lived by his wits (and the douaniers' lack of them). But he had had no occasion to return since. He cursed the bad luck that had brought him here now. There were no taverns, no people and no houses; just a dusty track winding up the hill, and a mid-summer stench that made breathing a torment.

He had not noticed the effort of the hour's walk to this point. But his legs were like lead as he climbed the last quarter mile to the Montfaucon plateau. There the air was even more foul, and the sight of the lakes of sludge made it worse. Beyond them he could see several figures standing next to a shed. He headed for them.

Two of them were from the municipal police. They were unmistakable in their three-cornered hats and dusty frock-coats. They stood awkwardly in the afternoon sun, shifting from one booted foot to the other.

Some paces away from them, and sheltering in what little shadow the shed cast, were Jacques Meulnier and Joseph. The lad was crouched on the ground; he still seemed dazed from the previous day's discovery. Meulnier stood immobile, and watched as Delourcq approached.

The final member of the group was Alphonse Catelan, the owner of the knacker's yard. A squat barrel of a man, he stood only as high as Meulnier's shoulder. He was now in his sixtieth year, and strands of pomaded grey hair fringed a glistening bald dome. He too wore a frock coat, but this had not been issued five years ago by the police stores. As he hurried forward to meet Delourcq, he dabbed a kerchief against his perspiring brow.

"You must be from the Prefecture of Police. My name is Catelan. I have run this yard for ten years in conformity with all the requirements of the police. This is the first time that there has been any incident here, and in any case the body was found in the soil pits, and I have no doubt that the crime was committed well away from here and the villains simply used the yard, or rather the pits, to get rid of the evidence. I am sure that you will want to concentrate your efforts elsewhere, Monsieur -- ?"

The agent waited while Catelan recovered his breath after this outburst. He knew the reputation of the Montfaucon knacker's yard. He had heard that horse-meat from sick animals slaughtered here made its way into the stew-pots of the slum-dwellers in the Faubourg du Temple. Catelan's belly strained against the buttoned waistcoat that he wore; he was not a man who would leave carcasses for the rats if he could exchange them for the sous of the poor.

"Delourcq." He cleared his throat and spat on the ground. "You must excuse me, Monsieur Catelan, I have swallowed so much dust on the way here."

Catelan had taken a step backwards. "Of course, of course. It is a long journey on a day like this, especially if you come on foot. Can I offer you an eau-de-vie? I have a flask in my own carriage," and he motioned towards a vehicle standing further off.

"You can drink your own filthy eau-de-vie," Delourcq mumbled. Then, more loudly, he asked: "Who are these men here?"

Before Catelan could answer, they heard the sound of a horse pounding up the slope to the plateau, and a rider clattered into view, following the route which Delourcq had taken. He rode straight up to them.

"Boizillac, of the *Sûreté*. Which one of you is Delourcq?"

The agent stared up at the new arrival on horseback. The sun was behind him, but Delourcq could make out the long flowing hair, the tailored coat and breeches, and even the gloves, yellow gloves, of the type of "young lion" that he saw riding along the Champs Elysées when he was stupid enough to agree to go there with Françoise. Canler was right; here was a mummy's boy who wouldn't raise a glass in the *Chien Fou* in case he got a stain on his gloves. Delourcq wished that he was still back in the tavern, on his third bottle of wine.

"Daniel Delourcq, Captain Boizillac. I have just begun to talk to Monsieur Catelan here, the owner of the yard."

Boizillac swung round in the saddle and jumped lightly to the ground. He signalled brusquely to one of the municipal police. "Hold my horse. Don't give him any water from here." Then to Delourcq: "Let me put the questions."

Catelan dabbed his forehead. "A pleasure to meet you, Captain Boizillac. My name is Catelan, Alphonse Catelan. I took over the proprietorship of this establishment on the first of January 1842, and I have always ensured that it is run in conformity with all the requirements of the law. --"

"Those do not include the reception of human remains," Boizillac interrupted him.

Catelan became flustered, and rubbed his brow hard enough to remove the epidermis. "No, no, of course not, Captain. But, as I have already explained to Monsieur Delourcq, the body was found here, but I am sure that the crime was committed in the city itself, and the body was then brought out here."

"Why are you sure of that?" asked Boizillac.

"Why?" the other man repeated. He looked vacantly at his interrogator for several seconds. "But, Captain, for ten years I have run this yard without incident, and in strict conformity with --"

"Did you find the body?" Boizillac cut into his words.

"In strict conformity -- why, no, I was notified of its discovery, but I did not find it myself. It was

Meulnier, Jacques Meulnier - an exemplary worker, who has been with the yard since before I entered into the proprietorship, and has never given me any cause--"

"Where is this Meulnier?"

"He is over there, Captain. Of course, I wanted to ensure that you would be able to speak to him as soon as you --"

Boizillac ignored him and walked to the figure indicated. Delourcq was at his side. Catelan scuttled to keep up with them, his kerchief flapping around his temples.

"Are you Meulnier?"

The horse-butcher paused to take stock of Boizillac. "Yes, sir, Jacques Meulnier."

"And who is the boy?"

"Joseph. Joseph Vincent. He works with me."

"You found the body?"

"Yes, sir. Yesterday afternoon. I was cleaning up for the day. I saw something floating in the lagoon, over there. I took a pole and hauled it out. It was the body of a man, with the head cut off. I left it on the ground, until Monsieur Catelan came."

"So you only found the body at the end of the

day. Did you see nothing unusual earlier on?"

"No, sir. Joseph and I were very busy yesterday. I had no time to look around until I finished."

"And the other workers, in the yard here, and at the cess-pits? Did they notice anything?"

Catelan stepped into the space between Boizillac and Meulnier. "As you would expect, Captain, I notified Monsieur Ronceville, the operator of the waste reception, of the discovery of the body, and he has in turn questioned all his workers, and advised me that none of them noticed anything out of the ordinary yesterday."

"And the other men who work in your yard?"

"Alas, Captain, I regret to say that none of my men saw anything unusual, except of course for Meulnier and Vincent."

"The body was decapitated?" Boizillac asked of Meulnier, who looked unsure of the question. "There was no head?"

"No, sir. It had been hacked off with a blade."

"And Monsieur Ronceville has dragged all the lagoons with nets, but the decapitated body part - the head, you understand - has not been brought to light."

"The head won't be here, Captain Boizillac,"

Delourcq offered. "The killer cut it off so that no-one could know who the dead man was. He probably buried it in the woods somewhere, or threw it in the Seine."

"Then the eels will have fed well." He turned back to Meulnier. "And what did you do with the body?"

"I followed Monsieur Catelan's orders."

Catelan wiped his forehead again. "It was a most distressing sight, most distressing. But I got Meulnier to wash the body, and then we wrapped it in a heavy oil-cloth and placed it in a barrel which we filled with water and salt. I realised that the legal authorities would need to see the remains, and I wanted to make sure that --"

"Where is this barrel?"

"The barrel? Of course, of course - it is in the shed here."

"Bring it out here, and lay the body on the ground."

"Why, of course, Captain. Meulnier, do as the Captain directs."

Joseph started to his feet, and edged away from the shed.

"Does Joseph need to stay any longer, sir?"

asked Meulnier. "He doesn't want to see the body again."

"He was with you all the time, and saw nothing that you did not see?" Meulnier nodded. "Very well," Boizillac agreed, "the boy can go." Meulnier rubbed Joseph's head with his large hand, and the boy hurried away. "You," Boizillac called to the second municipal policeman, "help this man bring out the barrel."

Meulnier went first into the shed. The policeman followed him slowly, and stopped at the door before plunging in. Catelan became even more agitated, rubbed the kerchief over his bald head, down his neck and around the inside of his collar, and then blurted out: "Forgive me, Captain, unless you insist that I am present for your examination of the remains, I would very much prefer to return to my carriage for the duration. I have a number of documents which I need to study, with your permission." His breathing grew laboured, and he swallowed hard. "A thousand apologies, Captain, but I have a delicate stomach, you understand --" They could hear the dragging of the barrel across the floor of the shed, and the grunts of the two men who were moving it. "Please excuse me, Captain." Meulnier emerged into daylight, holding either end of a thick rope that ran round the middle of the barrel. He pulled, and the wooden vat appeared. "May God have mercy," Catelan fluttered. "My papers, I must look at my papers --" And without waiting for Boizillac's approval he scuttled away to his carriage, threw himself inside, and slammed the door shut behind him.

"You'll need to stand back, sir. We'll have to tip the barrel over, so the water can run out."

Even though Meulnier used all his strength to tilt it over, at the last the barrel dropped heavily against the ground, and the brine burst out of it and flooded over the dust. It carried with it most of the large package which had been in the container.

"Fetch it out, then" Boizillac commanded, " and remove the oil-cloth."

Meulnier obeyed. The policeman backed away. There was a cord around the package which the horse-butcher untied, so that he could unwind the cloth. Delourcq had the sudden impression that, amid the loathsome stench from the cess-pits, he could detect an even more fetid smell that flowed out of the shed. It put him in mind of that battlefield where he had been wounded more than three decades before. Then he had seen horrors of mutilation, and smelt the foulness of decay and death. He had come through that; he would not flinch at the sight of this corpse. But what of Boizillac? He looked sideways at this dandy. He'd taken no nonsense from Catelan. But how would he respond to the sight of the remains that were rotting inside the cloth?

Meulnier stood up quickly. He had seen it before, but his face was like ash.

The corpse lay exposed. It was bloated by

saturation with water. It was oddly discoloured, and black patches of bruising spread alongside red areas of chafing. But it was recognisably a human form, and a man.

"We should cover his nakedness," said Boizillac. He took the scarf from his own neck and placed it over the groin of the corpse. Then he crouched by its side, and looked it over carefully, from shoulder to foot. "Can you turn him, so that I can see his back as well?" he asked.

Meulnier closed up the package, turned it through a half-circle, and laid it open again.

Boizillac completed his examination. "Come here, Delourcq." The older man had stayed back, watching Boizillac rather than giving any attention to the corpse. This young officer was not what he had expected. "Look at this wound." He pointed to a gash below the right shoulder-blade. "A deep stab, and a recent one. I think that this man was killed by a knife-thrust from behind, and his head was cut off once he was dead." He indicated the corpse's neck. "The decomposition makes it difficult to be certain, but I would say that there were only two incisions to remove the head. What sort of instrument could achieve that?"

"A meat cleaver?" Delourcq suggested.

"Or a sword that had been sharpened for the purpose."

"To chop heads off?"

"One thrust to burst the heart. Two cuts to sever the head. Three blows, and the victim is dead and cannot be recognised. Except --" Boizillac took hold of the right arm of the corpse and raised it up slightly, supporting the fingers of the right hand. "A further cut was needed, to take off the little finger."

Delourcq saw that the hand had been slashed to remove the little finger; the stump was a red sponge. "Why do that?"

Boizillac lowered the lifeless arm, and stood up. His gloves were wet and stained. "What if the man was wearing a ring that was too tight to be pulled off?"

"It must have been a ring that was worth a fortune."

"Or else that meant that the man could be recognised, even after his head had been cut off." He spoke to Meulnier. "I have finished. You can put the cloth over him again." The other man did so. "Now, be good enough to fetch the proprietor here."

Catelan returned; Delourcq caught the tang of alcohol on his breath. He stepped gingerly around the damp ground where the water had flooded. "So, Captain, you have been able to see the victim for yourself."

"Yes, you need not preserve the body any

longer. I trust that you can arrange for it to be buried."

"Of course, Captain. There will of course be a certain expenditure involved, which in the circumstances should by rights fall to the proper authorities to incur --"

"I am not a clerk, Monsieur Catelan." The yard-owner flushed, and began to stammer an apology. "You will wish to pursue that matter directly with the Prefecture. I have only one more question. There is a hut by the way-side at the entrance to this site. I assume for a night-watchman. Can you tell me who he is, and where I can find him?"

"The night-watchman. Yes, of course --" Catelan paused, and rubbed the dome of his head with his kerchief. "Meulnier, you know him, don't you?"

Meulnier responded. "Gobillot. He lives in the shack down below, at the foot of the hill, with his sister."

Boizillac nodded his thanks. He took the reins of his horse back, mounted and began to ride off. "Are you coming, Delourcq?"

The older man looked over the others on the site. The two municipal policemen had turned away and were talking to each other in low voices. Catelan was very flustered; he covered his nose and mouth with the cloth, then twisted it despairingly in his hands. Only Meulnier stood impassively. Delourcq spat on the ground once more - and, as he did so, he noticed that the gloves that had been on Boizillac's hands had been discarded next to the covered corpse.

He hurried after the rider. "Captain, you --", and he stopped in mid-sentence. Boizillac was wearing another, unsoiled pair of gloves. Delourcq said no more. No matter that a pair of gloves like that cost as much as a month of dinners at Ma Friche's; no matter that Meulnier had found the gloves, and was picking them up uncertainly. They had held the limb of a dead man who had been soused in night-soil. If Boizillac wanted to get rid of them, Delourcq understood.

It was not hard for Delourcq to keep up; the rider kept the horse to a slow pace. They progressed in silence, until they had left the plateau and started down the hill.

"How long have you been in the *Sûreté*?" Boizillac asked.

"Oh, I'm an old lag. I joined in 1836."

"And did you lose your eye in the service?"

Delourcq was by the right flank of the horse. He realised that Boizillac had been observing him. "In service, yes - but serving the Emperor, not Louis-Philippe."

Boizillac pulled the horse up to a sudden stop, and looked down at Delourcq. "You fought in

Napoléon's army?"

"I enlisted in my fifteenth year, when he came back from Elba. It was only for the last campaign, and I took a piece of British metal in the face at Waterloo." He tapped the left side of his face. "That was the last thing I saw with the eye I was born with here."

There was silence. Boizillac spurred his horse on again. Then he asked: "But did you ever see *him*?"

Over the years, scores had asked Delourcq the same question. His answer had developed from the original grain of truth into a lush field of story-telling. But now, whether it was because there was no pitcher of wine at hand, or because this tall young man on horseback had something in his voice that defied deception, Delourcq answered honestly: "I was only a simple foot-soldier. I saw him in the distance, watching the battle-field with his commanders, up on the brow of a hill. And then the fighting swept over us, and within the hour I had been hit and was left for dead."

"But you did see him," Boizillac confirmed. "All I can say for myself is that I was born the year before he died. For one year, I was on this earth and breathed its air while he still did. But that is little enough --"

"Aye, if he came back now, I'd enlist again, old and blind as I am," Delourcq said, as much to himself as to the other man.

"But we have his nephew as President," Boizillac commented. "There is hope for new glory for France."

"The glorious Badinguet," Delourcq thought to himself. "He has all the courage of that tame vulture he carried when he landed in Boulogne ten years ago." But he kept this scorn to himself. Spitting away from the horse, he cleared his throat and asked: "Are you looking for military service, Captain?"

The younger man smiled briefly. "If we were fighting to enter Vienna or Berlin again, to raise our Emperor above the Kings of Austria or Prussia, yes, I would return to the Army." His face lost its momentary enthusiasm. "But I spent seven years in the drought and the storms of Algeria, and that was long enough for me."

They had reached the bottom of the slope. Opposite them, scarcely visible behind a high tangle of bramble hedge and nettles, was a low shack built out of ill-fitting boards. Its tin roof had partially subsided, like a hat on the point of slipping from a man's head. The small windows lacked glass, and were covered inside with sacking. There was no front door; a tarpaulin had been nailed above the opening, and reached to within a foot of the floor.

Boizillac jumped down to the ground. "The desert Arabs of Algeria have better houses than this. Does anyone really live in this hovel?"

Delourcq shrugged. "It may not be very pretty, but it gives them a roof over their heads - although I doubt if they have to go outside to feel if it's raining." He looked around; there were no other houses nearby. "This must be *Maison Gobillot*."

Boizillac tied the reins of his horse around the stem of a birch-tree. He took the riding-crop, which he had not used on the horse, and slashed at the grass and weeds that grew between the track and the entrance to the house. The two of them stood by the doorway. He pulled back the tarpaulin: "Gobillot?" He repeated the name more loudly. "Gobillot?"

"Leave us alone," a woman's voice shouted from inside.

They stepped past the tarpaulin. It took them several moments until their eyes had adjusted to the gloom inside, which was broken only by a few shafts of light that came from gashes in the roof. There was a single room. To the left stood a simple wooden table and two stools. On one sat a woman, holding a knife in her hand. To the right lay two heaps of straw, on which lengths of sacking had been thrown. But even before they could make out these details, their feet stumbled against a litter of bottles, some shattered, which had been strewn across the floor. Wine had been spilt on the boards and on the bedding, and its staleness hung in the air and mingled with the odours of the wretched, unwashed lives that were lived here.

"Leave us alone," the woman repeated. They

could make out her haggard face, and the leathery skin that was criss-crossed by lines of age. She had little enough hair left, but it hung haphazardly over her eyes. "Get out of this house."

"Are you the sister of the man Gobillot?" Boizillac asked.

The woman turned away from them. There was a crust of black bread on the table. She cut an inch or two off it, crushed it with the handle of the knife, scraped the crumbs together and put them in her mouth.

Before either Delourcq or the woman realised what was happening, Boizillac twisted the knife out of her hand and snatched the bread from the table. "Answer my question."

She jumped to her feet. "Who are you?" she hissed. As she thrust her face towards him, he could see bruises around the eyes and on the chin.

"I am Captain Boizillac, of the Paris Police."

The woman had been about to leap at him, like a cat on a bird. Now her anger turned to fear, and she backed away. "The police? Why have you come here?"

"What is your name?"

"Marie."

"The sister of Gobillot, the nightwatchman?"

She nodded. "And where is he?"

"Don't you have eyes?" she spat. "Over there."

They looked again at the bedding, and made out a prostrate form near the far wall. "Wake him up."

She gave a mocking laugh. "Sooner wake the dead, when he's drunk his skinful."

Boizillac nodded to Delourcq. He went over to Gobillot, rolled him on to his back, and shook him vigorously by the shoulders; but it was to no avail.

"Is he sober when he keeps watch up at the yards?"

Fear crept back on to the woman's face. "Always. He only drinks when he gets back here, and then he sleeps it off. Why are you asking these questions?"

"Was he at his post last night, and the night before that?"

"Yes, he was. He hasn't missed a watch in all the years he's worked there. Why do you want to know?"

"A crime has been committed. Did your brother tell you if he saw anything out of the ordinary the night before last?"

"What crime? Gobillot didn't do it - he's as honest as the day is long."

"I didn't say that your brother committed the crime. I asked if he spoke of anything unusual happening during his watch."

"If more of that horse-flesh has been stolen, it wasn't Gobillot. You can see for yourself." She gestured at the hovel. "There's nothing here, only some scraps of bread. Give me that back, now." She pawed at Boizillac, who tossed the crust back on to the table, and set the knife down next to it. She started to carve another slice.

"Answer my question!" The younger man's voice had risen. On the other side of the room, the drunkard groaned in his sleep, then his snores became louder. But his sister only scowled at her interrogator and chewed on the dry bread. "Do you want me to arrest your brother, and keep him in a cell until he is sober enough to answer for himself?"

"No, no, you mustn't do that." Her eyes moved from Boizillac to Delourcq and back. "Gobillot never says very much. I give him what food I can when he comes back after a watch. Then he slakes his thirst, and sleeps it off." She paused. "All I get from him is a curse or two - and perhaps worse if his stomach plays him up." She turned her back on them. "He was no different these last two days."

It was enough for Boizillac. With one last

pitying look at the woman and the place where she lived, he hurried back out into the light. He detached his horse's reins, got back into the saddle, and turned towards Paris. Delourcq followed.

There was silence between them for a minute or two. Then Boizillac spoke. "We wasted our time with those wretches. And I would guess that Gobillot is only slightly less drunk when he is on watch. If anyone knocked on the door of his shack up there, he would probably sleep through it."

Delourcq stood still, forcing the rider to stop too. "You may be right, Captain. But I have a sense about that woman. She was holding something back."

"Why do you say that? She seemed like a simpleton to me."

Delourcq shook his head. "Her eyes didn't match her words. I want to talk to her again. But it might be better if I went back on my own, if you don't mind. I'm more her kind than you, Captain, if you take my meaning."

"Agreed," said Boizillac briefly. "We'll meet up again tomorrow morning, at the *Sûreté* offices, and you can tell me if you learn any more." Delourcq nodded, and started back along the road. "Delourcq," called the young man on horseback, "I am pleased to have made your acquaintance." He gave him a salute, then spurred his horse on, back into the city.

Delourcq watched him for a moment or two. With that long hair and those fancy clothes, he looked more than ever like one of the young swells that rode in the Tuileries Gardens, catching the eye of the ladies in their coaches from the Faubourg Saint-Germain. But he hadn't flinched from examining the corpse, and he hadn't missed a detail of the wounds to that body - even if he had quickly run out of patience with the old woman.

He went straight into the hovel this time, unannounced. Gobillot had not moved from his bed. But the woman stood under one of the gaps in the roof, looking up at a rag that she was holding in her hands against the light. Delourcq's entrance caught her unawares. She stuffed the rag in her sleeve, and cried at him: "Why are you snooping around again? Where's that stuck-up ponce who was here before?"

"Listen to me now," Delourcq said in a calm tone, "the more you curse and swear, the less friendly we will become. Neither Captain Boizillac nor I came here with the idea that Gobillot had committed any crime - other than drinking too much, maybe. But a crime has been committed. A man has been murdered. And if you or your brother have seen anything unusual, or found anything unusual, it may help us to work out what happened."

"I've said all I'm going to say to you. Now get out of our house."

She scuttled towards him and tried to push him

out backwards. Delourcq grabbed her left hand, then tugged from her sleeve what she had hidden there.

"Give me that back!"

He ignored her, and stepped out into the daylight to see it more clearly. Whatever it was, it did not belong in this poor shack. It looked like a scarf; made of silk, it had intricate patterns of gold on a dark blue background. The original pattern was clear, even if Delourcq had seen nothing like it before; but its appearance was spoilt by a spatter of red-tinged watermarks.

The woman had stopped in the doorway, looking anxiously round the tarpaulin. He went in again, and sat her down at the table. Still he spoke without anger. "Now, Marie, tell me the truth. If you do, we won't arrest you, or your brother." The old woman's eyes were big with fear. "Did Gobillot give this to you?" She nodded. "Did he bring it back with him after his watch the night before last? Did he find it up at Montfaucon?" She nodded again. "Did he bring anything else back?"

"No." The fear gave way to self-pity. "The only time he's ever found anything up there. He brought it back for me. It was covered in blood - I washed it out, and dried it, and it was good enough to wear. And now you've taken it - to give to your woman, I suppose."

"Blood." He folded the scarf together and put it in his pocket. He took out a few sous and pressed them into the woman's hand. "You had no right to this, and we shall need it for our investigation. But fair exchange is no robbery, and I'm leaving you payment for it." He stepped back into the road. "And tell your brother when he wake up that he should drink less, if he knows what's good for him." As he headed back towards the city, the old woman remained where she stood, shouting insults after him even as she counted the coins he had given her.

Chapter Three

Wednesday 5 November - evening

Rue St Martin

Lucien had lived in Paris for two years, since his return from Algeria. He had modest lodgings in an older house in the Rue du Bac, about half-way between the Jardin du Luxembourg and the Invalides. It was a quarter of Paris bristling with military schools, barracks and stables; and the other lodgers in the house were all former officers like Lucien, who took comfort from the proximity of the army even though they had now left its ranks. Lucien was able to keep his horse in a stable only twenty paces away; and it needed little more than ten minutes' canter through the streets of the southern *arrondissements* before he reached open countryside and could spur his horse on so that the wind of their chase cleansed his mind of the dark memories of the city.

His military service in North Africa had reinforced his inclination to solitude, which had been a part of his upbringing in provincial France south of the Loire. Even in Paris, he spent his evenings with his books, studying the military campaigns of the Emperor who had died little more than half a year after his birth. The remains of that great man lay in the Invalides, a mile from his lodgings; and Lucien felt both sorrow and pride in this knowledge.

But in the last month a change had come into his life. Nicolas de Montholon, a fellow lodger in the Rue du Bac, had insisted that Lucien come out of his shell a little and join him at the "varieties". They had gone to the *Théâtre Drolatique* - a stage and auditorium squeezed into a site on the Rue St Martin like an overfilled purse jammed into a narrow pocket. The performance had been much as expected - loud, louche, and laughable. But the highlight had been as Nicolas had predicted - the two young actresses who had played sisters exposed to every sort of moral peril that the court of the Louis XIV could produce. Laure Cerise, the brunette, could flash her eyes coquettishly, but often had an air of reverie in the midst of the intrigues around her. Delphine Ramille, the blonde, was all flirtation, and every line of her frame spoke cunning. Nicolas favoured Delphine, but Lucien was immediately drawn to Laure.

Both actresses had several protectors - overweight merchants twice Lucien's age who sat in boxes opening on to the theatre stage itself, and who drove the girls away after the performance in their own carriages. Nicolas had contrived to introduce Lucien and himself to the actresses, in the mêlées which flooded on to the stage when the curtain came down at the end of the evening; and there had been a sparkle in their eyes which promised more than was said in the ritual exchanges of words. Then, as the theatre emptied, Delphine and Laure had been shepherded away by their sexagenarian beaux, and the two young men had returned to the Rue du Bac sharing oaths of admiration.

Tonight, at last, Nicolas had said that he had arranged a private supper with the two actresses after the performance. And, although Lucien had at first smiled ruefully and suggested that they were unlikely to make much headway against the influence of the wealth of the protectors, Nicolas had talked long enough about the charms of Laure that in the end he had agreed to take the chance.

The play that night was a comic melodrama, set in an imaginary Levantine sultanate. Laure acted the part of an Oriental princess, and Delphine her maid-servant and confidante; and the drama turned on the princess' efforts to thwart her father's intention of marrying her off to a rival, elderly potentate, and to give herself instead to a young man born into a noble family but scorned by the sultan's court. The story was little more than a pretext for the costumes - both Laure and Delphine wore brilliant silk outfits, with crossover jackets that were open in an inverted triangle from the shoulder almost to the waist, and trousers that fitted closely down to the knee and then splayed out in long ribbon fringes. Their hair was swept up on their heads, and shaped by glittering tiaras. Their eyes shone with the light reflected from the chandeliers above the stage, and their cheeks and mouths had the glow of the rouge that had been applied.

Nicolas had secured seats in a first-tier box for Lucien and himself. He pointed out the empty seats in the stage-side box, where the actresses' protectors usually sat. "It's Delphine's work," he said, "she's spun them a tale to keep them away tonight!" But the theatre otherwise contained the usual motley collection of admirers, enthusiasts and detractors who accompanied the performances with cheers and boos, and flooded on the stage at the end, leaving a flotsam of bouquets, cards and insincere words.

The two young men from the Rue du Bac made their way from their box down one flight of stairs to the theatre foyer, into the auditorium and then up two more flights of stairs behind the stage to an attic corridor where the actresses had their changing room. They knocked at the half-open door, and Delphine called to them to come in. They stepped into a space little larger than a lumber-room. Along one wall stood three large wardrobes, from which costumes spilled out. On the opposite wall was a wide mirror, above a table on which were scattered pots of make-up and powder, brushes, sticks and pencils, as well as a clutch of wigs and hair-pieces and two brilliant candelabra. The narrow aisle between contained two upright chairs: Laure sat on one of them, changed out of her Oriental disguise into a relatively demure evening gown, wiping her face clean of the last traces of stage-paint. The other chair supported a middle-aged man unknown to either Lucien or Nicolas; using his left hand to convey a cigar to and from his mouth, he attended to the tangles of Laure's hair, or the ruffles of her gown, with his right hand. A second stranger was the elderly woman who was helping Delphine: the two stood next to the door and by a wardrobe, and the dresser was fastening the actress's gown at the rear as Nicolas walked in. The glimpse which he caught of Delphine's chest before the gown was tightened spread a blush across his face which would have served him well under limelights - and provoked a peal of laughter from Delphine. "Nicolas," she cried, "I am glad that you arrived in time for an appetiser!"

The young man recovered his self-composure. "I begin to realise just how hungry I am," he countered. Noticing that Lucien had remained in the corridor, he ushered him in. "And I have brought my fellow diner - Monsieur Lucien de Boizillac."

Delphine, who was now decent, linked arms with both of them. There was no longer any space to move in the room. "What a pleasure to spend an evening with two such men, instead of our 'uncles'. What do you say, Laure?"

Only now, when the other girl was satisfied that she had completed her demaquillage, did Laure turn from the mirror, look carefully at Lucien and then reply to Delphine: "If only I had your talent for lying..."

"Lying?" protested the other girl. "I simply explained the theatrical superstition, that the protectors' box must be empty for a premiere - and you know how powerful superstitions are."

At this the third man in the room rose from his chair. "It is a new superstition to me, who have spent fifteen years in the theatre. Allow me to introduce myself. I am Victor Verdant, the manager of the *Théâtre Drolatique* - and protector of the protectors." He drew deeply on his cigar, and blew out a cloud, then extended his hand over Laure's head. "I am pleased to meet you, Monsieur de Boizillac - and Monsieur de Montholon."

"Victor is like his cigar," Delphine vouchsafed to her two companions. "He produces a lot of smoke, but after half an hour he's completely burnt out. He will be joining us for dinner, just to make sure that we don't do anything stupid. Won't you, Victor?"

The manager smiled. "The gentlemen will understand that Delphine and Laure represent a considerable investment for the theatre, and that the management has a duty to safeguard that investment against what we might call undue depreciation. But I assure you that I shall be discretion itself at the dinner-table. You will no more notice me than the floral centre-piece."

"Except that the flowers smell a lot sweeter," rejoined Delphine. "Come, Yvette, give me my cloak." The old woman wrapped a thick black cloak round the actress's shoulders. Laure stood up and let herself be enveloped as well. They left the dressing-room in a gaggle with Nicolas and Lucien, and Victor Verdant followed in their wake.

Nicolas stepped out on to the street first, and hailed a cab. He gave the driver the name of a restaurant a short way to the north of the Palais du Louvre, then opened the door to allow the actresses to climb in. Delphine sat facing backwards, and Nicolas quickly settled in by her side. Laure sat opposite, and

Lucien took his place next to her - only to feel the pressure against his left side of the theatre manager's form. "I shall study the crowds in the street, " he announced, and held his gaze fixedly out through the window as the cab jolted on its way. Delphine laughed, and fell into conversation with Nicolas which was at times intimate, at others raucous. But Lucien found it impossible to talk easily in that company. Laure heard his stuttering efforts at small talk - and unexpectedly placed a finger on his lips and breathed: "Save your words until later, when we have all drunk some wine." She leaned her head against his shoulder. They completed the journey in silence.

Driver and horse knew their way. It took little more than fifteen minutes to clatter over the cobbled surfaces, until they swung into the Place des Victoires. Seeing their surroundings, Delphine theatrically distanced herself from her companion and asked in a loud voice: "What victories are you hoping for tonight, Monsieur de Montholon? And who will be the conqueror, and who will be conquered?"

Nicolas was equal to her. "We have already seen the victories which you, and Laure, won on the stage tonight. The audience was completely vanquished."

"You flatterer!" she laughed. "But I shall put you to the test again. Who had the greater triumph - Mademoiselle Cerise, or Mademoiselle Ramille?"

"That's an impossible question, Delphine. It's

not possible to separate the two of you."

"In our acting, perhaps not - but don't imagine that we are always together in our performances off the stage!" She wagged a reproving finger at him. Nicolas paused as he considered what she had said, and then roared with amusement. But Lucien's embarrassment was only deepened by the exchange; and, seeing the look on his face, Laure called to the other actress: "Shame on you, *ma soeur*, we are with gentlemen tonight, not with some stage-door gigolos."

Delphine stuck her tongue out. "Just listen to the voice of conscience -"

She was interrupted by the theatre manager. "We shall have to listen some other time. We have arrived." The cab juddered to a halt. The driver dismounted and opened the door. Cold droplets of the night mist stung their faces as they stepped down. Victor Verdant gathered up the actresses. "Come, my dears, let us get inside quickly, before the chill reaches you." Nicolas paid the fare, and the two young men strode after their companions.

The *Auberge Dijonnaise* was the choice of Nicolas. He had grown up near Dijon; and on the rare occasions when his salary as a riding-master allowed him to eat in style, this was the restaurant he favoured. It was on the first floor of a house in the Rue Croix des Petits Champs. Spurred on by their flight from the coldness outside, the five of them hurried up the stairs and arrived breathless at the door of the restaurant. A fire of massive logs burned at the further end of the room. They were guided to a table whose trailing linen cover glowed with the reflected orange of the fire. Delphine clapped her hands with delight: seizing a spill from the hearth, she held it in the flames until it took, eased a cigar from Victor's pocket, lit it in her own mouth and then passed it to Nicolas. A curving sofa ran along the wall behind the table. Seated at the fireside end, the two of them continued their pantomime, as the girl threw the spill back into the flames and Nicolas puffed furiously to produce clouds of smoke.

Victor indicated that Laure and Lucien should occupy the other places on the sofa. He pulled a chair to the further corner and sat down there. Looking round, he commented contentedly: "Well, this is a welcoming place. I think that I shall enjoy communing with a good Burgundy." He winked at the others. "Monsieur de Montholon, are you happy to allow me to order?"

"My dear Monsieur Verdant," Nicolas replied, "I am sure that you know what the young ladies like to eat and drink. Please order accordingly."

The manager summoned the waiter and instructed him carefully in what he was to serve - beginning with the immediate production of champagne for the others, and a vintage Beaune for himself.

Delphine took her glass. "While my head is still clear and before my tongue is tied in knots, I want to drink a toast to our companions tonight. Close your ears, Victor! When I was a child, I had to spend every morning six days a week scrubbing the floors of the institution where I grew up. But just once a week, on Sunday, I had no cleaning duties, because we spent the morning in devotion in the chapel.

"And I was so happy to be in the chapel. The light shone through the stained glass and sparkled on the candles, and I used to think just how beautiful life could be, and forget about how hard my life really was.

"And here I am back in the chapel." She swept her elegant arm in an arc. "The light shines from the fire, and sparkles here on the candles on the table, and it's a special day, and I can forget about all the other days when I have do all my rubbing and polishing with my drab old 'uncles'..." She laughed, and raised her glass. "I can hear Laure telling me off, even though she's not speaking. But I drink to you, Laure, whom I love so much - and to you, Nicolas, and to you, Lucien, whom we may yet come to love." She emptied her glass, and sank to the sofa to drape her arm around Nicolas.

Lucien turned to Laure. "Was Delphine an orphan?"

"Today, she was an orphan. Tomorrow, she will be the child of a noble Polish family sent to live in France when their castle was burnt down. Next week she will be a runaway who escaped to Paris from the boredom of life in the Jura." She drained her glass. "I have heard her tell enough stories for twelve lifetimes. Delphine is an actress, and she knows her audience."

Lucien considered for a moment. "And you are an actress too. So if I ask you about you questions, will you shape your answers according to the audience?"

"Doesn't everyone do that?" She laughed. "I shall ask you some questions, and we'll see what you do. Here's the first one. Why are you in the police?"

He thought of his enthusiasm to support the Government led by the nephew of the great Emperor, which had guided him to Paris on his return from Algeria two years earlier. He remembered the pride which he had felt when he rode out along the streets of the capital with the sash and sword of his office. And he recalled the events of that day, and the inspection of the headless corpse at Montfaucon. There was a large gulf between supporting President Bonaparte and clearing up everyday crimes, but he still took satisfaction from the knowledge that he was serving a regime that promised to revive France's old glory.

"Lucien?" Laure asked. "How long do you need to 'shape your answer'?"

"Forgive me, I think that I have not been asked that question before, and to answer it fully would take a long time."

"Go ahead," she said, "I shall be happy to listen to your voice all night."

Victor cut in. "Well now, my friends, you may

think that you can exist on sweet talk and champagne, but I know different. You need full stomachs as well. If you will excuse me, I shall address myself to our waiter and ensure that our meal is brought to us sooner rather than later." He stood up. "And please begin eating if the food arrives before I return. I always like to look in on the kitchen." He made his way across the restaurant, as Delphine and Laure exchanged a knowing look.

With Victor gone, and Delphine and Nicolas absorbed in their own company, Lucien found that his tongue was loosened. The meal was served; the theatre manager failed to re-appear; but Lucien noticed little of this as he took Laure along the pathways of his memory and told her about his provincial childhood, his years in Algeria, and his life in Paris. He wanted her to know all about him, to share his past and his present; for the future, who knew. In his keenness to speak, he neglected the meal set before him; and from time to time, Laure halted him in mid-sentence by pressing a finger to his lips, and forced him to eat.

At last they ended the meal. Nicolas and Delphine were drinking cognac. There was still half a glass of red wine in front of the other two; Laure sipped from it, and then held it to Lucien's mouth for him to taste as well. He had been speaking of his experience in the police, of the drunkards and villains that he had pursued along the dark gullies of filth in the east of the city, and of the fresh air and sunlight of his rides in the countryside beyond.

"And don't you think that these criminals would

be better people if they could enjoy the fresh air of the countryside, instead of the gloom of city streets?" Laure asked, suddenly.

"But they have chosen to live in the city, and to live a life of crime."

"Have they? And have their children asked to be born into the same streets, rather than out in the country?"

He paused. "I have done nothing but talk about myself - and still you are asking me questions! It must be my turn to ask you about yourself now."

Laure looked into the wine-glass. "There is nothing in my life to match yours, Monsieur de Boizillac - no fine upbringing in the provinces, or campaigns in the army, or patrolling the streets of Paris."

"But you have a talent which all the world admires."

She turned her gaze to him. "All the world? Oh no, Lucien. The men admire us only so long as our looks remain - and the women hate us when we are successful, and scorn us when we fail."

"If that is what you think, why did you choose to be an actress?"

"Did I choose?"

"Tell me. You must provide the answers now."

Delphine's voice rang out. "Oh look, here comes Victor at last. He has found a lot to talk about in the kitchen!"

The manager looked flushed. "Excuse me, Monsieur de Montholon and Monsieur de Boizillac, but your companions must make a rapid exit from the stage of this restaurant."

"Victor?" Delphine asked in a sharp tone. "Have you disgraced yourself?"

"Don't be foolish, Delphine. This is nothing to do with me."

"But Monsieur Verdant," Nicolas intervened testily, "we are not ready to leave yet."

The manager flapped his hands in nervous reassurance. "I understand your feelings perfectly, Monsieur. But please understand mine. I happened to glance through the window just now, and saw Monsieur Hipployte Boulanger emerging from a carriage. Even now he is climbing the stairs and will shortly come through that door."

The actresses had already stood up and were preparing to go.

"But" protested Nicolas, "who is this Hippolyte

Boulanger?"

"He is the business partner of my 'uncle'," Delphine explained. "If he sees us here with you, there will be all sorts of recriminations. We must leave at once."

Nicolas screwed up his napkin and threw it angrily on to the table. "Recriminations! Let him speak to me, and I shall deal with them."

"I cannot allow you to do that," Verdant insisted. "I should be impugned, my theatre would be ruined, and your charming companions would lose their fame and their future. I undertake that we shall arrange another meeting, very soon - but now the three of us must leave. Come, my dears, I shall guide you through the kitchen. Monsieur de Montholon, Monsieur de Boizillac, my compliments!" He bustled away. Delphine blew Nicolas a kiss, and followed.

Laure took Lucien's hand for a moment. "The next time, I promise to answer." Then she too had skipped away.

Nicolas loosed a military oath. The door to the restaurant opened, and an elderly bourgeois came in with a young woman on his arm. "Damn it! I've a mind to slap that old dotard's face for spoiling our evening."

Lucien restrained him. "Sit down, Nicolas. Finish your cognac, and then we can pay and go home." The other man slumped down on the sofa, and drank with a bad grace. "If you court an actress, you must learn the art of patience."

"Patience be damned! But aren't they wonderful? Did you see Delphine's eyes, and her mouth? And did you hear the things she said? I've never met a woman like her. Well, old comrade, are you glad I persuaded you to join me tonight?"

"Monsieur de Montholon," said Lucien, with mock formality, and raising his wine in a salute, "I am deeply indebted to you."

They drained their glasses, paid the bill, and returned to the Rue du Bac.

Chapter Four

Thursday 6 November - morning

Ile de la Cité

Delourcq lived in the Faubourg Saint-Antoine, in the east of Paris. For some years, he and Françoise had rented three rooms on the first floor of a tenement block opposite the barracks in the Rue de Reuilly. He joked with Françoise that this would give her the chance to admire all the soldier-boys as they marched up and down. She gave a savage laugh and said that they were only fit to shoot at the poor people of the city who rose up to demand food and work. Françoise was no friend of governments.

Even at Delourcq's swift pace, this meant that he had a forty-five minute walk to the Ile de la Cité and the *Sûreté* offices. It was his habit to break his fast at one of the taverns, like the *Chien Fou*, at the end of this journey. A glass of red wine drove out the damp of the autumn mornings, and was often served with some useful information about the latest villainies.

But today he headed straight for the *Sûreté* building, cursing inwardly. He had been stupid enough simply to agree to meet this young Captain "in the morning". Did that mean at first light, or after a proper intake of food and drink, or when? He might be standing around for several hours while this Boizillac was still sleeping. What a fool he was. He spat on the mire that lay underfoot.

It was a surprise for him to see Boizillac standing outside their building, waiting for him. He was on foot, having left his mount in the stables of the Palais de Justice; but, wrapped in a fine long coat, with top hat, yellow gloves and polished boots, he stood out from his surroundings as clearly as if he had still been on horseback. "I got him wrong again," Delourcq thought to himself. "He dresses like a peacock, but he's as eager as a hawk."

The two men met. "Well, Delourcq, was it worth your while going back to the nightwatchman's sister?"

"It was, captain." He felt in his pocket. "I got this from her." He produced the rag that he had taken from the woman. Boizillac held it between his gloved hands and examined it.

"Well done," he said. A fine drizzle had begun to fall. "Is there somewhere we can go out of this weather, Delourcq? Not the *Sûreté* - I have no love for those dried-up clerks behind their desks."

Delourcq hesitated. "Well, I know most of the taverns around here, and they know me. But, with all due respect, captain, they're not the sort of places for your sort of person."

"They are this morning. Lead the way."

Delourcq did as he was told. And so, despite his initial expectations that he would have to do without his breakfast, within five minutes he found himself in the *Chien Fou* after all, at his normal table, sharing a pitcher of red wine with Boizillac, and catching the inquisitive and admiring glances of Ma Friche at the young man's back.

Now that he was out of the rain, Boizillac was oblivious to his surroundings. He had nodded briefly to acknowledge the glass of red wine that his companion had filled from the pitcher and placed in front of him, but it remained undrunk. He had spread the scarf out on the table and was examining it closely. After several minutes, he looked up. "What do you make of it, Delourcq?"

The older man swallowed the liquor that he had been rolling noiselessly round his mouth, and wiped his lips with the back of his hand. "I reckon it belonged to the killer, Captain. That poor devil in the shit-pond had been stripped of all his clothes, so it can't have been his. I reckon the villain who did for him brought him up to Montfaucon, slipped him into the pond, and then cleaned his hands on that rag. Why he didn't take it with him, I can't say." He remembered how Boizillac had left behind his gloves at Montfaucon. "Maybe he didn't want to take away any traces of the killing. But that's what I reckon."

"I agree. Look at the size of the material. I think that the killer wore this wrapped around his face, as a mask -"

"So that no-one would recognise him?"

"Possibly, but he must have been operating in the darkness, so a disguise was not so necessary. I wonder whether he wanted to protect himself against the stench from the waste pits. When his work was done, and he had got rid of the body, he needed to clean his hands. It would have been a matter of seconds to pull the scarf from his face, wipe his hands, and then ride off. And then, as you say, he may have thrown the cloth down in disgust, or it may have slipped from his hands and been lost in the darkness."

"Until Gobillot woke up from his drunken stupor and tottered out and found it."

"And he found nothing else?"

"No, captain, I'm sure I got all there is to get out of Gobillot and his sister."

Boizillac took a drink from his glass. He winced involuntarily. "You know, Delourcq, I've drunk stronger than this out of a water barrel."

The older man laughed. "Ma Friche has been known to confuse her barrels of water and wine - but this is what she always gives me. There's enough wine in it to warm my blood, but not enough to cloud my thoughts."

"In that case, I'll drink to your warm blood and

clear head. But I don't expect to acquire a taste for it."
He caught sight of the proprietress watching them, and
raised his glass to her. Then he turned back to
Delourcq. "But what of this pattern - have you ever
seen anything like this before?"

"No. My Françoise would have some idea. But
it's new to me."

"I've seen fabrics like this before - when I was
serving in Algeria. It's an Arab design."

"Arab? You mean, the killer is an Arab?"

"I don't know. There are thousands of
Frenchmen who have done military service in Algeria,
as I did. Any one of them could have brought back such
a scarf with him, and covered his face with it before
dumping a corpse at Montfaucon. On the other hand..."
He rubbed the material between his thumb and finger.

"What is it, Captain?"

"There's something different about this fabric.
It's somehow richer than any cloth I saw in Algeria -
not the sort of thing that an Arab would happily give up
to a foreigner." He stood up suddenly. "Come on,
Delourcq, we must pay a visit to General Vauzuron."

The older man seemed stuck to the bench.
"What has he got to do with all this?"

Boizillac took a leather pouch from an inner

pocket of his greatcoat. He folded the scarf up and put it inside the pouch, which he returned to its pocket. "I served under Vauzuron in the campaign of 1846 against Abd-el-Kader. He came back to France three years ago, at the same time as I did. All I brought back with me was my captain's uniform, and the promise of a position in the Paris police. Vauzuron brought back a glorious reputation, a carriage full of ornaments and furniture, and a retinue of servants whom he recruited from the Arabs of Oran."

Delourcq finished the wine that remained in the pitcher, left some coins on the table, and followed Boizillac to the door. "And he lives here in Paris, with a household of Arabs?"

"He has a house in the Rue de Chaillot - at least, that is the address from which he has written to me, although I haven't visited him. But I intend to go there and seek his agreement to show the scarf to his retinue. They'll know a great deal more about Arab fabrics and patterns than I do, and they may be able to tell us where this scarf came from."

Delourcq hung back. "Captain, I'm not dressed to go visiting a General of the French Army."

"You are acting on official business, and you are assisting me. That will be good enough. Now, let's find a cab." He dived off into the downpour, and the other man made haste to keep up with him. They splashed through the mud as far as the Quai des Orfèvres and climbed into a cab there. Their route ran parallel to the Seine until the Pont du Champ-de-Mars, where they crossed to the right bank. Boizillac travelled in silence. Delourcq looked out of the window at the sodden figures scuttling along the streets, and the barges on the river, and wondered silently whether the Captain's confidence in the reception which they would be given was justified.

The Rue de Chaillot was at the western edge of civilised Paris, a line of villas built during the thirty or so years since the Bourbon Restoration on land that had previously held small farms and market gardens. No.23, a sandstone mansion whose ground floor windows were enveloped by spindles of climbing rose trees, bare and skeletal at this time of year, stood well back from the road. The cab followed a rutted mud drive to the main door.

Boizillac got out, paid off the driver, and knocked at the door. Delourcq stood a few paces behind him.

It took some time for the knock to be acknowledged. The drizzle had soaked into the men's shoulders when the door at last was pulled open. Despite their conversation in the *Chien Fou*, Delourcq was not prepared for their reception. A domestic stood before them in the flowing robes of an Arab tribesman, and his hooded eyes and copper skin colour spoke of the fierce heat of North Africa. Delourcq cursed softly in disbelief, and spat on the ground.

"Is this the house of General Vauzuron?"

Boizillac demanded.

The Arab servant nodded briefly, but his eyes relaxed their scrutiny of the visitors for less than a second.

"Then would you let the General know that I, Captain Lucien de Boizillac, of the Prefecture of Police, would like to speak to him urgently on a matter of public security."

The other man spoke for the first time. "It is very early in the day, Monsieur de Boizillac. The General is not used to receiving visitors at such an hour."

Delourcq saw that the younger man drew himself up in irritation. "I served with the General in Algeria. He was always one of the first to be on horseback in the morning when an expedition had to be launched. An interview at ten in the morning will cause him no difficulty, unless he is ill. How is his health?"

"Perfect, Monsieur."

"Then waste no more time, and announce me. And allow us to shelter indoors while we wait to be presented." He entered the house, forcing the servant to step backwards to admit him. Delourcq followed, and shut the door behind him.

They were in a wide hallway, from which a staircase rose centrally, turning once to the first floor.

The walls were hung with paintings of scenes from the Algerian campaigns of the last decade, and with arrangements of knives, scimitars and pikes which bore the marks of Arab workmanship. And there was a sweetness in the air which reminded Delourcq of the masses that he had attended as a child.

"Please wait here for a moment. I shall go and announce you to the General." The words were spoken in a flat and courteous tone, but the speaker's eyes flashed, as if they reflected the anger which Boizillac had displayed. He turned and moved swiftly and noiselessly up the stairs; the swaying of his robes showed that he was barefoot.

"Am I getting a fever, Captain, or is this place damnably hot?" Delourcq had wiped the rain from his brow, but the sweat had immediately broken out on it. He ran his finger round his collar.

The younger man had set his hat down on a side-table; now he unbuttoned his coat. But his companion was struck by the fact that he kept his yellow gloves on his hands. "No, you're right, Delourcq. It's almost like the heat of North Africa - and that smell, I remember it from their holy places. It's an incense that they burn."

"How long was the General in Algeria?"

"Longer than me. He must have spent at least ten years there."

Delourcq breathed in deeply, then shook himself. "I reckon he's tried to make a little Algeria here in the Rue de Chaillot. Does he have a family?"

Boizillac considered a moment. "He was married before he went to Algeria, but his wife died in Paris in the cholera outbreak of 1842. I never heard that they had any children." He fell silent. The Arab servant was already moving softly back down the stairs towards them. "Prepare yourself, Delourcq."

"The General will receive you in the drawing-room. Please follow me."

The servant led them to the first floor. While his words were courteous enough, there was no mistaking the reserve between him and the intrusive visitors. He mounted the stairs with the ease of practice. Boizillac took them two at a time to keep pace, but Delourcq had to pause for breath at the turn, and reached the top puffing, while the other two stood waiting for him. "Sorry, captain - it's the heat, it's slowing me down."

A set of panelled double doors faced them. Opening one, the servant spoke to the interior of the room to announce their arrival, and stood to one side to let them pass.

The salon into which they stepped extended across the front of the house, above the main door. The further wall was punctured by a row of windows, but the murky daylight which they admitted was further obscured by the heavy velvet curtains that hung from them. Illumination of the room was provided by the flickering candles that stood in candelabra at either end of the salon, and by the log fire that burnt in the hearth to their right as they entered. A chaise-longue, over which a Persian rug was draped, stood in the immediate radius of heat from the fire; and its brightness lit up a man seated on the chaise, smoking a cigar.

"De Boizillac? What the hell are you doing here?"

The captain paused for a moment. He remembered Vauzuron from the Algerian campaigns, when he had been a wiry, tanned figure in uniform, sitting proud in the saddle of his horse. Now he was looking at a grand bourgeois, in a silk dressing-gown, whose face was puffy and dappled with the flush of excess. But it was after all the same man.

"General," he began instinctively, "since I left service in Algeria, I have been an officer of the Paris police, and I come to you today in that capacity."

"The Paris police!" Vauzuron snorted. "Saving your presence, de Boizillac, there's rarely been much to choose between the police and the villains they're supposed to prosecute."

As Boizillac advanced into the room, Vauzuron caught sight of his companion. "And who in God's name have you brought with you?"

"May I introduce Monsieur Delourcq, also from

the Paris police?"

"No, you may not. What on earth do you think you're doing, trailing riffraff from the streets through my salon?"

Delourcq was unsurprised by his reception, but saw Boizillac's shoulders stiffen. "General Vauzuron, Delourcq has given good service to the Prefecture of Police for fifteen years - and in his youth he fought at the Battle of Waterloo."

"On which side?" the older man asked. He threw his half-smoked cigar into the fire and spoke his next words to the flames which devoured it. "Very well, de Boizillac, the army needs its foot-soldiers. But tell him to stand on the far side of the room, by the windows - he carries the smell of the Faubourg Saint-Antoine with him."

Delourcq was only too pleased to follow these instructions. There was a pool of chill air alongside the windows, which lifted him out of the torpor that seemed to drift on the heat through the rest of the house. As he crossed the room, he caught sight of the expression on the captain's face; it was anger, triggered by the conduct of his superior officer. And he noticed Vauzuron's feet for the first time; he too was unshod. Delourcq wondered what other practices he shared with his Arab servants.

"Well, keep this brief, de Boizillac. I have papers to attend to this morning, before my engagements later in the day." He remained seated. There were no chairs for the visitors.

"Of course - and my thanks for allowing us to disturb your day without prior notice." Delourcq could hear the flat tone in the captain's voice. Vauzuron, who missed the irony, gave a flick of his hand to acknowledge the gratitude expressed. "Two days ago, a corpse was found at Montfaucon - the body of a man who had been murdered."

"How?"

"He had been stabbed, and then beheaded."

"And what was the name of this corpse, when it lived and breathed and walked the streets of Paris?"

"We don't know. We haven't found the head, and the body had been completely stripped of clothes."

"And no-one has come to the police looking for a missing person - no wife, or mistress?"

"No-one."

Vauzuron clicked his fingers. The Arab servant, who had been standing in the shadows by the door, hurried to his side carrying a box of cigars. The general took one out and held it in his mouth while the servant lit it with a taper from the fire. He took a mouthful of smoke and then blew it towards the hearth. "Then why in God's name are you concerned with this matter? It would be better to spend your time hunting down the socialists who are plotting to plunge the country into chaos than wasting it on some nameless vermin who was loved by no-one when he was alive, and is mourned by no-one now that he's dead."

It took Boizillac several seconds to compose an answer. "In the first place, General, I have been ordered to investigate this case and to discover the culprit. And in the second place, someone is walking the streets of Paris who two or three days ago took a knife to one of his fellow-men and put him to death. The law forbids murder, and, if killers are not found and punished, then the law is worth nothing."

"Your devotion to the law does you credit," Vauzuron returned. "If only I was convinced that those whose deaths you investigate were worthy of the law's protection. Still, I have no time to argue this further. Why has your investigation of this case brought you here today?"

Boizillac produced the leather pouch from inside his coat. Vauzuron watched him indolently, as though he was indifferent to the answer which his question would receive; but Delourcq could observe a quickening of interest on the part of the fourth person in the room, the Arab servant who had remained behind the chaise-longue.

"Permit me to show this, General. It was found at Montfaucon, where the corpse was discovered. I believe that it was left there by the murderer." He displayed the scarf.

Vauzuron did little more than glance at the material in Boizillac's hand. "That's all fine and well, de Boizillac, but what possible concern is it of mine?"

"Look more closely, sir." He held it nearer to the seated man. "Do you see the pattern? This is an Arab design, of an unusual quality and character. I can tell as much from what I recall of my service in Algeria, but that is all that I can tell. But my hope, and my request, is that you will allow me to show this scarf to one of your household, in case they can tell me more about the material used. That is why I have come here today."

Vauzuron made a signal to the servant. "Ben-Ahmed, light my reading candle and bring it over here." The Arab moved to a writing desk at one end of the room, lifted up by its metal base a heavy candle that stood there, started it burning with the flame of the candelabrum, and returned to the older man's side. Vauzuron gestured to Boizillac to bring the material directly under the candle, although he made no attempt to hold it himself. After studying it for some moments, he waved both scarf and light away, leaned back in the chaise and drew at length on his cigar. Then he looked back at Boizillac. "You're right, captain. It is Arab. So are we to assume, then, that it was an Arab assassin who finished off your Montfaucon vermin?"

"I cannot say, sir. As your own house shows -" and Boizillac nodded at the rich hangings on the walls of the salon, "it is quite possible for a Frenchman to have many Arab possessions. But my question, to you, General, or to your household, is this - do you recognise the pattern, or the material? Does it come from a particular town, or tribe?"

"And if it does, how will that help you?"

"It might mean that either the killer, or the dead man, or both of them had spent time in that part of Algeria, and that, by speaking to other old soldiers who served in the same area, I could find out if one of their number had suddenly gone missing from his local haunts."

Vauzuron snorted contemptuously. "If you ask me, you'd have more success looking for a gobbet of spit in the Seine - and spend your time more usefully too! But, you have your orders, I know, and I certainly have no wish to stand in the way of the Paris police. For myself, I have no special knowledge of such material that could help you. But there is another pair of eyes here." He signalled to the figure behind him. "Ben-Ahmed, you have heard what Captain de Boizillac has told me. Have you ever seen a fabric like the one that he is holding?"

Boizillac proffered the scarf again. The Arab slid round the side of the chaise longue and took the material from him. Turning his back to him, he held it close to the fire, to inspect it against the radiance of the flames. It was as he raised his head suddenly, as though he had made up his mind, and swivelling to face

Boizillac spoke the words "I cannot help you, Captain", that the scarf slipped from his hands and fell into the fire. But, almost before the material began to shrivel in the heat and break into flame, Boizillac had plunged his hand into the fire and retrieved it. It was singed, but only slightly.

"Good God, de Boizillac! Have you hurt yourself?" Vauzuron was sufficiently startled by the incident to rise from his seat.

"No, sir. You see --" and he held out his hand, "I am wearing gloves."

The general dropped back on to the chaise, and turned his attention to his servant. "And you, Ben-Ahmed, what in God's name were you thinking of?"

The Arab had stayed in front of the fire as Boizillac had recovered the scarf. He glanced towards the captain, before bowing in obeisance to Vauzuron. "A thousand pardons, sir. I fear that my grasp was loosened by the heat from the fire."

"I'm sorry about that, de Boizillac. Did you manage to save that wretched scrap of material?"

"Yes sir. But may I confirm that your man also has no knowledge of this fabric or design?"

"Is that what you said, Ben-Ahmed?" Vauzuron asked.

The servant had slipped back into the comparative darkness behind the general's seat. His eyes glittered as he repeated: "I am sorry that I cannot help the captain."

"I see," said Boizillac. "And are there any other members of your household to whom I might also show this scarf?"

"No point in doing that, de Boizillac. They all come from the same region as Ben-Ahmed, and he's the best of the lot of them. If he tells you that he doesn't recognise the design, you can be sure that none of the others would either." There was a moment's silence, as Vauzuron settled back into smoking his cigar, and Boizillac, after observing the Arab briefly, folded the material back together and replaced it in the pouch.

"In that case, General, I thank you again for receiving me, and Monsieur Delourcq, and I shall take my leave."

"Did you ride here?" Vauzuron asked.

"No, sir, we hired a cab."

"A cab? Never use them - they reek of vomit and scent. Did you pay the cab off? Ben-Ahmed, has Albert got my carriage ready? Tell him to bring it round to the front, to drive Captain de Boizillac into town." The servant bowed and hurried from the room.

"I appreciate your kindness, sir, but it isn't

necessary."

"Nonsense. There are advantages to living out here - but the distance to the Palais Bourbon is not one of them." He tossed the end of his cigar into the fire. "So, what will you do now, de Boizillac? I fear you've had a wasted journey out here."

"There may yet be others we can ask about the scarf. And, even though no-one has come to the Prefecture to report a missing person that would match the body we found, we have contacts that we can use to make further checks."

"So be it. But I repeat - I trust that the police will keep this sort of crime in perspective, and not lose sight of the real enemy in our midst, the forces of anarchy that we have been fighting to repress for the last three years." He signalled to his servant, only to realise that he had left the room. "De Boizillac, I am a little pressed this morning. Could you - and your companion - find your own way out? I am sure that Albert will be round at any moment. I do have some urgent papers." None were visible. Vauzuron had clearly decided that the interview was at an end, and he sat now with his gaze fixed on the fire.

"My thanks for your time, and for arranging our transport back into Paris. Come, Delourcq." They stepped out of the salon with no further exchange of words and went down the stairs.

Ben-Ahmed stood at the bottom. He handed

Boizillac his hat. "I must again ask to be forgiven for my clumsiness in allowing the scarf to fall into the fire."

"No harm done," Boizillac responded lightly. "I hope that General Vauzuron will not be angry with you."

The Arab's eyes sparkled. "No--" he said forcefully, checked himself, and went on quietly. "I think not." He opened the door to the driveway. "Albert has brought the General's carriage round. May I lead you to it?"

Boizillac and Delourcq climbed into the vehicle and were borne off to the city. The Arab servant watched until the carriage disappeared entirely from view, then closed the door with particular firmness.

"A double disappointment, Delourcq", said the young captain as they jolted away. "No intelligence about the scrap of material, and a fine army commander gone soft on the fruits of retirement." He fell silent for a few moments. "And as to his behaviour towards you-- "

"Say no more about that captain. In any case, I paid more attention to that servant of his. Didn't strike me as a very trustworthy type, if you take my meaning."

"No? You may be right, Delourcq. But we must look elsewhere if we are to make any more progress with this case."

***

Thursday 6 November - evening

Rue St. Honoré

Trégonnec - General Louis-Bertrand Alexandre de Trégonnec - had held command in Algeria too. But he was an older man than Vauzuron, and his relatively brief tour of duty in North Africa had only added to the reputation which he had already established by the middle years of the Orleans monarchy as an energetic - some said ruthless - organiser of military personnel and resources. With the collapse of the regime which had promoted his career, he had not chosen to retire into a largely private world simply to enjoy the fruits of his soldiering. Instead he succeeded in getting elected to the National Assembly as a representative of his native Finistère in Brittany, and allied himself with the forces who looked for a return to the past, of a royalist France. This made him no friend of the Republic, but also no admirer of Louis-Napoléon whose claim on the destiny of France seemed to Trégonnec and his allies no stronger than a thief's on the jewels which he has stolen from a family house.

Trégonnec's own house - a centuries-old mansion in the Rue St. Honoré - glittered with the silver sheen of chandeliers and candelabra that blazed in the great dining-room on the first floor. The general and his wife, Marguerite, gave frequent dinner parties, for those with whom they had social and political affinities.

Tonight there were eight diners seated around their table: the host and hostess; Vauzuron, and a third Algerian veteran, General Charles Grandchamps, who largely shared Trégonnec's outlook without following his example of active political involvement; Godefroi de Lieusaint, another member of the National Assembly with a sense of political self-importance inherited with the estates near La Rochelle which Louis XVIII had restored to his father thirty years before, and his wife, Adeline; Pierre Franquelle, a writer for the legitimist paper *La Voix du Pays*; and Henri d'Amboise, also an elected member of the Assembly, with both feet in the royalist camp, but with a network of contacts throughout the chamber.

The host was at the far end of the table from de Lieusaint, but this did not stop him from booming a reprimand over the intervening clutter of glasses and plates: "You weren't in the Assembly today, Godefroi - you missed some important business." Trégonnec was bald, but made up for this with thickets of hair that grew on his cheeks, below his nose and above his eyes, which shone fiercely through the tangle of his eyebrows.

"Family reasons," de Lieusaint responded vaguely, and drank from his glass. "But I was hoping to hear from you, or d'Amboise, about what happened."

"Not another invasion by the mob?" asked Vauzuron, who sat between the host and d'Amboise on the left hand side of the table.

"Calm yourself, Maximilien, the conflict was philosophical, not physical."

"Not yet," observed Franquelle acidly, from the other side of the table.

"We launched a proposition asserting the right of the Assembly to call upon the armed forces to defend it."

Adeline de Lieusaint sat to the immediate right of the host. "To defend it against what, my dear Louis-Bertrand? Against a mob invasion?"

D'Amboise leaned towards her. Barely forty, he was a younger man than the others at the dinner, and gave the impression of even less maturity because of his plumpness, above all because of his clean-shaven baby-face. "A mob invasion doesn't frighten me, Madame. If the sans-culottes break into the chamber, our good friend Trégonnec will stand up and shake his whiskers at them, and they will turn and run!" There was laughter.

"Whiskers be damned!" Trégonnec thundered. "I'd lay about them with my sword. But to answer your question, Adeline, our concern is not to be protected against the hovels, but against the palaces, and against one palace in particular."

"A palace?" Madame de Lieusaint repeated in a puzzled tone of voice. Unlike her husband, she was happier on their rural retreat in the West than in Paris, and had never been able to understand the intrigues of the capital, or the pleasure which Parisians took in them. "What do you mean?"

Noting the wry smile that passed between d'Amboise and Franquelle, Godefroi de Lieusaint felt it necessary to intervene. "The Elysée Palace, my dear. Bonaparte's nephew has no love for the Republic, or for the Assembly which the Republic has elected."

His wife turned again to Trégonnec. "So you think that Louis Bonaparte might send the troops into the Assembly and lock you all up? Godefroi as well? It's not possible!"

The smiles turned into loud laughter at the righteous indignation in her voice. Only the military veterans remained serious. Trégonnec spoke, at first to Adeline de Lieusaint, and then to the table generally. "If only it were not possible. But look at what has happened. Bonaparte has sent his famous message to the Assembly, arguing yet again that we should change the electoral law so that every hovel-dweller in the land should be able to vote. What infamy!" he boomed. "Bonaparte no more wants to see the revolutionaries elected to the Assembly than we do, but he strikes a pose to see if he can tempt the weak-minded. And Saint-Arnaud, our new Minister of War, has sent a circular to the army in Paris, saying that his word - or the word of his master in the Elysée - is law. Well, we shall see. Saint-Arnaud has his answer in our proposition. I only hope that the Assembly as a whole will agree it, when we debate it in ten days' time."

"Saint-Arnaud!" It was the first contribution to the exchanges which Grandchamps had made. If North African service had been the making of Vauzuron, it had started Grandchamps on a slow decline. He had completed his tour of duty with success, but his health had been undermined by two bouts of dysentery; and, in the five years since he had returned to France, he had suffered permanently from nausea and stomach pains. His grey, gaunt features contrasted with the ruddy solidity of the others at the dinner. Trégonnec had invited him out of comradeship, not in the expectation of conviviality. "A worm who thinks he is a viper. Well, worm or viper, he will be caught by the nephew of the eagle, chewed up, and spat out again." His eyes rested on the flames of the candles, avoiding the gaze of the others.

"Did you serve with Saint-Arnaud in Algeria?" Godefroi de Lieusaint asked.

Still looking at the table, Grandchamps spat out his reply: "I did."

"And what can you tell us about your former comrade-in-arms?" de Lieusaint asked provocatively.

"No more than a lame, broken-down old horse can tell you about a snake. Ask the others!" It was all that Grandchamps would say.

Franquelle had been observing the flow of conversation with amusement. Any stranger to the gathering would have immediately marked the writer out as an outsider. While the generals and their wives sat proud in the knowledge of their achievements, Franquelle was hunched and folded into the crumpled layers of his threadbare clothes, and had the furtive glance of a creature of the streets. He had proved his value to the legitimist cause by the power of his pen, and he had been granted admission to the houses of the cause's supporters because they both admired and feared that power. But he was not liked. When Grandchamps' spat-out command to Lieusaint checked the discussion momentarily, Franquelle intervened.

"I can help you, Monsieur de Lieusaint. We have all seen how General Saint-Arnaud has climbed to the pinnacle in the last three years, over the corpses of the Arabs of Algeria, women, children, and - well, there may have been some men fighting his troops as well. All in the name of the Republic, and its Bonapartist Prince-President. But he began his military career thirty years ago, in the service of King Louis XVIII. Unfortunately, his devotion to the King's service came to an early end when he fought a duel with his commanding officer and was dismissed. He left the country in search of glory on the battle-fields of Greece, but it seems that he went to the wrong address.

"So - to the eternal benefit of France - he returned once more to the motherland, and I understand that spent several years enlisting, deserting, and re-enlisting in the Army, and being allocated to such prestigious duties as jailer and stores-guard. What better preparation could there have been for his more recent triumphs? At last, we have as Minister of War a man whose loyalty to his monarch lasted no longer than the period of credit on his gambling expenses, who put his military service on and off as frequently as he changed his clothes, and who developed his military strategy in the company of prisoners and victuallers." He paused, and his eyes raked his audience. "I would say that General Grandchamps was being generous to General Saint-Arnaud when he called him a worm."

Adeline de Lieusaint made a sharp intake of breath. "Monsieur Franquelle, is this all true?"

The writer smiled at her, showing a mouthful of stained and misshapen teeth. "Madame de Lieusaint, the reputation of my commentaries, whether written or spoken, is beyond reproach."

No-one around the table gainsaid Franquelle. Even if they had not known as much about Saint-Arnaud's background, they were united in their contempt for his unprincipled support of the Bonapartist cause.

"Well," gasped Madame de Lieusaint, "I am shocked to learn about the real nature of General Saint-Arnaud, and even more shocked that Louis Bonaparte should choose such a man for so important a position. But surely the President has other advisers of better character about him?"

Again, Franquelle was the first to speak. "There is his other new appointment, as Prefect of Police,

Monsieur Maupas --" He paused, and then looked across the table. "But surely, Monsieur d'Amboise, I speak of one of your associates."

For a moment there was a deeper flush to the pink complexion of the younger man, discomfited at the implication of a close link with one of Bonaparte's trustees. Then d'Amboise mastered his reaction and smiled at the journalist. "As ever, Monsieur Franquelle, you assume that I know the secrets of *le tout Paris*. But I have met Maupas, yes. My family has an estate near Toulouse, where he was Prefect until his recent summons to Paris."

"Was he, indeed?" commented Vauzuron. "And what manner of man is he?"

"He is of fairly humble origins, but he has made the best of the hand which life dealt him, and discharged his official responsibilities with zeal and efficiency," d'Amboise explained.

"He's a functionary, a damned functionary," Trégonnec rumbled. "He's thrown his weight around as Mister High-and-Mighty Prefect in Toulouse and, before that, in Boulogne, stuck his nose into military matters that are best left to the army commanders, and sucked up to his Bonapartist masters. I trust that you are not offended by my plain speaking, d'Amboise. I cannot imagine that you regard this jumped-up little clerk as a friend!"

D'Amboise's smile was undaunted. He was no

more troubled by the anti-Bonapartist tone of that evening's conversation than he had been by the mockery of the legitimists that had flowed around the table at which he had eaten the previous night, in Maupas' house. "Monsieur de Trégonnec, for me to take offence at your words would be like shaking my fist at a thunderstorm." He beamed in all directions. There was a moment's silence, and then Trégonnec and all the other guests save Grandchamps burst out laughing.

Vauzuron sat next to d'Amboise. As the laughter died down, he turned to him. "So you know Maupas, do you? Next time you see him, you might mention what happened to me today. I was visited - at ten in the morning, would you believe - by a young captain who served in Algeria when I was out there. De Boizillac, that's his name. He's with the Prefecture of Police now. He appeared this morning, out of the blue, with a sidekick who looked as if he'd slept the night in the sewers."

D'Amboise was intrigued. "And why did this young captain call on you so suddenly, General?"

"Strangest story. It seems that they found a corpse a couple of days ago - no clothes, no possessions and no head even. Only thing they did find was a scrap of material, with an Arabic design. De Boizillac knew I had Arab servants, so he got it into his head that they might recognise the design. Complete idiocy, in my view - and I told him so."

"And your servants --?"

"Knew nothing about it. I told de Boizillac he should be locking up villains and anarchists, not wasting my time. If you see Maupas, tell him about it. He's in charge now - he should see to it that his police go after the villains, not come knocking on my door!"

"Well, certainly, General, if I bump into Prefect Maupas, I shall indeed mention your concern to him."

"But there's always Morny," Trégonnec boomed down the table. "He's a different kettle of fish."

"Louis Bonaparte's half-brother?" asked Adeline de Lieusaint.

"But he's the worst kind of turncoat," her husband countered. "For ten years there was no more loyal supporter of the Orleanist monarchy. Even when Bonaparte was first elected President, I remember Morny still talking about paving the way for the eventual return to the throne of the Comte de Paris. And now suddenly this year, we see a rapprochement between Hortense de Beauharnais' sons from both sides of the sheets, and Morny has thrown his lot in with Bonaparte."

"I didn't agree with Morny when he supported the Orleanists, and I don't agree with him now," Trégonnec thundered. "But, unlike Saint-Arnaud and Maupas, he knows what he's doing."

"He certainly does," agreed Franquelle. "Who do you think put the idea of re-introducing universal suffrage into our dear President's head? But Morny served in Algeria too, some fifteen years ago. Is there no-one at this table who knew him then?"

"He never advanced beyond the rank of lieutenant," commented Trégonnec, "but he showed himself brave enough, rescuing Trézel when he was shot at the siege of Constantine in '36."

"A blaze of glory to cover his rather hurried abandonment of the military profession," Franquelle commented acidly. "But are there not rumours that his behaviour in Algeria before his moment of fame was less glorious? Have I not heard --?"

He was prevented from completing his sentence by an unexpected outburst from Vauzuron. "Really, Trégonnec, this is too bad! I have no time for Morny's politics, but the man was given the *légion d'honneur* for his bravery. We should not be dragging his military reputation through the mire."

Grandchamps was moved to intervene again. "Tell me, Monsieur Franquelle, what military service have you yourself completed?"

"Alas, General, I have a medical condition - a deformity of the spine - which has always made me unfit for active service. I have been compelled to fight my battles with the pen, rather than the sword."

D'Amboise leaned across the table. "And do you believe that the pen is mightier than the sword?"

Franquelle saw the trap, and stepped round it. He offered the broadest possible smile to D'Amboise, showing the wreckage of his teeth to their full extent. "You pose a false contradiction, my dear sir. The pen and the sword must be allies, and join battle against a common enemy."

D'Amboise leaned back again. But Vauzuron was not placated. "Well, if you ask me, there are far too many words being written, and spoken - and not enough action! Someone needs to step in and put an end to all this scribbling and squabbling, and bring the country back to its senses!" There was a momentary silence, as all eyes turned to the agitated figure of Vauzuron who gripped his dinner knife and banged it repeatedly on the table as he spoke.

"But Maximilien," Trégonnec responded at length, in an unusually restrained tone, "that is exactly what Bonaparte is planning to do."

Vauzuron looked at Trégonnec with a baffled expression. He raised the knife again, to underline a point that he was about to make. But he too was blocked, for at that moment Grandchamps groaned loudly and pressed both his hands to his stomach. He rose unsteadily to his feet and gasped to his host: "Forgive me, Trégonnec, but the pains have become too much. I must return home."

It was the end of the evening. Marguerite de Trégonnec, who had said nothing during the meal, took charge, helping the ailing man from the table, ensuring that he was enveloped in a travelling cloak, and seeing him into his waiting carriage. Vauzuron was only too happy to take this as his cue to depart as well; and d'Amboise and Franquelle wasted no time in leaving too. Godefroi and Adeline de Lieusaint, to whom the Trégonnecs were closest, lingered after the others, allowing the men to talk more privately about developments in the Assembly. When they took their leave, the heat of the dinner-table discussions had cooled, but their concern about the manoeuvring of the Bonapartists was undiminished.

Chapter Five

Sunday 9 November

Barrière d'Italie and beyond

The frustration which Lucien felt at his failure to shed any light on the murder of the Montfaucon corpse still weighed on his mind the following Sunday. But two things raised his spirits as he paced about his lodgings that morning. The first was that the day had brought a change in the weather; the rain-clouds had rolled away, if only briefly, and there was a clear blue sky above the city. The second was that he was to see Laure Cerise.

It was only four days since their meeting at the *Théâtre Drolatique*, but Nicolas de Montholon had already contrived a second assignation with Delphine Ramille. He had talked at length to Lucien about his "triumph" with the actress, remembering only as an afterthought that Delphine had passed on a message from Laure, saying that she could escape the supervision of Victor Verdant on Sunday afternoon, and proposing the Quai des Fleurs as a meeting-place.

The sunshine, and the recollection of his conversation with the actress in the *Auberge Dijonnaise*, gave Lucien the idea of an excursion. There was a barouche at the stables where he kept his horse; it was free, and he arranged to hire it. And so it was that, when Laure stepped down from a cab which had conveyed her southwards through the city and across the Pont Notre Dame, she saw a chestnut-brown horse trotting towards her pulling a small open carriage driven by Lucien.

"Good day, Mademoiselle Cerise," he called, as his gloved hands drew the horse to a standstill. "May I offer you the opportunity to enjoy the fresh air of the countryside?"

"Are you hoping to save me from a life of crime?" she laughed and, without waiting for a reply, took the hand that he extended towards her and climbed on to the driving platform to sit on the bench beside him.

"Are you comfortable there?" He asked. "Will you be worried about falling off?"

"If I feel myself slipping at all, I shall take hold of your arm again." She leaned against the back rail. "Drive on!"

Lucien cracked the whip to set the horse off again. They drove straight across the Ile de la Cité to cross the Petit Pont, then turned eastwards to follow the left bank of the Seine as far as the Jardin du Roi; leaving the river behind them, they followed the Boulevard de l'Hôpital past the forbidding bulk of the Salpetrière; and finally reached the Barrière d'Italie. Lucien paused for a moment at the tollgate. "Are you sure you want to abandon the safety of the city?"

The breeze that had buffeted them had left Laure's face flushed. The excitement could be heard in her voice as she urged him on. "Now is not the time for faint hearts. Spur your steed forward. On into the unknown!" It was a quotation from one of her roles. They both laughed at the moment of theatre, then drove on through the gateway.

They had passed through Paris at a steady trot. Now, catching Laure's enthusiasm, Lucien whipped the horse up to a faster pace as they headed southwards along the Mélun road. After half an hour's swift driving, the road brought them alongside the Seine, upstream of Paris; and at Choisy they crossed the toll-bridge from west to east, leaving the flatter open land behind them and swinging south again on a winding road which hugged the line of the river, below the wooded hills that rose towards Créteil. Again, Lucien drove the horse forward, and the little carriage bounced round the corners of the route and jumped over the ruts in the surface, forcing his passenger to make good her promise to seize his arm and secure herself from being ejected.

It was mid-afternoon when Lucien guided them up from the valley and into the Forêt de Sénart. The sky had lost its brightness and the air was becoming heavier. As they advanced more steadily between the stands of oak trees on either side, a wind began to blow through the leaves. Laure gave a sudden cry, and touched her cheek. "A drop of rain," she exclaimed, and now they could hear rain starting to beat on the canopy of the trees.

They were approaching a cross-roads within the forest. "Go to the right here," the young woman urged.

Lucien slowed the horse. "But that's just a track running into the woods."

"Perhaps," she countered, "or perhaps there's a charming little *auberge* at the end of it, where we can shelter from the storm."

"And if there isn't?"

"Then we shall get very wet!"

He stopped the carriage for a moment. There was no-one else in sight, either on horseback or on foot. He had ridden the route to Mélun several times, and they would need at least another fifteen minutes to reach Corbeil, where he knew of inns and hostels. Perhaps it was better to stay under the partial protection of the forest while the rain still fell. He shook the reins and turned them into the side track. It was little wider than the carriage, and its wheels slid into parallel grooves which had been carved into the ground and which held the vehicle as though it was on rails.

They turned a corner, brushing against the ferns that splayed out at the base of the oaks, and began to go down hill. It was growing darker; and, though little rain fell on them from above, the ruts in which the wheels turned had started to run with water, and splashes flew from the hooves of the horse.

But Laure's instinct was right. Only a hundred yards further on, they came to a clearing, where the full force of the downpour made itself felt. Alongside the track was a rambling structure which seemed to drape itself from the high central chimney stack like some great tent made of stone and wood. The chimney was smoking; there were lights in the windows; a sign above the front door announcing the *Auberge des Chasseurs*; and a rough-hewn stable-block into which Lucien guided the horse.

They scampered through the open to go in at the door of the inn. It was a simple enough place: the ill-shaped stones which made up the walls presented no less rugged a face to the interior as outside; the floor was a fretwork of wide slates embedded in the beaten earth, and scattered with straw; and the tables and chairs had been hammered together from wood cut in the forest. But a fire burned in the hearth that faced them as they entered; a section of tree-trunk as long as a man is tall rested on the fire-irons, its underside an incandescent red; and Laure and Lucien felt the blaze of heat drive the dampness out of their clothes, and flush their faces.

"Driven down from Paris, monsieur, madame?" The brilliance of the fire had blinded them to an older man who had been standing to one side of the hearth, and who now came forward, smiling. "Welcome to the *Auberge des Chasseurs*. My name is Jean Plessis."

"Monsieur Plessis," Lucien replied, "we are

very pleased to have discovered your inn. For the past ten minutes or so, we have been driving through a downpour."

"And is your carriage in the stables?" Lucien nodded. Plessis shouted to the back of the room: "Christophe - go and take care of the horse in the stables." Plessis was a good deal shorter than Lucien, and stouter as well. He had a full, red face which was framed by a luxuriant beard. "Give me your coats, now, and make yourselves comfortable. I shall be back in a moment." He took the capes which both the travellers from Paris slipped from their shoulders and carried them off into the shadows.

They looked round. There were a dozen tables packed into the room, but no other visitors. Laure laughed. "We may be the only people who have ever found our way to this inn!"

"Where shall we sit?" asked Lucien.

"There!" Laure had spotted a rustic sofa behind a table to the left of the fire; the frame and base were assembled from branches that had been sawn and hammered, but then made more comfortable by draping a coarse cloth over the frame; and the seat had been padded with straw. They sat side-by-side.

Plessis returned, carrying on a round wooden tray a pitcher of red wine, two glasses and a basket of coarse black bread. "Fire is good, but wine is better. And this wine, which is grown by a cousin of mine in

Burgundy, is one of the best." He filled their glasses. The younger people paused for a moment, toasted each other with their eyes, and then drank.

"Ah," said Laure, "if only I had a cousin with a vineyard. This is wonderful."

Plessis smiled and looked towards Lucien for confirmation. "I think that the autumn weather has given an edge to my appreciation - but I agree, monsieur Plessis, this is a wine that it is certainly worth driving for two hours to drink!"

"I shall leave you to enjoy it. I need to check that Christophe has attended to his duties. But, if you wish to order something to eat, I shall be back in a few moments to check with you." He left them.

"Are you hungry?" Lucien asked.

"I am always hungry," Laure laughed. "Delphine says that I have the appetite of a medieval pope - which is not very respectful, but you know the way she is."

"Nicolas is very fond of her."

"Is that what he says?" his companion asked over the rim of her wineglass, but went on without waiting for an answer. "Well, Monsieur de Montholon is a fine young man, and he and Delphine clearly enjoy each other's company a good deal. But if Delphine is free with her favours today, he should not expect that she will be tomorrow."

"Do you mean that she is only playing with Nicolas?"

"All of Delphine's life is a play, on the stage and off it. Come, come, Monsieur de Boizillac, don't look so disapproving. Delphine is an actress, and she has to play the parts which others write for her - the dramatists, Victor Verdant, her 'uncles', and now Nicolas de Montholon. But all these performances last for only a few hours. Now, why are you looking so sombre?"

"Because you are an actress too." His gaze rested on Laure's dark-green eyes, wondering what thoughts lay behind the brightness and laughter.

She leaned forward suddenly and her cheek brushed against his as she whispered in his ear: "But I am not Delphine, and if you win my favour, it will not be for a drama lasting a few days --" She drew back modestly, with a blush which Lucien could see even in the dim light of the room, as Jean Plessis returned.

"All is well in the stables, monsieur. Now, can I bring you something to eat?"

Laure had recovered her composure sooner than Lucien, and responded: "Thank you, monsieur Plessis, we are both hungry from our drive. What can you offer us?"

"Well, it is my good lady wife who is in charge of the kitchen, and I can assure you that she knows how to cook all the fine dishes which you might get in the grand restaurants of Paris." He patted his waistline in emphasis. "But, if you would like a meal that is both delicious and nourishing but rests rather more easily on the stomach, I would recommend one of Mère Plessis' omelettes, made with duck eggs, mushrooms from the forest floor, and a touch of wild onions and honey-sweet garlic. They are *extraordinary*!"

"Then that is what we shall have," Laure affirmed. Plessis beamed at them, topped up their glasses, gave a little bow, and retreated to the back of the room taking the empty pitcher with him. "I hope you'll like it, Lucien."

He thought for a moment. "If I don't, I think that our host will throw me out of the inn, and that would never do. So I have decided that it will be magnificent, even before I've tasted it!"

"Now, wasn't I clever to find this place?"

"Very clever indeed," Lucien replied, "-- unless you've been here before. Have you, Laure?"

"Do you think that handsome young captains drive me out into the countryside all the time, then?"

"Why not? What better things could they find to do with their time? But I know very little about you, Laure. When we met last week, I told you about my family and where I grew up. What about you?"

Laure looked at her glass now, and her eyes no longer glittered. "Well, monsieur de Boizillac", and she gave just enough emphasis to the particle before his name to suggest the difference in their upbringings, "you must realise that I was not born into a family with a country estate and a tradition of service to the *patrie*. Do you really need to know any more?" She turned her eyes back to look at him questioningly. "Are you sure that you won't be so appalled by my history that you will realise your mistake in paying court to an actress?"

"I know that I have not made a mistake. Trust me, Laure."

"I am a child of Paris, through and through. I was born within a stone's throw of the Porte Saint-Denis, I grew up on the streets between the Temple and the Hôtel de Ville, and now I act in the theatres of the Rue Saint-Martin. If my skin is as white as milk, that is not the effect of powder, but the natural result of an existence spent in the gloom and fog of the city's alleyways and thoroughfares. And the light that shines into my life is not the sunshine of the French countryside, or event the heat of the African desert, but the brilliance of the candles in the theatre. I first saw that light when I was sixteen, my *début* on the stage, and for the past six years it has been that light that has kept the darkness at bay for me."

"And how did you become an actress? Are there others in your family --?"

"My family?" She looked at him for a moment. "Yes, I had a family at first, although I pray that I may be forgiven for having so little memory of most of them. My father had already abandoned us before I could talk. My mother earned what she could by cleaning and washing for other people, but it was scarcely enough to pay for one room in a hovel by Saint-Denis. There were five of us in that room - my mother, Marc and Luc, my brothers, Marie, my sister, and me, the youngest of the lot. That was how we lived until I was three. And then cholera swept through Paris, like a great flood, and left Marc and me behind, and carried off Luc, and Marie, and our mother." Her voice had become hard. "I remember the men, with cloths over their mouths, taking my mother's body out of the house, and Marc holding my hand and telling me I had to stay with him. It was very dark, then."

"How old was your brother?"

"Marc? He was ten or eleven."

"And was there no-one else to look after you? What about your father?"

"Marc always said that our father died as well from the cholera. But later on, I realised that Marc wanted nothing to do with our father, or with other adults, and he made up his mind to fend for himself and for me without help from anyone else. And he did. He worked from dawn until midnight, fetching and carrying and running errands for one of the wine-houses near the Temple, and in return they let us live in the basement and gave us food and drink. We lived there for five or six years, and in the end I used to help Marc with his errands. I know my way around those streets with my eyes closed. But then that way of life ended too." She fell silent.

"What happened then?"

"The army happened, monsieur de Boizillac - your army happened. Marc was fifteen or sixteen. He'd had enough of being everyone's dogsbody. There was a general recruitment for service in Algeria, and he enlisted. He agreed to send money to the landlord of the wine house, to pay for me, and then he was gone - for ten years. And he sent the money back regularly, and it went straight into the pocket of the landlord. As for me, one week after Marc left France, the landlord spoke to someone he knew who spoke to someone else, and I was taken to the *Orphelinat du Temple* and entrusted to the care of the orphanage sisters."

Jean Plessis re-appeared, carrying a tray with two large plates which were covered with the omelettes cooked by his wife. He placed them carefully in front of his two visitors, gave them each knife, fork and napkin, and wished them "*Bon appétit*". Refilling their glasses, he left them to their meal.

Laure shook off the pensive air with which she had recounted her childhood, and purred with pleasure as she ate the first mouthful. "Cheer up, monsieur de Boizillac," she teased Lucien, "all's well that ends well, and my story has ended with one of the best meals I've ever had. Here, taste it!" And she speared a slice of omelette with her fork and held it up for Lucien to eat. It jolted him out of his thoughts.

"No, no, I don't need to eat your food, I have my own." He began eating as well, and for a minute or two they both consumed their meal, communicating only with murmurs of approval. But Lucien felt obliged to question Laure again. "So you were no more than ten when you entered the orphanage, and sixteen when you became an actress. But did you go straight from the orphanage into the theatre? Did the sisters agree?"

Laure burst out laughing. "Still more questions! And from a captain of police with egg on his face!" She laughed even more at Lucien's embarrassed expression and dabbed the egg off with her napkin. "Well, I think I've answered enough of your questions. I'll tell you no more than that I went first from the orphanage into service in the house of one of Parisian society's grandest personages - and no, I shall not tell you his name - and from there to the theatre. And it was Victor Verdant who took me under his wing when I was sixteen, and gave me a new name, and made sure --"

"A new name?" Lucien interrupted.

"Did you think that Laure Cerise was my real name?" She laughed more loudly then before, but stopped when she saw how crestfallen Lucien appeared. "No, it is a stage name, just like Delphine Ramille. My mother called me Laure, but my father was a Carreleur, and Laure Carreleur is the name which I received when I came into this world."

"And Marc Carreleur, your brother? What has become of him? He must have returned to France three years ago, when I did as well."

For a moment the laughter faded from Laure's face. "I can tell you very little of him."

"But he lives in Paris? You saw him when he returned?"

"I saw him. It was a shock for both of us. I thought that he was dead, or had forgotten about me after so many years. It took him several weeks to find me, since I had gone from wine-house to orphanage to mansion to theatre, with several other stops on the way. But the ten years that we were apart changed both of us completely. Where he lives now, and what he does, I cannot tell you." She swirled the wine in her glass, and drank it in one. "And so you see, monsieur de Boizillac -- Lucien," and she touched the side of his face gently, "I am a child of Paris, as I told you before, and I have no family other than Paris itself. So, give me some more wine, and top up your own glass, and let us drink to Paris."

He did as instructed, and they clinked glasses and toasted the city. An hour had passed since they arrived at the *auberge* and, though they spent a second hour there, enjoying the warmth of the fire and the wine, Laure resolutely refused to say any more about the years before she was taken up by the theatre manager. They talked instead about the plays in which she had performed, and the actors and actresses with whom she had shared the stage; and, when Jean Plessis came to tell them that the rain had stopped and that dusk was not far off, Laure drew him into their conversation too, and prised stories out of him about his rare visits to Paris when even he had seen a variety performance.

But in the end, and with even greater reluctance on the part of Lucien than Laure, they paid for their food and drink, wrapped themselves in their cloaks, and climbed back into the barouche. Christophe lit the lanterns on either side of the bench, Lucien whipped up the horse, and they rode, gently at first through the forest, then more rapidly back along their route to the capital. It was little later than seven in the evening when the carriage reached the house in a side-street off the Rue Saint-Martin which was owned by Victor Verdant and where Laure and Delphine had their rooms. Laure had rested against Lucien as he drove; now they kissed briefly, she breathed to him that she would arrange to see him again soon, and then stepped down from the barouche and disappeared into the shadows. The return to the Rue du Bac should have taken fifteen minutes, but Lucien drove round Paris for an hour...

Chapter Six

Monday 10 November

Ile de la Cité

Lucien slept poorly that night. The memory of the hours spent with Laure mixed uncomfortably with thoughts of the corpse at Montfaucon; in his dreams, he unwrapped shrouds from around prostrate forms only to recognise the face of the young woman from the *Théâtre Drolatique*. He rose early, lit a candle, and sought to control his mind's activity by reading again in his descriptions of the Napoleonic campaigns.

It was still murky some two hours later when, enveloped in his long coat and hat, he took his horse from the stables in the Rue du Bac and rode to the Ile de la Cité. Fog spread across the Seine and spilled out on either side, seeming to absorb any weak daylight and transfer the river's dank chill into the streets. Unusually, Lucien found that the ride had a soporific effect, and it was fortunate that his mount knew the way to the Préfecture de Police even through the muffled streets.

He left the horse in the police stables and walked to the entrance on the Quai des Orfèvres. A bell tolled eight in the distance. In the doorway stood the now familiar figure of Delourcq; he had an old woollen scarf wrapped around his face but his hair, uncovered against the weather, was wet and lank. "Morning, captain," he said. He coughed suddenly, then spat enthusiastically into the street. "Seem to have half the bloody Seine in my throat this morning."

Lucien paused as he removed his hat, and scrutinised Delourcq. Here was a man who, if not actually twice his age, looked it, and more. Great hanks of unkempt hair hung down from the bald dome of his head like seaweed trailing from a rock. His face was rough, red and pitted, and, even though his right eye often gleamed with an animal cunning, the fixity of his false left eye gave an impression of stupidity, even malice. He had neither beard nor moustache, but his jowls were always so dark that it was impossible to tell whether he had shaved or not. And his clothes, if not dirty, were so shapeless and worn that a layer of grease might actually improve their insulating qualities. If a man like Delourcq appeared on the Boizillac estate near Valençay, he would be driven off the land by the steward, and the *garde champêtre* would be notified that there was a suspicious individual in the area. But this was the man that he, Lucien de Boizillac, had been given to work with in Paris.

"You look a bit under the weather yourself, captain" said the older man. He reached inside his battered jacket. "Maybe you'd like a drop of this - it helps to stoke up the fire on a cold morning like today."

Embarrassed to be interrupted in his thoughts, Lucien took the small metal flask which was held out to him, unscrewed the thimble-mug that served as a stopper, and sniffed. "What is it?"

A smile cracked Delourcq's face. "Eau-de-vie, captain. It's saved my life a few times, I can tell you. You need to drink three thimblefuls straight down. Go on, now."

He did as instructed. He had swallowed the first dose and just emptied the second into his mouth when he felt a sudden burst of warmth erupt. Startled, he gulped down the second mouthful and, as the flames within rose up and filled his head as well, he handed the flask and stopper back to the other man. Shaking his head, and laughing in spite of himself, he gasped: "My God, Delourcq, how have you lived to be so old?"

Delourcq drank off several tots himself. Then, kissing the flask before hiding inside his jacket again, he winked his good eye at Lucien and said: "I've been well preserved!"

Lucien felt obliged to lean against the wall for a few seconds until his head cleared. "Delourcq, you know this building better than me, and just now I think that your eau-de-vie has done nothing for my memory. Can you lead the way?"

"It will be my pleasure, captain. Follow me."

The two men walked in silence through the long corridors that ran back to the offices of the *Sûreté*. Lights fixed to the wall by brackets burned at intervals, but served only to emphasise the surrounding darkness, and the November chill seemed to burden the atmosphere inside the Préfecture even more heavily than the streets outside. To Lucien it felt almost as though they were heading downwards, under the Seine, which might burst in through the ceiling above them and flood the passageway.

They were not kept waiting. The clerk who was Canler's doorkeeper indicated with a nod of the head that they should go straight in. Although Lucien had met Canler before, he had not visited his office. It was almost as obscure as the corridor that led to it. Overshadowed by the high walls of the justice building, the windows were no more than rectangles of grey mist. Maps of Paris hung on the walls, above cabinets filled with ledgers and box-files that were crammed with details of the underworld and *demi-monde* of the city. But Lucien could discern these only through a glass darkly, for the only lamp stood on the desk in the centre of the office and illuminated the small, bald figure of the *Sûreté's* chief. He remained seated. There were other chairs in the room, vaguely perceptible in the darkest corners; but Canler launched immediately into his remarks without inviting them to sit down.

"Captain Boizillac, Monsieur Delourcq, we need to take stock of your investigation into the discovery of the murder victim at the sewage lagoon of Montfaucon last week. I have here -" and he tapped a manuscript on the desk in front of him "- a memorandum which you wrote last Friday, Captain Boizillac. You make it clear that you examined the body thoroughly, and you have carefully noted the unusual injuries which the victim suffered. And you have also recorded the substance of the conversations which you had with those present at the lagoon, and also with the sister of the night-watchman. The detail is admirable. But what are your conclusions?"

"I am afraid that, so far, we have discovered nothing that points a finger at an identifiable culprit. I believe that the murderer must have killed his victim in another part of Paris and then conveyed him to Montfaucon on horseback. So, in addition to our investigation at the site itself, we need to make inquiries elsewhere in the city as well."

Canler's eyes glittered as they stared across the room at Boizillac and Delourcq. "Including at the house of General Vauzuron, I understand?"

"When Delourcq spoke to the night-watchman's sister, he got from her a scarf with an Arab design which her brother had taken from the murder site. I hoped that the General's Arab servants would recognise the design. You will have read my explanation in my report."

"Yes, I did read your report, on the day that you wrote it - which was why I was not surprised to be summoned to speak to Prefect Maupas on Saturday, when I was treated to what I may call some critical observations on the behaviour of my agents. They were variations on the theme that members of the *Sûreté* should be filling the gaols with villains and anarchists rather than wasting the time of distinguished representatives of the French Army."

"Piss-pots!" grumbled Delourcq, in a voice that was scarcely audible.

"Monsieur Delourcq?" Canler asked. "Do you wish to respond to the Prefect's comments?"

Delourcq shook his head, and said nothing more.

"Captain Boizillac?"

"I served under General Vauzuron in Algeria. There was a time when he had a keen sense of his own duties and those of others, when he recognised that upholding the law, military or civil, was a higher priority than sticking to social etiquette. But times have changed So, it seems, has he. Now he --"

"Thank you, Captain Boizillac. I asked you in today to make you aware of the Prefect's concern, not to pass judgement on those personages who may have provoked his concern. You and Monsieur Delourcq, indeed the *Sûreté* as a whole, will not be able to carry out our work if our methods draw complaints from such personages."

"But this complaint is unjustified. The only reason for my calling on General Vauzuron was to obtain information that might help to identify a murderer."

"But you did not obtain that information, and

you have not identified the murderer." Canler picked up a pen and began to write in red ink on the memorandum in front of him. "And with that in mind, I have decided that --"

He was interrupted by the entry into the room of the clerk. "Monsieur Canler, I have just been handed this letter, by a messenger from the *commissariat* in the XIIth *arrondissement*. It is urgent."

Canler put down his pen, took the letter and broke the seal. He spread the page out in front of him on the desk and read it through. Lucien and Delourcq watched him in silence. When he finished, he retrieved his pen and struck through the few words which he had written at the top of Lucien's report.

"To resume, gentlemen, I have decided that you are to continue your investigation in the XIIth *arrondissement*. In the early hours of this morning, one of the stockmen at the Abattoir de Villejuif disturbed an intruder, who ran away from what has been identified as a man's corpse. The local *officier de la paix* has noted that a deep incision has been made into one side of the man's neck. I would hazard that the murderer was interrupted in the act of decapitation." Canler sighed softly. "I would have thought that our fellow citizens would be happy to leave it to the authorities to separate villains from their heads, but it seems that we are not doing enough to satisfy at least one inhabitant of Paris. Well, do you know the Abattoir de Villejuif?"

"I know it," said Delourcq. "I've not seen it that

often, but I've smelt it enough in summer."

"Make your way there at once. See whether this killing was done by the same hand that butchered the corpse at Montfaucon. Above all, make sure that you advance this investigation. Let me have a further report by the end of the week." He waved them out of the room.

Boizillac needed no guidance from Delourcq this time. He strode swiftly back to the main entrance to the building, with the older man scuttling to keep up with him. Though the morning was as damp and dreary as before, his torpor had lifted, and a light glinted in his eyes. He paused at the door and turned to his companion. "Where is the abattoir, then, Delourcq?"

"At the southern edge of the city, Captain. The butcher's yard is no more than a hundred paces from the Barrière d'Italie - the *barrière de sang*, they call it. When there are heavy rains in the spring, the drains in the yard overflow, and the blood from the slaughtered cattle washes back along the road to the city-gate. Helps to harden the soles of your shoes." He grinned.

"The Barrière d'Italie..." Lucien recalled his excursion of the day before with Laure, How long after they had returned through the gate had the murderer brought his victim to the abattoir? "Come on then - we must find a cab."

They bundled themselves into a cab on the Quai des Orfèvres, crossed the Seine by the Pont St. Michel, and wound south and east through the city, finally along the crowded squalor of the Rue Moufetard. Climbing down outside the Abattoir de Villejuif, Lucien paid off the driver and involuntarily glanced down at the road. It was wet, but with the dampness of mist and the traces of mud and manure. There was no blood.

Setting his hat firmly on his head, and pulling his gloves taut, he led Delourcq through the yard-gates. The entrance passage-way was wide, to accommodate the herds driven in, and it was flanked on either side by two long, single-storey buildings set back behind rough-hewn verandas that were raised a yard or so above the ground. A second set of gates spanned the passage-way between the further end of the buildings, and beyond them could be heard the sounds of the cattle, booming plaintively; and the damp air was made even heavier with the powerful stench of the animals' excretions of sweat, urine and dung. But the ground in the passage-way between the two buildings was cleaner than the road outside, and fresh straw had been spread out to be swept away after the next influx of cattle.

A figure stepped out of the building on the right and stood on the veranda above them. "My name is Massenier. I am the manager of this yard. What is your business here?"

Lucien jumped on to the veranda and went up to him. "Boizillac, of the *Sûreté*. And this is my colleague, Delourcq." The older agent stayed in the passage-way, and nodded briefly in acknowledgement. "We have come to inspect the corpse."

Delourcq noted that, tall as he was, Boizillac had to look up to meet the gaze of the other man. Massenier had a head of silver-grey hair, and a lined face, that showed his fifty years of life; but he stood straight-backed in his long black frock-coat, and put Delourcq in mind less of a butcher than of a bank-clerk. His face darkened, and he spoke rapidly. "Monsieur - or is it Captain - Boizillac, I would be grateful if you would lower your voice, and follow me into my office. And could I invite your colleague to join us there as well?"

Boizillac gave a sign to Delourcq, and they both stepped into the office. There was little enough to see in the room; if Massenier kept papers and records of the abattoir's business, they must be held elsewhere. There was no desk as such, merely a high wooden lectern behind which Massenier now stood, as he stood during most of the working day, so that he could see out of the windows of the office at the same time as making notes in the ledger-book which rested on the lectern's top. Massenier never sat down in his office; and there were consequently no chairs. But what was most clearly missing from the premises was a corpse.

Boizillac bridled a little. "I repeat, Monsieur Massenier, we need to see the corpse that has been discovered. What is the purpose of a discussion in this office?"

The yard manager leaned heavily on the lectern, and frowned a little as he replied. Now Delourcq was reminded of the priests that he had been obliged to listen to in church as a child, and he half-expected to hear a sermon about the sins of mankind. As though he didn't already know enough about the subject! "I understand your impatience, Monsieur Boizillac, but I should like to explain the circumstances of the discovery. And you will understand that I do not want to air these details outside, where anyone might hear us. If you will excuse a purely commercial concern, it could be bad for business." Massenier looked extremely sombre; and, although Delourcq was momentarily amused by the turn of phrase, his humour was dampened by the thought that he should warn Françoise to give a fairly close examination to the packets of meat she bought over the next couple of weeks.

"Very well," Boizillac conceded. "But where is the corpse?"

"I had it conveyed to the cemetery beyond the *barrière*. It seemed more respectful, and..."

"Better for business?" Boizillac asked. He looked at Delourcq. "You know the cemetery?"

"Less than five minutes' walk, captain."

"We'll go there once we have heard your explanation, Monsieur Massenier."

"It is quickly told. Albert Dutoit, one of our older stockmen, has a billet in one of the outbuildings in the yard. He keeps his ears open for any intruders at night. A few years ago, before Dutoit took up his quarters, it was almost a nightly occurrence that some poor devil would break into the compound in search of freshly slaughtered meat. Dutoit's predecessor was either too cowardly, or possibly too drunk, to offer any challenge. We replaced him, and the break-ins stopped almost overnight. Dutoit fears no-one but God." The manager allowed himself a brief smile of self-contentment. "Word soon spread through the *arrondissement* that anyone trying to raid the Abattoir de Villejuif was likely to get away with nothing more than a broken head. But it seems that someone had not heard of Dutoit's reputation."

"You mean whoever was responsible for leaving the corpse here?"

"Exactly. It was at around three this morning when Dutoit heard unusual noises. Some of the cattle in the pens started up, and then he heard what sounded to him like a large sack being dropped over the inner gates. He rose at once, but could see nothing across the yard from his billet. It was dark, and foggy. He lit a torch, and went across the yard to where he could hear scuffling noises, and breathing. Whoever was at work must not have expected another human presence at that time of night, and had his back to Dutoit's approach. Albert came close enough to make out a dark figure hunched over a shape on the ground. But his torch suddenly flared and spat, and was reflected in the blade of a knife that the figure was holding, and even as Dutoit called out a challenge and hurried forward to tackle him, the intruder leapt away, was back over the gates in an instant, and disappeared into the darkness. And that was when Dutoit found the body of the murdered man."

"Unclothed?"

"Completely naked. The demon had killed him by stabbing him through the heart. And when Dutoit disturbed him, he was in the middle of cutting off his head." Massenier took a handkerchief from his pocket, and wiped his lips. "You seem less shocked by this crime than I am, Monsieur Boizillac. Is this the moral resilience of the police?"

"Your description of the criminal and his victim is reminiscent of the circumstances of another murder which we are already investigating, in which a decapitated corpse was found at Montfaucon."

"Montfaucon? Any association of my yard with those foul pits would be catastrophic! I must ask you to handle this matter with the utmost discretion, Monsieur Boizillac."

"We need to see the spot where the body was found."

"I can take you there, of course. But there is nothing to see. The body was moved to the cemetery two hours ago, and we have washed and swept the yard clean since then."

"That was unfortunate," Boizillac said tersely.

"Did you find anything left by the murderer - the knife, for example?"

Massenier shook his head. "There was nothing, no weapon, no clothing. Only the sack in which the body had been brought into the yard - and we used that to convey it out again."

"A sack," Boizillac repeated. "We must examine that as well. It is still with the body, I assume?"

"I trust so," Massenier replied, slightly unsure of his ground. "And Dutoit is at the cemetery also. I sent him there with the corpse, and told him to stay with it until further notice."

Boizillac nodded briefly. "That was well done." He turned towards the door. "Well, Delourcq, let us make our way to the cemetery. I see no point in spending any more time here."

Massenier moved quickly round his lectern as they left. "Two last observations, Captain Boizillac. Apart from yourselves and the local *commissariat*, only Dutoit and myself know of this murder."

"And the cemetery personnel too, I suppose."

"Yes, they too will know. But I have not spoken of it to any of the other stockmen here, and nor will Dutoit either. You must understand my concern to avoid knowledge of this spreading any further."

Delourcq could see the shadow of anxiety over the manager's eyes. In his own mind, he had no doubt that Massenier had as much chance of concealing what had happened as Delourcq had of flying to the moon; delivering a mysterious corpse to a Parisian cemetery was almost as effective as pasting an announcement on the walls of the town hall in getting tongues wagging. But neither Delourcq nor Boizillac would talk of what they had found.

"I understand," the captain responded curtly. "There was something else that you wanted to mention?"

"Yes." Massenier paused for a moment and stepped back behind his lectern. "I saw the corpse, but the poor devil's features were completely unknown to me. But Dutoit --"

"Recognised him?" asked Boizillac.

"I believe so," the manager said, with evident reluctance. "I must appeal to your discretion again, Captain Boizillac. In the four or five years that Dutoit has worked here, his behaviour has been impeccable. But that was not always the case. He told me in complete frankness that he had previously moved in rather different circles, and had some associations with the world of petty crime. I have respected his confidence, and there has been no reason for me to regret doing so. But this morning, after he had fetched me to the yard and taken word to the *commissariat*, he told me that he thought he knew the dead man's face."

"And his name?"

"I fear not. The memory was still indistinct. You will clearly want to question him further. But I would ask you to do so with discretion, and out of the hearing of anyone else. He is one of my best workers, and I would hope to protect his reputation here."

"Well," Boizillac began, "we cannot suppress our questions if --"

Delourcq gave a rasping cough. "Allow me to say something, captain." They exchanged looks, and the younger man nodded. "Monsieur Massenier, if we took exception to everyone who had got on the wrong side of the law at some time in their life, we would know as much about the real criminals as the sisters in the Couvent du Sacré-Coeur." He coughed again, frustrated at being unable to clear his throat inside the office. "What I mean is that there is at least one person in this room who also has a few murky deeds in his past. I mean me, sir, Daniel Delourcq," he added as Massenier's face clouded over. "So you can trust us to do the necessary to make sure that your man Dutoit tells us what we need to know, without being marked out as a former villain. If you follow my meaning."

The manager looked at Delourcq for a few seconds, and then nodded in assent. "I am grateful to you both. And I stand ready to help you further, if you require." He walked with them to the main entrance to the abattoir, shook hands, and left them to return to his office.

It was approaching mid-morning, but the fog and the chill had scarcely lightened during their interview at the abattoir. The two men walked side by side along the road leading to the *barrière*. Delourcq, the lower half of his face buried in his scarf, kept his own counsel. But, once they were out of earshot of the manager, Boizillac spoke up. "There's a man who cares more about the carcasses of his cattle than about a dead man."

Delourcq pulled down the top edge of the scarf, spat vigorously, and commented: "He can make a lot more money out of animals than men."

"Ah yes," the younger man replied, "money. I had forgotten that, since the death of the Emperor, the glory of France is money and not valueless things like honour, or courage, or self-sacrifice."

Delourcq snorted and rubbed his sleeve across his nose. "Well, now, captain, there are people who are born on estates in the country, and who get full plates of food two or three times a day, and who wear a brand-new coat every year. And for them, having money is like having air to breathe or water to drink - it's so natural that they don't even need to think about it." The older man kept his eyes on the road as they approached the barrier, though he could feel Boizillac's sideways gaze on him.

"And then there are other people who grow up in a back-street of the city, and most of the time survive on a bowl of soup and last week's bread, and who get their clothes from the flea-market at the Temple and wear them until they fall apart. And the only time that they don't think about money is if they ever get enough of it to drink themselves stupid. And then there are people in the middle, like our Monsieur Massenier. Maybe he was born on a country estate, and has lost his fortune. Or maybe he grew up in the shadow of Notre-Dame, and has made the best of himself. Either way, he knows that money doesn't come naturally to most folk, and if it is flowing in, because he is managing to sell the meat from his abattoir, he doesn't want something like this killing to dam the flow." They passed through into the land beyond the city limits.

"No-one is going to put up statues in honour of money-making, sure enough. But if you've never had much money, or if you've lost what you had - well, all I mean to say, captain, is that it does tend to prey on your mind." He still avoided looking directly at Boizillac, but he could tell from their slower pace that his words had struck home.

After a few moments, the younger man spoke up. "Explain one more thing to me, Delourcq. How is it possible that your eau-de-vie, which has muddled my thoughts, has given you such a clear head and a ready tongue?" They stopped momentarily, and joined in laughing.

Delourcq reached inside his jacket. "Would you

like another drop, captain?"

"Not for me, I think. Isn't that the cemetery over there?"

"It is." They resumed their progress. "But, if you don't object, I'll drink some myself. I find it helps." He took a swig and put the flask back as they reached their destination.

The cemetery outside the *barrière d'Italie* was a large rectangular site, carved out of the orchards that had grown there some fifty years before. Enclosed by a low brick wall, it was split into four square subdivisions by rough gravel driveways running in from the perimeter and intersecting at a central clearing where a simple chapel stood, next to an even humbler structure that included both the cemetery-keeper's lodge and a shed for grave-digging tools and for anything else that needed to be stored. The place was deserted that morning. Their steps crunched on the gravel as they made for the lodge, and they followed the tracks made by cart-wheels that had also rolled that way earlier in the day. They saw a hand-cart upended by the lodge; and, as they drew nearer, they saw two figures come out of the lodge and watch them approach.

"The one with his hand on the door is Saint-Pierre, the keeper," said Delourcq. "He's been here almost as long as the cemetery."

"Is his name really Saint-Pierre?"

"That I don't know, captain, but it's the right name for the job."

"So the other one must be Dutoit. I shall need your help to get as much as we can out of him." They were now within hailing distance. "I am Captain Boizillac, of the *Sûreté*, and this is Monsieur Delourcq. We have just spoken to Monsieur Massenier, at the Abattoir de Villejuif."

"Albert Dutoit, stockman at the abattoir." He was shorter than either Boizillac or Delourcq, but was powerfully built, with wide shoulders. His voice was firm, but the agents caught the same guarded look in his eyes as had been shown by his manager.

"And you are Monsieur Saint-Pierre?" Boizillac asked the other man.

The keeper moved away from the lodge to be clearly visible. For a moment, Boizillac was taken aback. The man was completely bald, and his spare features and sunken cheeks gave him a skeletal appearance, reinforced by the way his clothes hung on an emaciated frame. The only contrast was made by his hands, which were enormous and marked by blood-red patches on the skin. He spoke slowly, as if considering each word. "Saint-Pierre is good enough. Follow me." He walked the length of the lodge to open the double doors into the shed.

As he turned the corner of the building, a shower of gravel rained down on his head and shoulders, thrown by a couple of street urchins who had been lying in wait. He lunged towards them, but they sprinted away, laughing and shouting: "*Saint-Pierre, Saint-Pierre, mets ton cul dans ton lit de terre!*" He rubbed the top of his head, and, looking at Boizillac, muttered: "I shan't waste my efforts chasing them. If we get a cold enough winter, they'll be back here by the feast of Saint Simeon, in a box." For a moment, his face was split by a wide grin, then he took a key from the ring on his belt and opened the doors. "Here's what you've come to see," he said, and stood aside.

"It's pitch black in there", Boizillac responded. "Are there no windows?"

"Windows?" Saint-Pierre echoed sardonically. "For those little demons to throw stones at? We're not in the Tuileries gardens here, mister police captain."

"Then light a candle," the younger man bristled. "You may be able to see in the dark, but I can't."

The cemetery-keeper shot a poisonous glance at Boizillac, and seemed about to send a barbed remark after it. But he shrugged his shoulders and stepped into the shed to do as he had been bidden. It was just possible to hear him murmur under his breath: "That's one less candle for you when you're in your box", but, as the candle took and illuminated the interior of the building, Boizillac was too attentive to what it revealed to take any notice of the old man's invective.

The corpse lay on a heavy wooden table in the

centre of the shed. A sack covered it. Boizillac took the candle which Saint-Pierre had lit and, holding it up high, pulled back the covering with his other hand. At first sight, the body was intact, although bruised and bloodied. Boizillac's rapid scrutiny told him that the dead man was shorter than average, five feet six at most, and with a well-filled belly that pointed to comfortable circumstances and middle age. He had a full head of black hair that might well have been carefully groomed in life, but now was tangled and matted with the blood that had flowed from the deep incision at the base of his neck. And something had happened to his face; the nose was crushed, and there were purplish contusions on the forehead and cheeks.

"He landed on his face when he was dropped over the fence into the stock-yard. It smashed him up." Dutoit had stayed by the doorway, but offered this explanation. "He was handled worse than a side of pork."

Boizillac said nothing. With Delourcq at his side, he completed his examination of the corpse. Raising the cold flesh, he noted the same stab-point in the dead man's back that they had seen on the Montfaucon corpse. He studied the incision which showed that the killer had been setting about the same task of decapitation when he had been disturbed by Dutoit. And finally he held up the dead right hand of the victim on the table, and saw that the killer had severed the little finger before abandoning the corpse. "It is as before, Delourcq, just as before."

"Like a savage beast, captain, except that this is a beast that plans and calculates."

Boizillac shifted the light a little. "What do you make of the sacking?"

Delourcq turned it from end to end, and looked it over both front and back. "Well, it's badly stained from this poor devil's blood, and it must have picked up some soiling from the abattoir hand-cart it came here in. But otherwise - it looks to me as though it hasn't been used before."

"A new sack? That is calculating."

"Captain?"

"A new sack has no identity. A used sack carries the traces of its cargo, and where it came from." They stood in thoughtful silence for a moment.

"Seen what you wanted?" asked Saint-Pierre's rasping voice. "Then perhaps you gentlemen would like to go back to where you came from, and leave me to show my latest guest to his room." The candle-light showed the sneer on the old man's face.

Boizillac spoke in an undertone to Delourcq. "I shall keep this old death's head busy with some questions. You talk to Dutoit." He turned to the cemetery-keeper. "We have finished here, Saint-Pierre. We can go to your lodge now, so that I can clarify matters with you."

"With me? What do you want from me? All I know about your friend on the table there is what size of box he'll need when I drop him into the ground."

Boizillac passed the candle to Delourcq. "I assure you that I shall be very interested in that information." Only his companion noticed as he slipped off the gloves that he had been wearing and replaced them with another pair. He took the old man's arm firmly in his grip and steered him out of the shed. "And I'm certain that you have other wisdom to impart as well." Saint-Pierre was so taken aback by Boizillac's determination that he offered no more resistance either of word or gesture. The two of them disappeared.

"He won't get anything out of Saint-Pierre," Dutoit observed to the older agent.

"The captain knows what he's doing," Delourcq replied. "Don't be misled by his appearance." He was still inside the shed; the stockman stood in the doorway, and Delourcq found it hard to see his face even against the dull light of the day. "Shall we close up this place?"

"It's up to you. I've seen worse than that. I'm happy to stay here if you have questions to ask."

"All right, but I must clear my throat." Delourcq stepped out for a moment, coughed vigorously and hawked up, then returned inside. He took a swig from his flask. "Can I offer you some?"

The other man shook his hand. "I have a day's work ahead of me."

"Is the work good?"

"I get paid, I have a place to sleep, what more could I ask?"

"And the manager, Massenier? Straight as a ramrod, eh? Wouldn't approve of you drinking?"

"Nor should he." There was a pause; Delourcq felt that he was being silently scrutinised. "No questions about the corpse?"

"We heard the story from your manager. But he said you might have something to add."

Another pause. "You don't recognise me, do you, Delourcq?"

The agent took the candle from where it stood on the table and raised it above the other man's head. It was a powerful face, with eyes glinting from the deep recess between the narrow forehead and the prominent cheekbones; but, even when Delourcq looked closely, it stirred no recollections.

"No. But you know me. Tell me why."

"You remember the Belleville gang? Back in '46?"

"The silver-stealers?"

Dutoit smiled. "Candle-holders, salvers, plates - anything made of silver."

"There were four of them. We caught them all when they cracked one of the big houses in the Faubourg Saint-Germain. They were sent down to Toulon. Were they friends of yours?"

There was a short burst of laughter. "Never friends, no. But they kept me in work for several years. I was the silversmith - turned everything they brought back into coin of the realm."

"And they didn't squeal on you?"

"I still had a stash of silver to convert when they were caught. If they kept me out of prison, it would still be there for them when they were free. Well, they have another five years left to serve, but I haven't got the silver any more. After they left Paris in the prison convoy, I had a word with your boss at the *Sûreté*. I handed over the stolen goods, he gave me a clean bill of health and a new name, and I got the job at the stock-yard. As far as the gang are concerned, I've disappeared."

Delourcq scratched the side of his face. "You got a good deal there. Strange that I never heard anything about this."

"Maybe it was a private transaction with your

boss. But it was at that time that one of the old lags in the Rue aux Fèves pointed you out to me, as the hero behind the capture of the Belleville gang. I never forget a face."

"And I never betray a confidence. You know my face - what about that one?" Delourcq gestured with the candle towards the corpse.

Dutoit nodded. "He came to my workshop a couple of times, to look over some of the gang's hauls. And I was sent to his lodgings once, with a set of silver thimble-cups that he had bought. His name is Jattée. I thought it was him even by torch-light, but when I could see him better in daylight, I was sure of it."

"And where are his lodgings?"

"I can tell you where I went five years ago. I don't know if Jattée was still living in them when this happened to him. It's not that far from here. You know where the Bièvre runs under the Rue du Jardin du Roi? There's a row of houses along the road, with a passageway through the middle of it. If you walk through, you come out into a field that goes down to the stream. Le Marais du Bièvre. There's a single house in the field. That was where I saw Jattée." He paused for a moment. "It was an abomination, Delourcq. I swore I'd never go back there."

"What happened?"

"Nothing happened. I gave him the silverware,

and left at once. But the stench, the filth -- I'm not sorry to see him go like this. Paris should smell a little sweeter in future."

"Well, there's a treat in store for me. And was there no-one else there - a wife, a family?"

"Not for Jattée. That wasn't his way." Dutoit paused again. "He used the back-door instead of entering at the front, if you follow my meaning."

"May God forgive him," muttered Delourcq. He had spent long enough inside the mortuary shed. He stepped out into the November chill, motioning the other man to follow him, closed the door behind them, and spat violently on to the gravel. "And what else can you tell me about him? Where did he get the money to buy silver? Who were his associates?"

"I heard it said that he inherited a pile of money, but I never believed it. He behaved like a common criminal, and if he came by money, it can only have been through villainy. As for his associates, I never met them and had no wish to do so."

"No ideas about his killer?"

"The devil had vanished into the night before I had a chance to see his face. But I wouldn't be surprised if there were scores of men who wanted to cut Jattée's throat. Listen, Delourcq, now you know everything I know about Jattée, and you know about my history too. But it's just between us, agreed? I don't want the rest of Paris to know that Albert Dutoit used to be the silversmith of Belleville."

Delourcq clenched his right fist and locked the knuckles against Dutoit's right hand. It was the handshake of the Parisian underworld. "You have my word."

"Well, you two look as thick as thieves." Boizillac and Saint-Pierre were just stepping out of the lodge door, and the cemetery keeper, whose natural ill-temper had been worsened by an apparently pointless interrogation, spoke sourly in the direction of the other men.

"I think that, by keeping company with the dead all the time, Monsieur Saint-Pierre has lost the knack of dealing with the living," Boizillac said loudly. "I have spent quite long enough with him, Delourcq. Have you completed your conversation?"

"Yes, captain. Our business here is finished."

"Good. Well then, Monsieur Dutoit, you are free to return to the stock-yard. And Monsieur Saint-Pierre is free to continue with his duties. Until we meet again." He raised his hat slightly, and set off along the gravel path.

"I hope you'll be in your box if we do," grumbled the cemetery keeper, and turned back into his lodge.

Delourcq nodded briefly at Dutoit, then joined

Boizillac.

"Did you learn much?" asked the younger man.

"A good deal."

"Well done. Look, I'm chilled through from the day and talking to that wretched death's head. Let's find an inn where we can sit down. Then you can tell me what you've found out."

"We'll find somewhere in the Rue Moufetard. That's the way we need to go, anyway."

Chapter Seven

Monday 10 November - midday

Plaine de Chaillot

His hand rested on the gold pommel of his stick. The gilt had been applied to a solid ball of lead, that gave lethal weight to what looked like a dandy's affectation. Only once had he been compelled to test its effect on a human skull, to defend himself against an athletic young man who thought that he was worth more. The boy had been felled like a deer riddled with shot. Since then, the stick was his constant companion.

Seated alone in his carriage, he had travelled the length of the Champs Elysées and on to reach the Barrière de Neuilly. His household, and his office retinue, had grown used to his excursions, which he might take even in the middle of pressing business, even in foul weather, far worse than the chilly fog which smothered Paris today. He said no more than : "I must ride out," and the carriage was summoned, and his man-servant brought his cape and his hat. Those around him told themselves and each other that he needed the fresh air to clear his mind, away from the pressure of reports and decisions.

They were wrong. His mind was always clear, even after discussions lasting half a day, or a night of debauchery. Nothing could blunt the edge of his insight and determination. If he rode out, it was in further pursuit of that determination.

Only Gianni, his driver, knew where he went on his excursions, where he stopped, and whom he met; but Gianni had been well-chosen. His loyalty was to his passenger and master alone, and he never spoke to the rest of the household about these outings.

Now the carriage turned off the main westward highway to travel in a southerly direction, across the Plaine de Chaillot. Gianni had followed this road before. It was broad enough, but its earth bed was heavily scored by the wheels of farm carts. He slowed the horses to little more than a trot; and after a mile, where the road rose and fell into a valley lined with willow trees, he halted the carriage altogether. He had noticed the figure standing back among the trees. Gianni kept his eyes on the road ahead, but he heard the carriage door open and felt the movement as a second passenger climbed in. The door fell shut. Gianni whipped up the horses, and they rode on.

Inside, it was still only the man with the gold-handled stick who was seated. The newcomer was kneeling, bracing himself against the swaying of the carriage, his head bowed down so that his gaze was on the floor.

"Give me your report."

"It is done, master."

It is done, the seated figure repeated to himself.

Adieu, Jattée, may the fires of hell burn long and bright on your bloated soul!

"But I fear your anger, master."

"Why? What has happened?"

The kneeling figure was little more than half the other man's age, and powerfully built. If they had fought, the younger man could have broken the other's neck in a matter of seconds. But they would never fight, for the younger man acknowledged a dominion which was not based on physical strength. His eyes remained downcast. "The man is dead, master. But I was surprised before I could take his head from his body, and I had to flee."

For a few seconds, the only sounds were from outside, the clatter of the horses' hooves and the scraping of the wheels on the earth and stones of the road.

"Was your face seen?"

"No!"

"Where did you leave the body?"

"In the place where the beasts are slaughtered, at the southern edge of the city."

They rode on again without speaking. Then the older man stood up, grasping his stick in one hand. The kneeling figure made no movement. The stick rose up; it struck five times against the carriage ceiling. Gianni, recognising the signal, slowed where there was firm ground alongside the road, wheeled the horses round, and headed back in the direction from which they had come. "Are you angry, master?"

"No. It is regrettable that the face of the dead man will be seen, but he at least can speak no more poisoned words. You have done well, my friend."

"And what would you have me do now, master?"

"Two of the devils are dead, but there is a third one who still lives. I have spoken of him before. It is still my wish that you should ensure that he meets the same fate as the others. And it must be done soon. But wait until I send you word, as before. Then strike fast!"

"As you command, master."

No more words were exchanged. Gianni stopped the carriage as it arrived back at the line of willows. The door opened and closed, and the second passenger had disappeared even before the sound of its slamming reached Gianni's ears. They returned to Paris.

The man inside had thought through all the implications of what he had heard, and decided on what steps he needed to take, by the time they passed through the Barrière de Neuilly for a second time. Now he must pick up official business again...

***

Monday 10 November - early afternoon

Le Marais du Bièvre

They were an oddly assorted pair. The younger one stood upright, protected against the weather by his tall hat, his long, close-fitting coat and his boots. His older companion bent like a tree in the prevailing wind, bare-headed, the only covering over his workman's clothes the well-worn scarf that was wrapped round his neck. While they took a simple lunch of bread, meat and wine in one of the better-looking establishments on the Rue Moufetard, the day lost some of its chill, but only as the mist turned into drizzle and then a steady downpour. As they sat at table, Delourcq had relayed everything that Dutoit had told him. Outside once more, they said nothing, but walked purposefully up the Rue Moufetard, following the stockman's directions.

The Bièvre followed a diagonal course across the southerly limits of Paris, extending perhaps two or three miles from the Boulevard Saint Jacques to the point near the Salpetrière hospital where it issued into the Seine. As it entered the city, it was a small flow of muddy water, a rural stream that had lost its way. But by the time that it merged with the Seine, it had absorbed so much human waste, effluent from the Gobelin porcelain works, rubbish from the tanneries, and overflow from the Abbattoir de Villejuif, that it had become a thick broth that steamed continuously in the cooler months of the year. If it had rained heavily and the stream had risen above its usual course and then fallen back, the banks were lined with a bilious scum. Dogs would feast on the residue, before crawling away with pain in their bellies. And still the lowlands between the stream and the houses that stood proud along the roads were dotted with the hovels and shacks of families who had been forced by poverty to come to Paris for work, and now had nowhere else to go.

This was where Jattée had lived.

The passageway through the houses that Dutoit had mentioned took some moments to find. The entrance was closed by a gate, but it was not locked, and Boizillac and Delourcq walked through, taking care in the gloom to avoid the ruts and pits that pocked the ground. Emerging at the back of the buildings, they found that the land sloped down rapidly to a flat hollow whose floor lay well below the level of the surrounding streets. Le Marais du Bièvre was an elongated triangle of boggy turf which stretched perhaps a hundred and fifty metres from the broad base where they stood, to the apex where the traversing stream again passed under the streets of the twelfth *arrondissement* to carry its filth towards the Seine. A solitary house stood in the middle, rain coursing off its roof.

"Have you ever been here before, Delourcq?"

"No, captain. I thought I knew Paris, but for all

the times I've walked up and down the Rue Moufetard, I never once saw this place. God, it makes me feel ill just to look at the mud and the foul water." He took out his flask as a reflex action and drank a tot.

"Come on."

They had to take some fifty paces. They found that their feet sank into the ground as they walked. Boizillac's boots were equal to the challenge, but Delourcq's feet were soon sopping wet inside his battered shoes. The house was an odd construction. Solidly built of stone, but covered in grime and mould, the ground floor was a long rectangle with side-walls that were punctured only by small slit windows at eye-level. There was an upper floor, but this occupied a much smaller area so that the house had a stepped outline. There was an external staircase which ran up to the first floor. The two men had made their way to what appeared to be the main entrance, a heavy door on the ground floor facing the direction from which they had come.

Boizillac knocked. There was nothing to be heard, apart from the incessant beating of the rain on roof and ground. He knocked again and shouted against the door: "Is anyone there? We are from the Prefecture of Police."

A small flap in the centre of the door opened inwards, and a pair of eyes could be seen on the other side. A woman's voice spoke, harshly: "What do you want?"

"Is this the house of the man called Jattée?"

"He's not here. You'll have to come back another time."

"Jattée is dead."

"Dead? Jattée dead? How do you know that?"

"We have just examined his body. He was stabbed to death, and dumped at the Abattoir de Villejuif. Now open this door."

The eyes disappeared. For several moments, all Boizillac and Delourcq could hear was the sound of the woman muttering; she seemed to be arguing with herself over what she should do. Then, in a matter of seconds, she turned the key in the lock, swung back the door, and hurled herself out, pushing the two men aside and struggling away into the rain. Delourcq recovered from his surprise and ran after her. She knew the firm places in the ground; he did not. As his feet stuck and one of his shoes came off, she was away, up the slope and out into the street.

"Never mind, Delourcq", the younger man called out. "You can look for her later. Let's see what's inside."

Delourcq spat in disgust, extracted his shoe from the mire and wiped out the mud with his hand, then rejoined his companion. "I'm sorry, captain. If I track that she-wolf down, I'll let her know what I think of her hospitality!"

There was no artificial light inside the house. But, when their eyes had adjusted to the gloom, they realised that a central corridor ran the length of the ground floor from the entrance where they stood to the far wall, and that there was a series of doors flanking either side of the corridor. And they became aware of a dull rumour, the suppressed sounds of breathing, coughing and snorting.

"What sort of place is this, Delourcq?"

The other man said nothing. On a hook just inside the entrance hung an enormous key-ring with twenty or more keys attached. Delourcq took it down and went to the first door along the corridor. After several tries, he found the right key and unlocked the door. They looked in. The room, little more than a square three metres by three, was bare, except for straw scattered over the floor. Huddled in the far corner were some human forms. The light was too dim to make out their number.

"Who are you?" demanded Boizillac. There was no reply, other than a child-like whimpering.

"Let me try, captain." Delourcq went over and crouched down, talking in a low voice. As Boizillac's eyes adjusted, he made out the figure of a woman, leaning against the wall, and sheltering in her arms three children, all of whom looked to be under ten years old. They were painfully thin, and dressed in rags.

After a few minutes, Delourcq rejoined the captain, and they stood in the corridor. "She says that her name is Pialat, and she and her children are from the Auvergne. They came to Paris with the children's father two years ago, but he left them during the first winter. After several weeks, they were taken in here."

"By Jattée?"

"Or by the *concierge* we met when we arrived. The woman herself has never seen the *maître de la maison*."

"But this wasn't philanthropy?"

Delourcq spat violently out of the house. "No, captain, it wasn't. She had to pay for her lodgings by whatever means she could manage, mostly by scavenging on waste tips, sometimes with her body. And once or twice with her children."

"What do you mean?"

"There were occasions when the *concierge* took one of her children upstairs, to pay a visit to the *maître*." Delourcq's eyes gleamed savagely in the darkness. "I see now why Dutoit was glad that Jattée had been killed."

"I think that I agree with him," breathed Boizillac, feeling ever more revulsion at the thought of the house where they stood and its owner. "So Jattée's quarters are upstairs. What are the other rooms here?"

"More families like this one, captain. Jattée, or his harpy, must have raked them in, like windfalls from apple-trees, and then stored them away here for him to enjoy when he felt like it."

"But why did they stay here? They must have been let out during the day, to earn the few sous they needed to pay him. Why didn't this woman and her children run away?"

Delourcq coughed, to clear his throat. "Because lying in rags, sleeping on straw and seeing her children being corrupted was still better than anything else she could expect to find this side of death, captain."

Boizillac snatched the key-ring from the other man, and rushed along the corridor, unlocking the doors and shouting to the occupants: "You're free to go. Jattée is dead." But nobody emerged. Boizillac glimpsed the same wretched forms in all the cells, not moving, not speaking. At a loss, he turned back to Delourcq, still standing by the open front door. "What should we do?"

"We can tell the local *commissariat*, although they may already have known about this place and turned a blind eye. Maybe they can find places in orphanages for the children. And maybe it's better if these people simply stay here and have the house to themselves."

The younger man drew a leather purse from his pocket. He extracted several gold coins and gave them to Delourcq. "Give them these. At least they can feed themselves for the next few days."

His companion considered the coins in the palm of his hand for a moment or two. "If it's all the same with you, captain, when we've finished here I'll go and buy food with this, and bring it back here. This is a hundred times more money than any of these people have ever seen, and I don't think that they would be able to cope with it."

"Thank you, Delourcq. Now, before the despair of these poor wretches takes any more of a hold on my own spirit, let us investigate Jattée's own quarters upstairs." He stepped out in the sodden air with relief and hurried round the side of the building to stride up the steps. The older man spoke briefly to the family in the first room, and then followed.

The door to Jattée's apartment was locked. Either the man had left his home and been murdered elsewhere, or the assassin had committed his crime here and felt sufficiently confident to secure the scene behind him as he left with his victim. Boizillac took off his hat and gave it to Delourcq to hold, then rammed the door with his shoulder. The lock resisted the first shock, weakened with the second, and flew open with the third. They stepped inside.

A short passage-way ran between what were

little more than two closets: to the left, a cubicle with a wash-stand and soil-bucket, to the right an enlarged store-cupboard with a small wooden table supporting a half-consumed loaf and some cheese. Both these cubicles were cluttered with debris - cast-off clothes, mud-stained boots, empty wine-bottles, discarded paper - but it appeared to have accumulated over weeks and months, rather than being scattered by a recent intruder.

The passage-way led to the main room, which made up the rest of the apartment. It was plain that this was where Jattée had met his death. Curtains masking a bed at the left-hand end of the room had been pulled back; the sheets were twisted and crumpled, by the desperation of a man struggling furiously to resist an assailant; and his blood had pooled on the bed, then streaked down its side and on to the floor. The trail went no further. Clearly, the assassin had got the body inside the sack and then conveyed it out of the apartment.

Boizillac went straight across to the bed. There was no weapon, no scrap of clothing, that might have been left by the murderer. He spoke his thoughts. "Killed like a pig. He must have been asleep when the knife struck, and lived just long enough to flail around and fall to the floor. But how did the murderer get in? Was the door unlocked, or did he have a key?"

Delourcq was standing in the centre of the room. The floor at his feet was wet; there was a steady drip of water from above. "Maybe, captain. But that roof window isn't shut fast. That's another way into this place."

Boizillac walked over. "It's at least the height of two men. It would be hard to jump down from that height without waking a sleeping man only a few paces away."

"If it was the same man that Dutoit disturbed in the stock-yard, he was over the stock-yard gates in a matter of seconds. I couldn't do it, but a young man might. And Jattée was probably a heavy sleeper." He nudged an empty wine-bottle with his foot.

"But who was it? There's absolutely nothing here that tells us anything more about the murderer."

"It was the same devil that did for the corpse at Montfaucon, though, don't you think?" Boizillac nodded. "So there's a good chance that the other victim was an associate of Jattée. If I can get hold of that *concierge* again, I might get some sense out of her."

The younger man had been pacing round the room. Now he stopped at a narrow cupboard set into one of the walls. The door was not locked. Pulling it open, he discovered a pile of roughly folded blankets. "Look at this, Delourcq. He obviously liked to be well covered up in the winter."

"Or maybe those blankets are covering something else." The older man quickly emptied the cupboard, and then knelt down to examine the floor. The boards were loose, and came up in his hand. He reached down into a dark recess below, then fetched out a pair of candle-sticks, a tray and salver, and some thimble-cups all of silver. "Stolen goods, every one of them, I reckon, captain. Those must be the little tumblers that Dutoit told me about."

"Is there anything else down there?"

"Just this." Delourcq grunted as he hauled up a metal box whose weight was out of proportion to its book-like dimensions. The key was still in the lock. He opened the lid. There was a sheet of faded paper inside, which rested on top of a mass of coins. The agent gave a long, low whistle. "There's enough money here to fight the Russian campaign!"

"Let me see that piece of paper." Delourcq passed it to the young man. It was a simply written document, in an untrained hand. "*I, Jean Jattée, promise to hold the sum of one thousand francs for Louis Connassier, and to give them back to him when he asks for them. I shall keep only the sum of 10 francs for every year that I hold his money.*" There were two signatures: Jattée's name could be distinguished in one of them, while the other was no more than a series of unconnected marks. A date, in April 1846, also appeared.

"One thousand francs," said Delourcq, questioningly. "But there's far more than that here."

"And no other papers?" The older man shook his head. "We must find this Louis Connassier if we are to get to the bottom of Jattée's wealth and, I suspect, his murder."

"No other papers, captain. But underneath the coins I've found this." He passed a scrap of material to Boizillac. On it were sewn a series of metal characters: A 35 1182.

"This is a soldier's identification number. From Algeria." He put the material in his pocket. "How old would you say Jattée was?"

"Mid-forties?"

"So he could have done his twelve years in Africa as a young man, and then come back to France. And maybe Algeria has now caught up with him --" He picked up the box, locked it and gave it to Delourcq. "You'd best take this to the *commissariat*, Delourcq, and let them know about this place. Buy food for those wretches downstairs - and then we must find Connassier."

***

Wednesday 12 November - morning

Ile de la Cité

Boizillac and Delourcq had agreed that the older man was more likely to track down Louis Connassier, using his contacts among the low life of Paris; and reluctantly Boizillac accepted that his colleague would need at least a day to pursue his inquiries. The younger man spent the intervening day riding on horseback through the streets of the city, sensing more strongly than before the contrast between the elegant women and their beaux in the Rue de Rivoli and the ragged mothers and children of Saint-Jacques and Saint-Martin, and wondering what vile thoughts and impulses were hidden behind the masks of self-satisfaction that were the faces of the men. When he returned to his rooms in the Rue du Bac in the evening, he sat at his desk and began to write his report for Canler, breaking off only when he realised that the initial account of the examination of Jattée's body had turned into a description of the families held captive in the dead man's house and a denunciation of the failure of the local police to act against the iniquity of the place... He crumpled the paper up and threw it on the floor. His task was to find the murderer, not to stir up trouble. But he was sickened by what he had seen.

Delourcq proved his worth again. When the two of them met up outside the Prefecture, he had an address for Connassier. It was a lodging-house in the Petite Rue de l'Ambigu, beyond the Boulevard Saint-Martin, as far north from the city centre as the Marais du Bièvre was to the south.

They talked in the cab as they crossed the river and travelled along the Rue du Temple. "There were several of my contacts who knew Jattée, or knew of him," Delourcq explained. "A few years ago he splashed a lot of money around on gold and silver objects. Then he seems to have thought better of it, and kept his money to himself. But people still remember his spending spree back then."

"And did they know about his household? The women and children?"

"Seems not - although they knew he preferred men to women."

"And Connassier? Is he one of the men Jattée preferred?"

"It's a bit of a mystery, captain. None of the people who made sales to Jattée had ever heard of Connassier. The connection didn't come from them. It was only when I was talking to one of the river scavengers, old Taillefer who has a hovel by the Pont de Grainmont, that someone owned up to knowing 'Conna', and where he lives."

"So is he a scavenger too?"

Delourcq shook his head. "According to Taillefer, he's just a drunkard and a layabout, and tight-fisted these days - although he used to be a lot freer with his money. Maybe Jattée took his money and refused to give it back."

"Well done. We've got some questions to put to this man."

The Petite Rue de l'Ambigu snaked away from

the Boulevard Saint-Martin, following a narrow and twisting course towards the north. It was little more than a passage-way giving access to the outhouses and courtyards of the tenement blocks that lined the outer thoroughfares. The two men had to pay off the cab and make their way on foot along the cobbled switchback of the street. They were at first the only figures to be seen. Somewhere in the dark jumble of adjoining buildings, a child could be heard crying, answered by the shouts of a woman. Then the street was silent again, although it was a silence buffeted further off by the hubbub of the Boulevard and the perpetual noise of the city itself.

"Taillefer said that the house had no number, and that it was at the far end of the street," Delourcq explained.

Even the few years which Boizillac had spent in Paris had taught him that a lodging-house could be almost any manner of building, from a town-house of several storeys to a tumble-down shack. But none of the places that they had passed looked promising; they were scattered, single-storey hovels; several were abandoned and closed-up; the others looked on the point of collapse.

The street turned sharply to the right, and dropped down a slope. As they followed it round and downwards, they saw an old man sitting on a chair outside a rather larger building. A fire was burning fitfully in a brazier at his feet, and it lit up his coarse, weather-beaten face. He watched their approach.

"Taillefer?" Delourcq queried. "What are you doing here?"

The old man waited until the other two were standing over him. Without rising from his chair, he looked Boizillac up and down and then turned his gaze on Delourcq. "I thought you'd have some difficulty in finding this place, Dédé, so I came here to help you."

"Is this the lodging-house?" Boizillac asked, at the same time as Delourcq demanded: "Have you tipped Connassier off?"

Taillefer got up slowly, pulled a burning piece of wood from the fire, and held it up as a torch. "Come with me. I'll show you Conna's room. He's not there, but I didn't warn him off. I think someone else did that!"

"What do you mean?" Boizillac asked, but got no reply. The old man opened the door from the street and stepped inside.

"Where's the house-keeper?" Delourcq questioned.

"Ah, there you will be cross with me, Dédé. I came here yesterday, after you and I talked. And when I told Gueule-de-Bois, the housekeeper, about your interest in Conna, he ran off down the street like a rat being chased by a dog. He didn't even take his keys with him." Taillefer patted his pocket. "But I can find Gueule-de-Bois again, if you want him." He guided the other two to the staircase, and started downwards.

"You're right, I am angry. And don't spin us this yarn about being helpful, Taillefer. Once you knew that we were interested in Connassier, you behaved like a dog following the scent of a chunk of meat."

Taillefer paused on the stairs. The torch lit up the moisture and mould covering the walls. "If I were you, I should choose my words more carefully. There's been a good deal of butchering going on here. Look!" He was at the base of the stairs. Suddenly he thrust the torch downwards, to illuminate the rough stone floor. It glittered with pools of dampness that were fed by the cold sweat of the walls. But as the two police agents looked more closely, they could make out a swirling discoloration of the floor, dark, reddish-brown streaks that overlay the greens and greys of the stones, and that ran with the camber to the sides, joining a turgid scum-line at the base of the walls. "Blood", Taillefer said simply. "And there's lots more inside." He kicked open the door.

"Give me the torch," Boizillac commanded. The old man did so, and stood back as the others entered. There was a single room, and only three items of furniture. Table and chair had been knocked over, and lay in the midst of broken bottles and smashed plates and beakers. The bed stood where it always had, on the stone floor. But sheets and pillows had been twisted and thrown in every direction. And everything, grubby and soiled from the usage of months, was spattered by blood.

Delourcq looked back towards Taillefer, still standing at the threshold. "You've seen all this already?"

The old man nodded. "The door was unlocked. One look was enough for me."

The foul air made Delourcq gasp. He coughed vigorously, and hawked into the stairwell. "It smells like a pig-sty."

Taillefer chuckled. "It was no better when Conna was alive. He was a filthy swine."

Now Boizillac spoke. "How do you know that he's dead?"

"What do you think, young man? This is Conna's room. Where do you think that blood came from - the meat market?"

"Come on, Delourcq, vile as this place is, we must examine it. Taillefer, step in here and hold the torch up while we look."

Remembering his discovery at Jattée's house, Delourcq looked for any recesses where the occupant might have hidden something of value. But he found nothing, even after pushing the fragments of bottles and plates to one side and checking under the bed. Boizillac had meanwhile stripped the coverings from the bed and shaken them. He spoke tersely to Taillefer. "Bring the torch nearer." With his gloved hand, he picked up something that had fallen out of the bedding.

"What is it?" asked Delourcq. Then he recognised the severed stump for what it was.

Taillefer was watching too. "This is a hell of a lot of blood to come from cutting off a finger." There was no smile on his face, but the look in his eyes showed that he knew otherwise.

"So it must have been Connassier who was thrown into the sewage lagoon at Montfaucon." Boizillac checked himself for a moment. "We're not likely to find his head here --?"

"No, we've seen all there is to see here. Judging from the blood, this must have been where the head was taken off, but I'm sure the murderer got rid of it in the river. Why not the finger too?"

"Once he got the ring off, if that's what he wanted, why bother with the finger?"

"You're right about the ring," Taillefer interrupted again. "You couldn't miss it - a gold coin on a gold band. He always wore it on the little finger of his right hand, didn't matter how shabby his clothes were. And when he caught me looking at it once, he waved his hand in my face and said it was his *guarantee*. Of what, I don't know. But he called it his *guarantee*."

"You may spend most of your days knee-deep

in filth, Taillefer, but you have your uses," Delourcq said. "Make yourself useful again and light the way back out of here. We've finished, haven't we, captain?" He knew the answer already; he had seen Boizillac drop his gloves on the floor.

They made their way out of the building in silence. Taillefer threw the remains of the torch back into the brazier and sat down on the chair again. He gave the impression of a man who had just finished a good meal, and now wanted to take his ease. Delourcq had other ideas. "No rest for the wicked, old man. You said you could find Gueule-de-Bois again."

Taillefer's good humour was not dented. He patted Delourcq on the back. "Calm down, Dédé. How old are you - fifty? You're behaving like a school-boy. Follow me. If Gueule-de-Bois isn't in the tavern at the end of the street, I'll kiss Badinguet's arse." The scavenger started off, heading further northwards along the street. He dragged his right leg a little, and progress was slow. The two agents followed ten paces behind.

"What's wrong with his leg?" asked Boizillac.

"Nothing. He likes people to think that he's slower than he really is. And there's nothing wrong with his hearing, either. We should keep our voices down if we don't want him to hear what we say."

"Do you trust him?"

Delourcq reflected for a moment. "Yes, I do.

His is a vile trade - God alone knows what horrors he's dragged out of the river. But that's the way he's always made his living, and he's never tried to get a few extra *sous* by doing down his fellow-men."

"Unlike Jattée, and probably Connassier too, if we did but know the truth. And now both of them have been killed - and I believe that it was by the same hand."

"It's almost like the work of a madman, cutting off heads and dumping bodies at abattoirs and knackers' yards."

Boizillac thought for a moment. "He's a very clever madman, then, doing his work under cover of darkness and avoiding being seen by anyone. But perhaps there are such creatures - madmen who are clever." He pressed his hand against his forehead momentarily. "I have to tell you, Delourcq, nothing in my army experience has prepared me for this."

"No," the other man said simply. "And for all that I've spent half a century in this city, nothing has prepared me, either." They glanced at each other briefly. "But we'll find him, captain. I can feel it, in my *eau-de-vie*!" He patted the flask in his pocket.

As they reached the bottom of the slope down from Connassier's lodging-house, the street veered to the right again, and the buildings on either side closed in so tightly that a man walking with outstretched arms would have been able to touch both frontages. This was the final twenty or thirty yard stretch of the Petite Rue de l'Ambigu before it issued into the thoroughfare of the Rue du Faubourg Saint-Martin, and the tenements that lined the larger road crept back towards the hinterland here, turning the back alley into a chasm with grey stone walls and a roughly cobbled floor.

Taillefer had stopped walking, and stood where a double trap-door had been opened up into the street. As the other two joined him, they saw a neck-breaking flight of steps leading down from the opening, heard a grumble of men's voices, and smelt an outflow of sweat, alcohol and bad temper. "Welcome to the *Enfer de Saint-Martin*, gentlemen - the official residence of Gueule-de-Bois."

Delourcq turned to his companion. "Shall we get Taillefer to fetch him out, captain?"

Boizillac shook his head. "He might take to his heels again. No, we shall just have to descend into this hell. But I would be obliged, Monsieur Taillefer, if you would continue to act as our guide, and lead the way."

Without hesitating, the old man descended, turning sideways to get a better footing on the narrow stone steps. The other two followed his example. The last step was the threshold into the *cabaret*, the larger of a line of cellars that ran under the tenements. There were no tables or chairs as such; barrels of different sizes had been sawn in two to serve as seating for men or their glasses. The floor was beaten earth, scattered with sawdust. At the further side of the cellar, no more than fifteen feet from the door, stood two large barrels side-by-side, supporting a wooden board, which was the counter.

Hard as it was to see in the subterranean gloom, Boizillac could make out an opening in the wall behind the counter, which gave on to a second cellar. But even as his eyes adjusted to the darkness and began to pick out the sombre figures settled on their barrel seats, two things happened. One of the drinkers on the far side of the room jumped up and darted round the counter and through the opening, to be followed with equal speed by Taillefer, who seemed no longer to be troubled by a limp. And at the same moment another of the bar's customers reared up, spat the word "*Salaud!*" in the direction of the newcomers, and launched himself at Delourcq. The attacker used the *savate* fighting technique, in which feet were more important than hands. The onslaught caught the police agents unawares; the impact of the first kick from a heavy boot knocked Delourcq off-balance, and he slumped forwards on to one of the tables. The attacker was already preparing to drive his heel into the base of Delourcq's spine when Boizillac, overcoming his surprise, jumped forward, pushed the aggressor sideways so that he too tottered between barrels, and before he could recover landed a perfect uppercut on his chin. The man fell backwards and crashed to the floor.

Boizillac turned to check on Delourcq. "Are you all right?"

But his companion had only been winded. He stood up again, pressing one hand against the back of his leg where the kick had been aimed. "No permanent damage - but look out for yourself, captain!"

The warning was a second too late. Taking advantage of Boizillac's distraction, the attacker had scrambled to his feet and snatched a wine-bottle from a table. Even as Boizillac raised an arm to protect himself, the bottle smashed against it and, as the young police captain recoiled, the other man barged past him and was out of the door, up the steps and into the street before either of the agents could start a pursuit.

Boizillac brushed the glass fragments from his coat. He was uninjured, but his pride was hurt. There were still half-a-dozen drinkers in the bar. He barked a command at them. "Tell me the name of that man!"

There was a sullen silence, broken by Delourcq. "No need to ask them, captain. I know him. I put him away in prison five or six years ago."

"Who is he?"

"Bertrand Baudoin. I caught him breaking into one of the big houses on the Rue de Bourbon one night. He used his fighting skills on me, but I was prepared for him that time. He recognised me just now before I'd even seen him." He rubbed his leg ruefully.

"In other circumstances, I'd give chase and arrest him again, but we have something more important to attend to right now. But I'm afraid that we've been left in the lurch by Taillefer."

At that moment, the old man re-appeared in the doorway to the second cellar. His right hand gripped the twisted collar of the drinker who had bolted from the bar, and who was now struggling to free himself from Taillefer. "I caught the little weasel before he could vanish down some bolt-hole," the old man said happily. "Where would you like him?"

"I think I've seen enough of this hell," Boizillac commented softly to Delourcq. More loudly he called to Taillefer: "Let's go back up to the street. You need the eyes of a cat to see in this darkness, and I would rather question Monsieur Gueule-de-Bois in the light of day." He went to the bottom of the steps. "Where's the landlord of this place, by the way?"

Taillefer explained: "At the back. When he heard the fracas, he decided that he needed to check his stocks. Shall I fetch him out, too?"

"No need," Boizillac replied. Then, raising his voice: "But he should know that, if any more agents of the Paris police are assaulted on his premises, he will pretty quickly find himself out of business."

They climbed back up the steps. Taillefer held as fast a grip on his wriggling companion as he did on the finds that he hauled from the Seine. Gueule-de-Bois was a good head shorter than the old man, and several stone lighter. His natural instinct was flight, rather than fight, and though he twisted and turned under Taillefer's hand, he made no attempt to strike or kick him or the others. "Let me go, you old bastard! What have the police got to do with me? Why can't I sit and drink my wine, like the others?"

"We could ask you the same question," Boizillac replied. "You seemed to lose your desire for sitting and drinking the moment we came into the bar."

"The sight of a policeman always spoils the taste of the wine," the other man retorted. He wriggled furiously. "Let go of me, Taillefer. I hope you rot in that beloved river of yours!" But he could not shake free.

They were standing in the narrow chasm where the Petite Rue de l'Ambigu neared its end. Taillefer spoke. "I can hold this little pest for as long as you like, captain. But it's not very comfortable here in the street. Why don't we take Gueule-de-Bois back to his den? You can continue your discussion there."

Gueule-de-Bois shot a venomous look at his captor, but a last desperate struggle made it plain to him that there was no escape, and he kept step with Taillefer who, at a nod from Boizillac, led the way back to the lodging-house.

The two agents spoke quietly to one another as they followed. "Your river-scavenger is being very helpful, Delourcq. Is he looking for a reward?"

"I think that tormenting Gueule-de-Bois is reward enough for him. Did you see the gleam in his eyes when he hauled him out of the second cellar?"

"But won't word get round that Taillefer is a friend of the police? Couldn't that be dangerous for him?"

"Taillefer is a loner. He works on his own, and doesn't give a fig for what anyone else thinks. All he needs are his own broad shoulders and strong arms, and he can defend himself against anything's that thrown at him, by people or by the river."

They reached the house. Taillefer released his captive inside the front door, and stood to block any chance of escape. "Shall we go down to Conna's room?" he asked Boizillac and Delourcq.

The anxiety on Gueule-de-Bois' face turned to horror. "You can't make me go down there. I'll answer your questions, but not down there."

"So you know how the room looks," Boizillac commented. "What do you think happened there?" Gueule-de-Bois cowered against the door-frame and mumbled something inaudible. "Speak up, man!"

"Someone did for him."

"You mean, killed him? Is that what you mean?"

"Yes, killed him, killed him. Took a knife and slit the poor bugger's throat."

"Who was it?"

"I don't know. It wasn't me! I've never taken a knife to anyone!"

"No," Taillefer interrupted, "you're afraid to cut up a fish in case it bites you!"

"And you've got a mouth as big as a fish's, old man, and I only wish that someone would stick a hook in it!"

"So you don't know who killed Connassier. But do you know *when* he was killed?"

"How would I know that?"

"When did you last see him alive? When did you find his room in that condition?"

"When? When?" The little man rubbed his hands against his temples. "What's today?"

"It's Wednesday the twelfth."

"Wednesday the twelfth. Wednesday - that's right, It was last Wednesday I went down there, and saw -- and saw --" He closed his eyes and shuddered.

"A week ago." Boizillac looked at Delourcq,

then back at the other man. "So you haven't seen Connassier since then?" Gueule-de-Bois nodded his head. "But when was the last time before last Wednesday that you did see him?"

"I can't remember. I never kept his company, you know. He never drank at the *Enfer*."

"No, we could see that he drank in his room," Delourcq put in. "Did he ask you to get wine for him?"

"Sometimes," Gueule-de-Bois admitted. "Yes, now I remember. Sunday last, he got me to fetch half-a-dozen bottles of wine for him. That was the last time I saw him."

"Sunday last?" Boizillac repeated. "You mean, Sunday the second?"

"Ten days ago," the other man replied. "That was the last time I saw him."

Boizillac nodded briefly at Delourcq in confirmation. Connassier had been alive on Sunday 2 November. On Wednesday 5 November he was missing from his room, which showed signs of carnage. And on Tuesday 4 November Jacques Meulnier discovered a corpse from which the head and the little finger on the right hand had been separated. "And between the Sunday and the Wednesday, did you see him at all?" A shake of the head. "Did you see anyone who came to visit him?" Another denial. "Very well. You've answered all our questions." He made his way back to the street. "And thank you, Monsieur Taillefer."

"Is that all?" Taillefer asked Delourcq, with disappointment in his voice. "Isn't this little weasel going to pay a visit to the Prefecture?"

"Well, since he clearly doesn't want to go, and we don't want to take him - no." Delourcq's voice took on a sterner note. "But listen, Gueule-de-Bois, if you remember anything else that might help to explain what happened to Conna, you must tell me straightaway." He began to follow Boizillac, and motioned Taillefer to walk several paces with him. "You've done well, Taillefer. I shan't forget your help. And if you hear any more, let me know."

Gueule-de-Bois remained in the shadow of the doorway, watching the departing figures. Taillefer went back towards him and called out: "You have the luck of the devil, you little worm!" But before he could say any more, the smaller man slammed the door shut in his face. Taillefer laughed. "You can't lock it, Gueule-de-Bois, I've taken your keys. I'll leave them on the doorstep." He did so, then set off in the opposite direction from the police agents, once again dragging his right leg. The door opened suddenly, a hand came out and snatched up the keys, a shout of "*Vieux con!*" echoed along the street, and the door was closed and locked again in an instant.

Chapter Eight

Thursday 13 November - evening

Rue St. Honoré

The evening was well advanced. Marguerite de Trégonnec had sat at her writing table and waited until her husband and his companion had returned from the Assembly and then, as the drawing-room clock chimed ten, she retired to her bed-room. But Trégonnec and Lieusaint were still too flushed from the voting in the Assembly to draw a line under the day. They sat at either side of the fire, each holding a glass of cognac.

"A famous victory!" the host blustered, his eyebrows bristling like the raised hairs on a dog's back. "And a defeat for Bonaparte, and his proposal to restore universal suffrage! Raise your glass, Godefroi, to victory for the forces of order and good sense!"

They drank. "Yes, it was a victory," Lieusaint agreed. "But our side had only seven more votes than the others - the Bonapartists and revolutionaries. Seven votes out of seven hundred."

Trégonnec's cheeks glowed red with the heat from the fire and from his enthusiasm. "What does that matter? One vote would have been enough, so long as it gave us the majority. And after this drubbing for Bonaparte, we can expect to get the necessary support for our own proposition, on the Assembly's right to be defended by the armed forces." He drained his glass. "We vote on that on Monday. I'm looking forward to rubbing Bonaparte's nose in the dirt."

"I drink to success in Monday's vote as well. But I have less confidence in some of our colleagues than you do, Alexandre - and no confidence at all in the willingness of the President of this Republic of ours to bow to the decisions of the Assembly."

Trégonnec stood up. "If he makes a move against us, he must fear the worst." The fire spat out a glowing ember. He crushed it with the heel of his boot. "That's what we shall do to the little upstart!" He refilled his glass from a decanter, which he offered to the other man. "Pour yourself some more courage, Godefroi."

"Thank you. I wish I had your spirit, Alexandre. But these days I feel like an old man." He swirled the liquid in the glass and breathed in the aroma. "It's only two years since I reached my fiftieth, but I begin to feel as though I've lived two lifetimes, or even three. The first ended when Charles Bourbon was forced from the throne, the second when the Orleanist usurper fled the country, and the third has seen this country come to the brink of destruction only to be pulled back by the simple-minded nephew of the Corsican bandit." He drank. "How did we allow it to happen, Alexandre? We, or our fathers, how could we let the mob drive the true king out of the country?"

Trégonnec was silent for a moment, only to

explode into words once more. "Treachery and deceit, that's what it was. King's closest advisers poured poison into his ears, convinced him that his position was untenable, scared him - yes, scared him - with memories of Louis' execution under the Revolution. Kept him isolated from his real supporters, people like us, until it was too late. And then they took their pieces of silver to help the Orleanist to the throne, that little impostor with water in his veins and a bank deposit where his heart should have been. Divide and rule, that was their motto. And for twenty years we have suffered the consequences of being divided into different factions. But now we've learnt our lesson. Now we have the strength to fight back against the contagion of revolution, to reject a republic based on the votes of the gutter-dwellers. And we must build on our victory to bring back the rightful rulers of this country. To the king!"

"The king!" Lieusaint echoed, but his words lacked the conviction of the other man.

The door to the drawing-room opened, and Trégonnec's man-servant stepped in. "General, Monsieur Henri d'Amboise is downstairs and hopes that, despite the lateness of the hour, you are still willing to receive him."

"Show him up, Jean." He turned to Lieusaint. "Was d'Amboise in the Assembly today?"

"I saw him there, although I didn't speak to him. Why would he call on you now?"

"Nothing unusual in that," Trégonnec commented. "He often calls here of an evening - wants to hear what I think of political developments. Attentive sort of fellow."

The servant returned, announced the visitor, and withdrew.

"D'Amboise, come in and take a chair." Trégonnec indicated the seat which he had occupied.

"General, I am obliged for your courtesy. And I am delighted to find you here as well, Monsieur de Lieusaint. I hope that I may benefit from the observations which you both have on today's events." He sat down. His naturally pink complexion responded to the fire by glowing brightly; otherwise, his boy-like appearance contrasted sharply with Trégonnec's craggy and whiskered face, and the grey hair and sunken cheeks of Lieusaint.

"I was just saying, it's been a great victory. We're starting to turn the tide on Bonaparte. And we'll do the same again next week."

"And you agree, Monsieur de Lieusaint?"

The other man had been staring into the fire. He looked at his questioner. "Of course it's been a victory for us." He paused. Trégonnec's fiery words seemed to have lost their effect on him. "But I have difficulty being optimistic about the future. It was a victory by a small margin."

"Does that matter?"

"Exactly what I said, d'Amboise. Victory is victory."

Lieusaint ignored the younger man and spoke to Trégonnec. "Only seven votes, Alexandre. You yourself spoke about treachery and deceit. Such practices did not die out when the Bourbons gave up the throne twenty years ago. They are still around us." D'Amboise shifted slightly on his chair. "Think how much of the Exchequer's revenues Bonaparte has spent over the past three years on houses and estates for his followers and for those he wants to win to his cause. What would it cost him to buy seven votes? A mere fraction of what he has spent so far!"

Trégonnec flushed even more deeply. "Who can be bought, Godefroi? Not I - and not you! Who do you mean?"

But d'Amboise intervened before the reply came. "My dear colleagues, surely there is a greater danger than desertion from our ranks. We were talking about it in this house only a week ago. Let us assume that our ranks hold firm, and that we inflict further defeats on Bonaparte in the Assembly - what will he do?"

"We were talking about that as well," Trégonnec commented gruffly. "He has a history of attempted coups, at Strasbourg and Boulogne. If he tries another one, he will meet with the same response - decisive action by the military acting in accordance with their constitutional duty!"

"But he is no longer an adventurer returning from exile abroad, General. Now he is the President of France, elected by five and a half million of his countrymen. If the army has to choose between the President and the Assembly, can you be sure of the choice that it will make?"

The older man spluttered to reply. "I know the choice that I would make if I still held military command--"

"There's the rub, Alexandre," Lieusaint observed wearily. "You have left active service, so has Grandchamps, so has Vauzuron. Changarnier has been dismissed. Ultimate command rests with Saint-Arnaud, who is Bonaparte's creature. What can we expect?"

The exchange reduced Trégonnec to brooding silence. He shook his glass roughly and drained it in a single mouthful. D'Amboise watched him for a moment or two, seeing the doubts which the older man was unwilling to voice; then he spoke again. "Your mention of General Vauzuron reminds me of the conversation which I had with him here last week, when he told me of his concern about one of the captains of the Paris police. As it happens, I did see Prefect Maupas a day or two after that conversation, and I was able to pass on the General's concern. If you see him again, perhaps you would be good enough to let him know that I acted on his words." He smiled ingratiatingly.

Trégonnec grunted a response; he seemed still preoccupied with the questions which had been posed about the army's loyalties. Lieusaint was more attentive. "Alexandre may well talk to Vauzuron again shortly. I am unlikely to. But may I inquire further about your discussion with Maupas? He sees more of President Bonaparte than almost anyone. Did he give any indication of the way that the Presidential mind is working?"

D'Amboise sipped his cognac before replying. At the meeting of notables he had attended the week before, Maupas had been pressed to say what plans were being laid; but, with a glint in his eye, had limited himself to replying that "1852 will be a Happy New Year--". "No, gentlemen," d'Amboise commented now, "I am sure that Prefect Maupas knows a good deal more than he says. He must do, since he says almost nothing!"

"I'm not surprised," snorted Trégonnec. "If he opens his mouth, he's likely to put his foot in it!"

Only D'Amboise laughed at the remark. Lieusaint returned to the charge. "And how did he respond to Vauzuron's concern? Did he take an interest?"

"Oh, most assuredly, Monsieur de Lieusaint. He undertook to look into the matter. Indeed, he hinted that he was contemplating a number of changes among the higher echelons of the Paris police." D'Amboise gave a knowing look.

"Stuff and nonsense," Trégonnec interjected. "Probably intends to give positions to his relatives, or perhaps a bastard son or two!"

A note of reprimand crept into Lieusaint's voice. "Alexandre, I am no friend of Maupas, but we should not underestimate the man. Saint-Arnaud and Maupas are Bonaparte's two guard-dogs, and they are bound to want their own packs of curs under them. And it will not benefit their own families, but the Bonapartes!"

Trégonnec glowered at Lieusaint. "Must say, Godefroi, you and d'Amboise here have quite spoilt my evening!" He set his glass down on a side-table. "I'm feeling my age too. I must take my gloom to bed."

D'Amboise was on his feet in an instant. "I shan't impose on your hospitality any longer, General. I wish you goodnight, and to you as well, Monsieur de Lieusaint." He tipped his head towards them and left.

"Don't take it too hard, Alexandre," said Lieusaint as he finished his cognac and prepared to depart. "I may be taking too sombre a view of matters. We may well win the vote next week."

"We may," muttered Trégonnec. "We must! And we must keep our faith in the army. There are still some good men, as well as the men of straw like Saint-Arnaud. *Bon courage*, Godefroi!" He slapped him on the back, and saw him to the door.

***

Friday 14 November - morning

Ile de la Cité

Boizillac and Delourcq divided their forces again after their visit to Connassier's lodgings in the Petite Rue de l'Ambigu. The older agent redoubled his efforts with his underworld contacts to find out more about the two dead men and their associates. He went back to the *Enfer de Saint-Martin* before sunrise the next morning and tackled the landlord before the bar opened to its first customers of the day. He tried the other *cabarets* in the neighbourhood. And there was also the *Marché aux Vieux Linges* only a quarter of a mile away down the Rue du Temple. Delourcq had half-a-dozen informants among the stall-holders, barrow-boys and dust-collectors who made their living in the midst of the old clothes, bedding and furniture that were packed into the market. It was easy enough for him to snatch a few words with each of them, hidden behind the stacks of worn and shoddy goods being traded. Jattée's name was unknown at this northern edge of Paris, and the little that he heard about Connassier only reinforced what he already knew, that the man was a loner and a drinker liked by no-one.

Boizillac decided to take a different approach. The silk scarf left at Montfaucon had spoken to him of Algeria, even if he had received no confirmation from Vauzuron and his household. Now they had found a military identification number at Le Marais du Bièvre, which could surely be checked against the enrolment records of the Army. He knew that books with details of enrolments and discharges were kept at the Office of Military Registration, near the Champ de Mars. "A 35 1182" must denote the recruitment to the Algerian Army in 1835 of either Jattée or Connassier, and study of the Army's records might throw more light on the men and when they had returned to France.

But his visit to the Champs de Mars office was a waste of time. Arriving early on Wednesday afternoon, Boizillac had to wait for over an hour until the Registrar returned to his desk after an extensive lunch. The Registrar gave the young captain of police a mellow enough greeting at first, but assumed a stonier expression when it became clear that Boizillac wanted to look at the records for 1835, 1836 and 1837. It was impossible, he said. The books for those years were in poor condition, because of careless handling, and they were being re-bound at an army depot near Lille. He did not expect that they would be returned to Paris for some months, and they could be requisitioned for examination only on much higher authority than a captain of police. He was sorry, but there was nothing he could do. His eyelids closed, indicating an end to the discussion and a surrender to the torpor induced by his meal. Boizillac left in disgust.

Canler wanted their report on Friday. Boizillac spent most of the intervening day drawing up a full memorandum to present to his superior. After several false starts, he completed his manuscript as evening fell on the Thursday.

"Report on the Investigation by Captain Lucien de Boizillac and Monsieur Daniel Delourcq into the Circumstances Surrounding the Deaths Discovered at Montfaucon on 4 November 1851 and at the Abattoir de Villejuif on 10 November 1851, with Proposals for Further Investigation...

"I, Captain Lucien de Boizillac, Inspector of the Sûreté of Paris, was instructed to go to the Sewage Lagoon at Montfaucon on Tuesday 4 November 1851, to investigate the Discovery of a Corpse. I was joined in my Investigation by Monsieur Daniel Delourcq, also of the Sûreté. We were shown the Corpse of an Adult Male, who had been killed by stabbing, mutilated by the Removal of the Head and of the little Finger of the right Hand, and thrown into the Lagoon. Questions put to the Discoverer of the Corpse, Monsieur Jacques Meulnier, a Worker in the Knacker's Yard, and to Monsieur Alphonse Catelan, Yard Manager, were of little Avail save to prove that no-one had seen the Assassin responsible, and to indicate that Deposition of the Corpse had very likely happened during the preceding Night.

"Monsieur Delourcq also posed several Questions to Monsieur Gobillot, the Montfaucon Night-watchman, and his Sister. The Man Gobillot had failed to see any Intruder to the Yard (in my Opinion, because of Inebriation), but he had discovered a Scarf, stained with Blood, which he had given to his Sister. Examination of the Scarf showed that it was of an Arab Design. While I was unable to obtain an Opinion on the Origin of the Design from the Arab Servant of General Vauzuron, whom I consulted with the Agreement of the General, I believe from my own Experience gained there that the Scarf is of Algerian Origin, and that it was left at Montfaucon by the Assassin.

"On Monday 10 November 1851, I, with Monsieur Delourcq, was instructed to go to the Abattoir de Villejuif to investigate the Discovery of a second Corpse. After discussion with Monsieur Massenier, Manager of the Abattoir, we were directed to the Cemetery near the Barrière d'Italie, to which the Corpse had already been conveyed. We encountered there Monsieur Albert Dutoit, Stockhand at the Abattoir, and the Keeper of the Cemetery, Monsieur Saint-Pierre. The Corpse which we were shown was again that of an Adult Male who had suffered the same Fate as the Corpse deposited at Montfaucon, showing Stab Wounds and the Severing of the little Finger of the right Hand, save that the Head remained on the Body. Monsieur Dutoit explained that he had

disturbed an Intruder in the Stockyard during the previous Night in the Act of severing the Head. While Monsieur Dutoit had surprised the Assassin, he had been unable to see any of his Features before the Man fled in the Darkness.

"Information provided by Monsieur Dutoit enabled us to establish that the Victim deposited in the Abattoir de Villejuif was JEAN JATTEE, resident at Le Marais du Bièvre, in the XIIth Arrondissement. I and Monsieur Delourcq went to the Victim's House on the same day. I shall not dwell on the odious Circumstances of the Household, save to state that Jattée had kept a Number of Women and Children as Captives in his Power for his own unnatural Purposes. Our Examination of his private Rooms discovered all the Signs of a Death-Struggle with the Assassin who very likely forced an Entry into Jattée's Apartment through a Ceiling Window. We also discovered Papers revealing a financial Association with LOUIS CONNASSIER, and a military Identification Number indicating Service with the Army in Algeria.

"Monsieur Delourcq was able to determine that Connassier was resident in the Petite Rue de l'Ambigu, in the Faubourg Saint-Martin. On Wednesday 12 November, I, with Monsieur Delourcq, went to that Address. With the Assistance of Monsieur Gustave Taillefer, a Seine River Scavenger who had provided

Information about Connassier's Whereabouts, we inspected the Lodgings. We found no Occupant, but the Room again showed Signs of a violent Struggle, above all the Spilling of much Blood. Close Investigation revealed a severed Finger.

"The Housekeeper to the Lodgings is an Individual who goes by the Name of Gueule-de-Bois. The Questions which I put to him confirmed that he had last seen Connassier on Sunday 2 November, and that he had discovered his Lodgings in the State previously described on Wednesday 5 November. However, he was not able to shed any more Light on the Identity of the likely Murderer of Connassier.

"I draw the following Conclusions from my Investigation:

"primo, that the Corpse recovered from the Sewage Lagoon at Montfaucon was that of LOUIS CONNASSIER, who was murdered in his Lodgings in the Petite Rue de l'Ambigu on Sunday 2 or Monday 3 November;

"secundo, that Connassier was killed by the same Assassin who murdered JEAN JATTEE a week later, on Sunday 9 November, in his House at Le Marais du Bièvre, before depositing his Corpse at the Abattoir de Villejuif. In both Cases, Death was inflicted by Stab Wounds to the Heart, and accompanied by

Mutilation of the Corpses;

"tertio, that there was at least a financial Connection between Connassier and Jattée, which cannot at present be clarified;

"quarto, that either Connassier or Jattée (or Both) served in the Army in Algeria, and that their Murderer may have an Algerian Connection, which also cannot yet be clarified.

"I propose that the Investigation should be continued in order to resolve the Aspects so far unclarified. On the one Hand, Monsieur Delourcq should exploit his Contacts among the criminal Classes to gain more Information about the Victims and their Manner of Life. On the other, I should be granted Authorisation to study the Records kept by the Army relating to Connassier and Jattée, which may point to other Associates and possible Reasons for these recent Crimes.

"Signed, this thirteenth day of November 1851, by Captain Lucien de Boizillac, Inspector of the Sûreté of Paris."

Boizillac carried this rolled up memorandum in an inside pocket of his frock-coat as he met Delourcq at the Quai des Orfèvres on the Friday morning. Standing just inside the entrance doorway, he drew the scroll out and proffered it to the other man. "You'll want to see my report."

Delourcq glanced across without taking the paper in his hand. "If it's all the same, captain, I'll leave it with you. I read what I have to in this life, and that's little enough. It'd take me ten times as long to read your report as it took you to write it, and we wouldn't want to be standing here all morning. So you go ahead and present it to the boss, and I'll speak up when necessary."

Boizillac nodded briefly, then led the way into the building, still carrying the report in his hand. He strode eagerly towards the distant office. At the start of the week, Canler had been poised to end their investigation and assign them to other duties. But the second killing, which Boizillac was certain had been carried out by the same man, had stayed his hand. Now they had established who the two victims were, and that they were linked with one another. Canler would see that they were building a chain of discoveries which was bound to lead on to finding out who the killer was, if they were allowed to take their investigation even further - above all, if they were given access to the Army records.

The building was as gloomy as ever. They approached Canler's office. "Well, that's a first," Delourcq muttered. When Boizillac looked at him quizzically, he went on: "The empty desk. Every time I've been here before, that damned clerk's been sitting behind it."

They paused for a moment, but there was no sound of anyone approaching. There was no sound at all. "Well, we're expected," said Boizillac. "We'll go in." He knocked briefly on the door and stepped into the room.

It was empty. The maps hung on the walls, and the cabinets of papers were arrayed around the perimeter. But no candles burned on the desk at the centre of the room, and no-one sat in the chair behind it.

"It is Friday today, isn't it?" Boizillac asked his companion, who confirmed it. "I don't understand. We were told to report here today. What's happened?"

Just then they heard footsteps clattering along the corridor outside. The younger man went back to the door, as the clerk arrived, breathless and anxious. "Captain de Boizillac, I apologise for being late. I have a letter for you." He reached inside his coat and brought out a sealed paper, which he handed to the other man.

"A letter? From whom?"

"Monsieur Canler. I have come from his house, to deliver it to you."

"But why is Monsieur Canler not in his office?" Boizillac asked sharply.

The clerk lowered his voice almost to a whisper to reply. "This is no longer his office."

"What do you mean?"

"Yesterday afternoon Monsieur Canler was summoned to see Prefect Maupas, and returned here only to inform me that he had been dismissed as Head of the *Sûreté*."

"But how is that possible?" asked Boizillac.

The clerk shook his head. "I cannot answer your questions, Monsieur de Boizillac. Perhaps the letter can." He fell silent.

"Who's moving into this office?" Delourcq asked.

"I have not been told," the clerk replied. "Monsieur Canler has advised me to continue with my duties here--" and he pointed to his desk in the corridor, "until his successor arrives."

Boizillac broke the seal and scanned the letter.

> *"Monsieur de Boizillac*
>
> *"I regret that I cannot honour our Appointment and receive your Report today.*
>
> *"I have ceased to hold the Position of Head of the Sûreté de Paris. However, I consider it appropriate to address these Words to you.*
>
> *"I am aware of the Progress that you and Monsieur Delourcq have made in investigating the Deaths at Montfaucon and the Abattoir de Villejuif. I commend you both on your Zeal.*
>
> *"You will however recall that your Efforts have not been viewed with Approval on all Sides. I*

was reminded of the Concern expressed in this Respect during my final Interview with Prefect Maupas (although I assure you that this was an incidental Observation, unconnected with the Cessation of my Position).

"You will understand that, until my Successor has been able to review the Operations of the Sûreté in general and your own Activity in particular, the Continuation of your Investigation must be subject to Doubt. I must advise you to proceed with particular Circumspection.

"To be blunt, if you now continue, you and Delourcq act on your own Account!

"Signed, this fourteenth Day of November 1851, Paul-Louis-Alphonse Canler, Paris."

He looked from the letter to his companion. "Come, Delourcq, we are wasting our time here. What was the name of that bar - the *Chien Fou?* Let's have a drink there." He made his way out of the building even more rapidly than he had entered, Delourcq hurrying to keep up with him.

It took only a few minutes along the dank and muddy streets of the Ile de la Cité to reach the bar, but it was long enough for the younger man to relate the contents of Canler's letter. Delourcq stepped in off the street first and made sure that his usual table near the door was available. Ma Friche preened herself as she caught sight of Boizillac stepping in behind him. She bustled over. "Bring us some of the wine you keep for special occasions," Delourcq said, "and then leave us in peace."

"What are you gentlemen celebrating?"

"Only getting a bottle of wine out of you that hasn't been watered down! Just do as you're asked, and make sure we're not disturbed." She scowled at Delourcq, and went off.

Once she was out of earshot, Boizillac spoke. "How is it possible, Delourcq? How can Canler be dismissed, at a time like this? Does Maupas understand what the work of the Sûreté is?" He paused, considering his words. He brought his fist down on the table. "I must go and see him, and tell him that he's made a mistake."

There was alarm in Delourcq's eyes and in his voice. "Forgive me for speaking out of turn, captain, but I don't think that would be a good idea. And I doubt that Monsieur Canler would approve either. Doesn't he talk about 'circumspection' in his letter? I'm not sure what that means, but I don't think it covers rushing into the office of the Prefect of Police."

They fell silent as Ma Friche returned to their table and deposited two glasses and an opened bottle of red wine. Delourcq dropped a few coins into her outstretched hand, and she left them.

"Yes, you're right," said Boizillac more calmly, as the other man filled the glasses. "But Canler has been done a dreadful injustice."

His companion took a first mouthful. "I doubt that you need worry about the Chief. He's done thirty years' service in the Prefecture. He must have seen scores of others come and go. He won't be surprised by his interview with Prefect Maupas."

"And what of us?" asked the younger man. "I thought that we would get Canler's agreement to taking our investigation one step further. And now he has told us to stop."

"Ah, but has he?"

Boizillac gave Delourcq a questioning look, then drew the letter out of his pocket and repeated to its final sentence: "To be blunt, if you now continue, you and Delourcq act on your own account!"

The older man contemplated his wine glass as he spoke. "Doesn't sound to me as if he's telling us to stop, only that we'll be acting on our own." He looked up. "I'm a bit more familiar with Monsieur Canler than you, captain, given the years he and I worked together. If he wanted something done, or not done, he said so straight out." He drank. "I reckon it's up to us to decide if we continue, or wait for the new man to tell us what to do."

Boizillac scanned the letter again. " 'If you now

continue--' " There was a gleam in his eye. "My decision is to go on. What's yours?"

"The same." He raised his glass. "To Monsieur Canler."

Boizillac smiled. "To Canler - and the success of our investigations!" They drained their glasses. The younger man's face fell. "But without Canler's approval, I shan't be able to study Army records."

"There must be other ways of skinning the cat," Delourcq commented. "Perhaps I'll find something more out about Algeria by talking to my contacts. And you, captain, surely you have former colleagues from the Army you could consult, apart from General Vauzuron?"

"Nicolas," the other man said. "One of my fellow lodgers in the Rue du Bac, Delourcq. He's spoken to me several times about the serving officers he regularly meets. I'll ask him. Your good health!"

By the time they finished the wine, Boizillac had recovered from the shock of Canler's disappearance, and was eager to press ahead. They parted company in the middle of the morning. Delourcq went to see if he could squeeze any more information out of the ranks of the underworld, Boizillac to wait in his lodgings until noon when Nicolas de Montholon returned from the Faubourg-Saint-German riding-school where he taught horseback skills to the sons and daughters of the old nobility. They agreed to meet again in the bar the following Monday.

It was doubly fortunate that Boizillac was in the house when Montholon returned. In the first place, the other man spent no longer in his rooms than it took to change his waistcoat and breeches, before leaving again to take lunch with an uncle who was a serving colonel in the Army with experience of Algeria in the 1830s. Montholon undertook to see whether he could help Boizillac towards the information he needed. In the second place, Montholon explained that Delphine had thrown him over the previous night, but not before she had passed on a note from Laure, which, smiling wryly, he gave to Boizillac. Slapping him on the shoulder, he was gone.

"Lucien - how long this week has been - come to my apartment at eleven o'clock on Friday night - 73, Rue du Saumon - Laure."

Boizillac stared at the note for some time. A bell tolling the quarter hour forced the realisation that he still had to wait almost half the day until he would see her again. He passed the afternoon riding his horse across Paris and back, going as far as Montfaucon in the north and the Barrière d'Italie in the south. He told himself that he was taking an opportunity to look again at the scenes of the crimes, but in fact it was no more than an attempt to speed the passage of the hours. In the early evening, he returned to the Rue du Bac. When Nicolas also returned, they shared a bottle of wine. His uncle had not recognised the names of the dead men, but would let Nicolas know in due course if he could discover anything. Lucien declined an invitation to join Nicolas for a meal in a restaurant near the Place de l'Odéon. He forced himself to read further in his books of military campaigns until the time came to see Laure.

Chapter Nine

Friday 14 November - late evening

Rue du Saumon

Lucien's impatience decided him to go on foot to the Rue du Saumon.

He stepped out of his lodgings shortly after ten. The fog was so thick and cold that it felt more like swimming through a channel of spume than walking along streets. The oil-lamps strung overhead burnt feebly, their light obscured by the dank breath of the city. The few carriages about emerged suddenly from the vaporous darkness, trailing streamers of fog behind them, clattered past, and were swallowed up again, sight and sound blanketed by the night air.

He followed the left bank of the river as far as the Pont-Neuf. As he crossed, he could sense rather than see the huge bulk of the Préfecture de Police and the Palais de Justice to the right. The mass of water flowing on either side of the Ile de la Cité could only be glimpsed through breaks in the wet gusts that it exhaled; but even at this late hour, when the city seemed to shiver under the first onset of winter, he could hear the sounds of oars in the water and boats creaking. He thought of Taillefer, perhaps plying his trade of scavenger even now. This must be a fruitful stretch of the river for him. Just a short way upstream was the pool formed by the Pont-au-Change and the

Pont-Notre-Dame, where the current was at its fastest. It was a place favoured by suicides - and perhaps by murderers. Anyone who entered the water there was dragged down and thrown up again only when all signs of life had been thrashed out of them.

But Lucien's route ran further northwards, along the Rue de la Monnaie, past the church of Saint-Eustache, and into the Rue Montmartre. There was more traffic here, and the movement seemed to have dispersed some of the fog. A couple of young men, their shirts open at the neck and wearing light jackets despite the evening, stumbled out of a side-street and bumped into him drunkenly. They spun into the carriageway and were lucky not to be run down by a barouche that sped past; then they were gone.

He reached the Rue du Saumon. It linked the Rue Montmartre with the Rue Montorgueil and, although he had often enough ridden along the two larger streets, he had never noticed this link before. It was lined with good, solid houses that gave off the same air of shared respectability that was no doubt displayed by the merchants and manufacturers who had made their homes there over the past thirty years. Flights of steps led up from the muddy streets to the front doors, below three or four rows of windows now hidden behind tightly closed shutters. It was just before eleven when Lucien turned into the street. It looked as though all the residents had already retired for the night.

Number 73 was at the further end. He paused in front of it to check that this was the right address.

Something dropped out of the sky, brushed his sleeve and fell to the ground. It was a bouquet. He looked up. At the very top of the house a figure was leaning out of a window. The dim light from the room behind made little impression on the darkness and the fog, but Lucien knew that it was Laure, even though all he could see was a silhouette.

She spoke only one word, and it was unmistakable: "Catch!" Something dropped from her extended hand. Lucien obeyed instinctively - and found a key in his hand. Laure gestured that he should let himself in, then disappeared from view. He glanced around him and, reassured that no-one had seen this nocturnal charade, hurried up the steps, unlocked, slipped through the doorway, and locked again quickly behind him.

He was almost completely unsighted. If there was a concierge in this house, she must have fallen asleep and failed to keep the lights burning. But even as he stood with his back to the door, trying to accustom his eyes, the darkness began to break up. A flickering light could be seen, coming down the stairwell at the end of the hall where he stood. Then Laure herself appeared, her face glowing in the light from the candle. She leaned over the banister rail at the turn of the stairs, and waved to him, without speaking. He walked across the hall - only to see her start away and run up the stairs ahead of him. Caught by her impulse, he gave chase. There were four flights; he had on a heavy frock-coat and boots; she wore only a freely flowing dress and satin slippers; and it was only on the top landing, as she made a show of setting her candle down on a small table outside her door, that he drew alongside her. She spun round as he rushed up, laughing at their exertions; and, before he could speak, she pressed one finger to his lips - then kissed him. It lasted no more than a few seconds, but it answered the all-important question that had been in both their minds.

She took his arm and led him inside her apartment. Tucked under the roof of the house, its ceiling was too low for a man as tall as Lucien. But the apartment was not a place for standing. Off to the left of the entrance corridor were a bathroom and a bedroom; to the right was a living-room, into which Laure now guided Lucien. There were two chaises-longues placed at right angles to each other; Lucien could see that Laure must have stood on the one below the window to spot him in the street below. The chairs were buried under a mass of rugs and cushions, which also spilt across the carpeted floor. All the fabrics favoured burgundy. A fire burned in the small hearth and spread more warmth into the radiant setting.

"This is my little nest in the sky, Lucien. More suited to a song-bird than an eagle, but it's comfortable, isn't it?"

Lucien compared it in his mind with the rigours of army accommodation, and with the cold simplicity of his own lodgings. He unbuttoned his coat against the heat. "It's charming, Laure." She took the coat from him, and hung it up. He saw another man's cloak on a hook. "Whose is that?" His voice sounded sharper than he had intended.

Laure looked at him. "The cape? It belongs to my 'uncle'." She paused briefly before speaking the last word.

Lucien gazed round the room. "And does this apartment also belong to him?"

"No, Lucien, it is mine." She still stood apart from him. "But he bought it and gave it to me."

"And what do you give him in return?"

She took his hand. "I know what you are thinking, Lucien, but I promise you that it isn't like that between us. My 'uncle' is more than twice your age. He is no longer interested in the pleasures of the flesh."

"Then what is he interested in? What reason does he have for supporting you?"

"He tells me that he just wants a friend. His wife died four or five years ago, and he says that he doesn't want to marry again - too many financial complications, he says. So he comes here most evenings, after the theatre, and sits beside me on the sofa, and tells me about his business - banking. And sometimes he falls asleep here, and lets himself out early the next morning. But mostly he drives off around midnight, back to his own house in Saint-Germain."

"And what are your - feelings for him?"

She glanced down for a moment. "I am grateful to him." She looked back at Lucien suddenly, and her eyes were blazing. "Without him I could be living in a cellar again, sharing my bedding with rats and lice, and at the mercy of any vile-tempered drunkard who stumbled in looking for somewhere to relieve himself. That was how I used to live, Lucien, and he saved me from returning to it!" Her voice became calmer. "So I am grateful. And he is a kind man, and gentle. He sits here and drinks a glass or two of wine, and then goes."

"So - is he a friend?"

"What do you call someone who gives you shelter, food and drink? Yes, he is a friend." There was a blankness in Lucien's eyes, as uncertainty drove out his initial enthusiasm. She cupped his face in her hands. "But you are my love." Their mouths met; her arms were around him; his doubts dissolved, and he embraced her.

When their passion had run its course, and they lay together in the bedroom, Laure sensed anxiety in the gaze which Lucien directed at her. "What is it, *mon cher*? Aren't you happy now we know each other?"

He kissed her again. "I'm sorry, Laure. I am happier with you than I have ever been in my life. But - I am worried. Worried about what is going to happen in Paris, and in France."

"You mean Bonaparte and the rest of them?"

She laughed. "They are all better comedians than I am. It's just a great spectacle for the benefit of the public."

"No, it's much more serious than that. They sacked the Head of the *Sûreté* today, the man to whom I report." He told Laure all that had happened during the preceding week. "But I don't want to give up my investigation, in spite of everything. Delourcq and I have already discovered so much about the two victims. If only I could learn more about their time in Algeria, I'm sure that we would get nearer to their murderer."

Laure was silent for a few seconds. "Perhaps I can help."

"You? What do you mean?"

"Well, not me exactly, but someone I know." She held his hand. "Lucien, you must promise not to betray this confidence."

"I do." He would have promised her anything.

"It is Marc, my brother. I know a little of what he does these days. I cannot tell you much, but he was in Algeria for many years - and he has made it his task to gather information about the Army in Algeria and those who served in it." She saw the puzzlement in Lucien's look. "He did not return from Algeria with pride in *la patrie*, as you did, Lucien. And what he does now puts him at risk of persecution from the servants of the State - from the police, like yourself. But, if you give me your word that you will not inform on him, I shall see if he can help you."

"But of course I give my word." He looked at her in admiration. "What a wonder you are, what a --" His words were lost as she pulled him to herself, and their bodies joined.

Chapter Ten

Saturday 15 November - evening

The Elysée Palace

"I still cannot be certain that the time has come!" His heavy-lidded eyes were fixed on the fire burning in the hearth, but his words were addressed to the listeners in his study. He fell silent again. His mind went back, beyond the last three years when he had been the head of state elected by popular will, to his long exile, his imprisonment, and the botched attempts to seize power in Strasbourg and Boulogne. Three years of power, after forty years of humiliation. He needed longer, he deserved longer to redress the balance, to re-unite the fortunes of his family and of his country. But was there no way other than force, and was there no time other than now?

"What further sign do you need?" Persigny spluttered with impatience. "Now that the Assembly has made their contempt for you crystal clear, why delay any longer? In two days' time they will vote to give themselves the right of command over the armed forces."

"The Army will never obey those prating lawyers!" The President's hooded gaze turned momentarily towards the speaker, a tall, slender man whose thinning hair had been groomed round his temples like a laurel-wreath. It was Saint-Arnaud, his own choice as head of the armed forces. "The Army recognises only one commander-in-chief, and he is here in this room." He bowed towards the figure in the fireside chair.

"How can you know the minds of all your officers, Saint-Arnaud?" The anxiety which Persigny felt made him even more careless with his words than usual. "And how can you be sure that none of them have had their pockets lined by the royalists? Hasn't military honour been measured in gold coins for the past thirty years?"

Saint-Arnaud flushed. "Whom do you have in your sights, sir?"

"Gentlemen, don't allow the pressures of the day to distort your judgement. We all know of the efforts which General Saint-Arnaud has undertaken to strengthen the loyalty of the Army. I raise my glass to him, and so should you, Persigny." Morny's glass caught the light of the fire as he sipped his cognac, and his cold gaze lay on Persigny as he reluctantly followed suit. "But our opponents in the Assembly will not win a majority again on Monday, not for this proposition."

"Are you sure, brother?" He had the President's attention.

"Yes, I am sure. I know them all. They may have felt bold enough to reject universal suffrage, even if they have done no more than build a sand-castle against the tide. But they will not dare to stand against the head of state, by setting their own private army against him. No, General, your men will not be required to face such a test of loyalty."

"So the need to act is not pressing..."

Persigny slammed his glass down on the desk. "No, no, you are playing into their hands. The longer we delay, the better our opponents will organise themselves."

"We have six weeks, gentlemen," said Morny. "The intelligence obtained by Monsieur de Maupas' agents shows that both sides - Ultras and Jacobins - are gathering their strength for action in the New Year. Nothing will happen in the next forty-eight hours."

"Then *we* must act before Christmas!" Persigny exclaimed. This time, Morny's only rejoinder was to incline his head briefly.

"Before Christmas," the President intoned. "Let it be so."

***

Sunday 16 November - evening

The Church of Saint-Jean-des-Champs

The fields where the Church of Saint-Jean had been built in the days of Louis XIV had long since disappeared under the bricks and mortar of the East End of Paris. On three sides it was hemmed in by the clutter and grime of the habitations of the poor, hastily built tenements that compressed sixty people into a space occupied by a single family in the Faubourg Saint-Germain. Until the turn of the century, the eastern end of the church had been spared encroachment; but then the remaining open space was sacrificed to a new, industrial temple, a tanning factory to produce the leather demanded in ever greater quantities by the capital. The spire of Saint-Jean still overtopped the factory chimneys, but it was the stench of the tanning process that spread through the streets, not ecclesiastical incense. And it seemed as though, when the tannery was built, it had blocked off more than the light from the east; even as the population of the *quartier de Saint-Jean* doubled and doubled again, the congregation of the church dwindled until the only ones left were the old women who could remember how it had been "before the factory".

"Lucien - go to confession at Saint-Jean-des-Champs, at six in the evening on Sunday - my brother can help you - with all my heart - Laure"

He had left the Rue du Saumon early on Saturday morning, and spent most of the day riding. The note was under his door when he returned to his lodgings in the Rue du Bac in the late afternoon. Now he stood inside Saint-Jean-des-Champs, making out the interior in the light thrown by the candles that burnt on stands around the nave and at either side of the altar. Lucien looked at the bronze figure of Christ; the suffering head seemed to him to be bent further forward than other representations he knew, the arms and shoulders to be twisted even more painfully. He could hear a low muttering, and he traced it to a huddle of shawl-clad figures who sat at the back of the church; their heads bowed, they recited the prayers of their youth. He could see no other living souls there.

The view of the altar was framed by two huge stone pillars which rose up at either side of the nave. Each supported a statue some fifteen feet above the ground, illuminated by a primitive chandelier that was raised and lowered on a rope that was lashed to a large iron ring set in the floor. The statue to the left was Saint-Jean, a bearded figure in dark, flowing robes who held a Bible in one hand and a sickle in the other. The pillar to the right supported the Virgin Mary; the whiteness of her robes could just be glimpsed under the soot of the centuries; and her hands were outstretched, as though beckoning to anyone who stepped into the church. At the base of the pillar stood the church's confessional boxes. Lucien walked across the flagged floor, his steps echoing through the void. The old women paid him no heed; he felt quite isolated, in this strange relic of an older Paris.

The confessional box had no ceiling; the flickering candles above the Virgin's head sent their uncertain light down; Lucien could see that the stones of the floor had been worn away by the knees of the devout, he could see that the wooden partition between the two cubicles had been darkened and streaked by the fingers of the poor as they pressed against the grille to unburden themselves of their sins.

"Boizillac?" The voice that spoke through the grille was soft and urgent.

"Who are you?"

"Carreleur. Are you alone?"

"Yes. Are you the priest here?"

There was a snort. "No. If you want the priest, you'll have to wait until tomorrow, when he's slept off the communion wine."

"We should not abuse the church like this. Come, we can go to an inn..."

"Stay where you are!" Carreleur did not raise his voice, but the peremptory tone was unmistakable. "You have won my sister's trust, but not mine. You can hear my voice, but you may not see my face."

Lucien stayed where he was. "Why? What do you fear?"

"You, and your kind - police, militia, all the lackeys of the state whose job it is to fight against the 'red spectre'. For that is the cause I serve, the cause that believes that every man has the right to a vote and the right to enjoy the fruits of his labour. And we believe that the same rights apply to the people of Algeria as to the people of France, and that the occupation of Algeria by the French Army is a crime which must be ended as soon as possible!" A passion had crept into his voice. He was silent for a moment or two, then continued more evenly: "Do you understand why I don't want to be seen drinking in a bar with a *commissaire de police*?"

"Laure told me nothing about this. Why are you prepared to help me?"

"It's Jattée you're asking about, isn't it? Jattée and Connassier? They were the biggest swine in the Algerian Army. As much as I hate this Government and all its henchmen, I hate those bastards and their kind even more. I'll tell you what I know about them so that, for once, the police can pick on the real villains."

"Laure must have told you that Jattée and Connassier are dead. I am investigating their murders, not any crimes they may have committed in Algeria. I want to find out who killed them, and that's why I need to know about their past."

"She told me. Understand this, Boizillac, I am talking to you today because Laure asked me to. We shall not meet again. I expect you to get to the source of these murders, no matter where that is. If I learn that you have given up - and you may be tempted to, I suspect - I shall use my influence with my sister to end your friendship. Do not doubt that I can."

Lucien bridled at the threat. "Are you telling me how I should conduct a police investigation? You have no right to do so!"

Carreleur waited for a few moments before replying. "I take lectures on my rights from no-one. Think carefully, Boizillac. Either you accept what I say, or our conversation ends now."

Lucien controlled his anger. It went against all his instincts to acknowledge the authority of a man who, by his own admission, was working against the military and civil powers of France. But Carreleur was Laure's brother; and it was clear that his understanding of her, as well as his knowledge of the men who had been murdered in Paris in the previous fortnight, were vastly superior to Lucien's. "I accept. Tell me what you know."

"I enlisted in 1836. I was too young according to the register of births, but I was tall for my age, and that was all that counted.

"Within six months I was shipped out to Algeria. There was snow on the barrack roof in Mélun when I left, but when I arrived in North Africa the sun was hot enough to blister my back. For the first few months, I thought that Algiers was paradise. It didn't last.

"Jattée was on the quartermaster's staff, at the regimental barracks. It's the best part of fifteen years since I first encountered him, but even now I can see those small black eyes and that puffy pink face, and his fat grasping hands. My sergeant warned me to keep clear of his hands - Jattée had a fondness for new recruits. So I knew what thoughts lay behind his gloating look, and kept my distance.

"My sergeant told me that Jattée was scum, and the lowest of the low. When I asked why no-one disciplined him, he said that Jattée was given special treatment because he had been a member of an Army patrol that was ambushed by Arab bandits. As a result, Jattée was invalided out of combat duties, and given an easy number in the stores. The sergeant was a simple enough man, but even he found it hard to believe that Jattée could have shown any courage under fire."

"How many men were in the patrol?" Lucien asked.

"I'll tell you." As the police agent strained to hear, he realised that the church was completely silent. The old women had stopped their muttering, and left. "There were five of them. Jattée, Connassier and one other private, all of whom were on mules; a sergeant, Beaupré, and a captain, Rousseau, both on horseback. They were transporting gold and silver coin from Algiers to Oran; the sacks were on the mules, Rousseau was at the front and Beaupré brought up the rear."

"A small enough escort for the coin."

"It wasn't unusual at that time. The smaller the numbers, the less likely they were to be spotted by the Arabs. But this time things went wrong. They were attacked some two or three hours' ride out of Algiers. Rousseau and Beaupré were killed, and their bodies hacked to pieces. The sacks of coins were taken. Jattée and the other two were wounded, but escaped back to Algiers by abandoning the mules and riding the dead men's horses. Jattée said that the Arabs had come at them from behind and shot Beaupré, who fell from his horse, dead. Rousseau rode back to them and dismounted, and then took a fatal blow. Connassier, who had a head wound, took Rousseau's horse; Jattée, who was hit in the left arm, took Beaupré's mount and carried the third man over the saddle."

"And yet he outran the Arabs?"

"He said that, once they got their hands on the gold and silver, they lost interest in the Frenchmen. The Army sent out a punishment patrol to pursue the attackers, but all they found were the remains of Rousseau and Beaupré. The tracks were lost in the desert, and the coins never came to light. So Jattée was transferred to quartermaster's duties, Connassier to the canteen squad, and Estève became a medical orderly."

"Estève was the third man?"

"*Les trois sodomites*, they became known as. After they had been transferred from combat duties, they spent more time indulging their vices than serving the cause of the Army. They publicly displayed their kinship by wearing a ring on the little finger of their right hand." Lucien saw again in his mind's eye the mutilated hands of the corpses. "And yet they were never reprimanded. It was if there was an invisible power that protected them.

"I stayed in Algeria for ten years. I saw the corruption in the Army and the way that the people and the produce of the country were abused and exploited, not to improve the lot of my compatriots back in France, but to swell the fortunes and the stomachs of the bastards at all levels of the French Army. But no-one was more corrupt than those three perverts. I was pleased when they finally returned to France, in 1845; the air in the Algiers barracks was a little less polluted. I came home in 1847.

"It's only since I came back that I have found out the truth about the ambush in 1836, and about so many other things that happened out there. When the meetings began here in Paris in 1848 and the people kicked out that fool of a king, I discovered that there were other ex-soldiers who were as sickened as me by what had gone on. Our meetings turned into an intelligence network, to share knowledge of what had been done in the name of France. So I was able to piece together the truth.

"Jattée, Connassier and Estève escaped because they were in league with their attackers. Jattée shot Beaupré, and took his horse. Rousseau fired off a couple of shots, which hit Jattée and Connassier, before they did for him as well. It was only then that they gave the signal and their Arab accomplices rode up to finish the work. Connassier roughed Estève up, so that it looked as though he had been beaten by the attackers. They left the sacks of coins with the Arabs, and then rode back to Algiers. I imagine that the butchering the bodies was done by the Arabs; Jattée may have been vicious enough to do it, but he was also very lazy.

"To avoid suspicion, none of the three sodomites could benefit from the gold and silver so long as they stayed in North Africa. But somehow, they arranged for their share to be transported to France, and when they came back in 1845 it was waiting for them. I discovered that all three of them had settled in big houses in the provinces when they first returned, trying to conceal their real identities. But the lure of Paris was too strong for two of them. Within twelve months Jattée sold up and moved to the XIIth *arrondissement* - into that vile place near the Bièvre - and Connassier quickly followed suit. And once they were back in Paris, they made no attempt to hide their real names."

"And Estève?"

"He's been cleverer than the other two. He had a place near Rouen, and was known as Stevane. Then he moved, a year or two ago. My network has no more intelligence about him."

"Near Rouen? Do you know exactly where?"

"Lyons-la-Forêt. But he may be here in Paris now, or he may have gone to the Devil. He hasn't been heard of for eighteen months."

"I shall have to find him. Either he is at risk of being murdered as well - or he may have done the first two killings."

"But there were other accomplices too. Until you find them, you cannot be sure of the truth."

"Who do you mean?"

"Why do you think that Jattée and the other got away with their vices? How do you imagine the transport of the gold and silver back to France was arranged? How could three soldiers of the lowest rank set up an ambush like that, and keep the truth hidden for nearly ten years, unless they were being helped by someone at a high level?"

Even as Lucien heard these words, he realised that Carreleur must be right. It was not difficult for him to think of the commanders and generals whose backs had been ramrod straight, and whose frames had been lean and spare, when they arrived in North Africa - and when they returned to France some years later were as soft and plump as suckling pigs. But would they have connived in the murder of their own officers? Would his own general have sacrificed him for a sack of gold?

"And you have no thoughts about who may have helped them?"

"No, that secret has been too well hidden. I hope that you do find Estève, and that he tells you the secret. But there may be little time left."

"And there is no more that you have to tell me?"

"Not about these men. There are many other crimes committed by the Army in Africa that I know of, and they will be revealed when the time is right. But that is not now."

Lucien reflected for a moment. "This network of yours - does it have intelligence about my service in Algeria as well?"

"It does. I made sure to check. I know that your service was honourable, according to the tests which the Army applies to such matters, and that, even if you were no friend of the Arabs, you did not treat them like beasts, in the manner of most of your fellow officers. But you are still the prisoner of your upbringing, Boizillac Your mind cannot escape beyond the bars of your cell, even though you do not see them - and unless you see them, you will never understand that the rules by which you live are simply the means by which the gaoler keeps you under his thumb."

"You confuse me. Who is the gaoler?"

"Who gets most benefit from the police's protection of people and property? Who derives greatest advantage from the offices of state? Who grows richest on the dealings of the banks? They are your gaolers."

"You're a dangerous man, Carreleur. Are there many who think like you?"

"Not enough for my wishes. But too many for

yours!"

"Well," said Lucien, "I thank you for the information which you have given me, and which I shall act on. But, although I shall do nothing against you, I cannot hope that you succeed in your endeavours."

"No, you cannot. Not until you see the bars of your cell. Now go. I shall wait until your feet have carried you back into the city. Then I shall leave." He said no more.

Lucien stepped out of the confessional into the silence, solitude, and deepening darkness. He left the church, with Carreleur's ideas flickering inside his mind like the flames of the candles hanging in the vault.

***

Monday 17 November - morning

Ile de la Cité

Lucien was late for his rendezvous with Delourcq. They had agreed to meet in the *Chien Fou* at eight on Monday morning, but Lucien had slept badly again. He had been troubled by a recurring dream in which he was alone in the immense darkness of a cathedral; he could hear footsteps behind him; and, although he saw no-one, the sound filled him with a panic fear that left him awake, and gasping for breath.

Delourcq was sipping at his wine when the younger man came in and sat at the same table. He saw the paleness of his expression. "Are you well, captain?" He poured a second glass and offered it to the newcomer.

Lucien drank unthinkingly, winced, and drank again. "Very well, Delourcq. At last, I've got some solid information about Jattée and Connassier." He recounted his conversation in the church of Saint-Jean-des-Champs.

Delourcq listened carefully. "I've never heard of this Carreleur, your informant, and I thought that I knew most of these types. How did you come across him, captain?"

"He's the brother of -- a young woman that I know."

Delourcq was watching Boizillac's face. "You trust the young woman.. But do you think you can trust her brother?"

Lucien played with his wine for a few seconds. "Can you trust hatred, Delourcq?"

"Hatred, captain?" The older man thought for a moment. "There've been plenty of examples of hatred in my lifetime. But the one that always stays in my mind is Ney - 'the brave of the brave', a man who would have died twenty times in battle if he hadn't had the luck of the devil. He was lucky to the end, until the

Emperor was finally defeated and sent into exile. And then, while the rest of us hid away until the King and all his family got over the shock of being back at Versailles, the hatred of the Bourbons saw to it that Ney was locked up in the Conciergerie, put on trial, and found guilty of treason. Two weeks before Christmas 1815, they took him out through the south gates of the Luxembourg gardens, stood him in front of a brick wall that had been built for the purpose, and riddled him with bullets." He drained his glass. "So, yes, true hatred you can trust."

"And I trust Carreleur's hatred of the *trois sodomites*. In fact, I think that I have come to share it."

"Well, captain, you've done better than me. I've found out nothing I didn't already know. But I've a mind to go and talk to Taillefer again."

"The river scavenger?"

"Yes. He knew where Connassier lived here in Paris. I reckon it'd be worth asking him if he knows anything about this Stevane, or Estève, whichever he calls himself."

"Agreed. But I don't think that he's likely to spare me the trouble of making the journey to Rouen, to make some inquiries locally."

The finished their wine. Delourcq left some coins on the table and nodded to Ma Friche as he followed the younger man out into the chill morning air. It was a brisk thirty minutes' walk to the Pont de Grainmont. They used the Pont Notre Dame to reach the right bank of the Seine, then walked upstream along the Quai de la Grève and the Quai des Ormes until they reached the Quai Morland. This was the point where the turgid flood of the Seine washed against the point of the Ile St. Louis and broke in two. But between the Ile St Louis and the outflow of the Bassin de l'Arsenal into the river there was still a smaller eyot, the Ile Louvier, separated from the Quai Morland by a narrow trench of leachate from the main flow. The Pont de Grainmont was the only solid link between the quay and the islet, which served as a wood-yard to central Paris.

A wagon loaded with roughly cut timber was negotiating its way off the islet as Boizillac and Delourcq approached. The two draught-horses advanced slowly over the cobbles of the bridge, and the wagon swayed from side to side. The timber had been piled up higher than the head of the driver who stood with the reins in his hands, shouting at the horses. As they turned right on to the quay, the load shifted and half a dozen lengths of wood clattered to the ground. The driver halted, jumped down cursing, and retrieved the fallen cargo.

"So where do we find Taillefer?" Lucien asked.

"We need to be nearer the river than this," Delourcq replied. The Quai Morland was some twenty feet above the surface of the water. Pegged into the slime-covered wall of the embankment was a descending line of stone sills; hanging next to them was a sodden, but solid, rope. Looking down, Lucien saw that they led to a craft that was floating in the trench; it had the hull of a barge, but the superstructure had been built up into a shack. There was a chimney, out of which smoke was billowing. "That's Taillefer's place. You can see what's happened to some of the timber from the Ile Louvier!"

Remembering his previous meeting with the old man, Lucien commented: "A man with a bad leg could never make his way up and down these steps."

"Shall we call him up here?"

"The man's twice my age!" Lucien exclaimed. "If he can do it, so can I. And besides, I'd like to see inside this floating palace of his. Come on."

He started down the steps. He regretted his enthusiasm almost at once; his long coat and boots were ideal for riding a horse, and adequate for walking the streets of the city; they had not been conceived for scuttling spider-like down a dank embankment wall. He gripped the rope firmly with one gloved hand, while the other held to the sill above as he moved slowly downwards. Delourcq watched until the younger man was at the bottom; took a mouthful from his flask; then followed him. It was not the first time that he had made this descent but, as before, he breathed a silent prayer of thanks when he completed it unscathed.

There was a door in the side of the shack that faced them. Lucien knocked on it, and pulled on the handle. It was locked. "There's no-one here, Delourcq."

The older man leaned against the wooden parapet that ran round the edge of the barge's deck and cupped his left hand to his ear. "Soon will be, captain."

Boizillac became aware of a rhythmic splashing, and the creak of a pair of oars. He looked upstream, through the frame of the Pont de Grainmont. Slowly a dark shape formed in the grey mist hanging under the bridge, and a small boat slid steadily towards them, propelled by the powerful arms of Taillefer. "Good morning," Delourcq shouted to him.

An answering call of "Good morning to you and your young friend, Dédé!" came back at once, though the oarsman did not pause or turn his head to look at them.

"Did you tell him we would come?" asked Lucien.

Delourcq shook his head. "Look at the stern of his rowboat, where the lantern is hanging. You see the mirror fixed there as well?"

Taillefer was alongside now. He shipped his oars, called out: "Can you catch a mooring rope, captain?" and, without waiting for a reply, tossed a hawse at the young man. "Tie it to the pin at the far end of the barge - and you, Dédé, catch this!" He hefted a wet sack over the parapet which landed at Delourcq's feet; water ran across the deck. Then, with a suddenness which took both of the agents by surprise, he swung himself aboard, took the mooring rope from Lucien, who had not moved since the rowboat came into sight, and made it tight at the bow.

"How was your night's fishing?" asked Delourcq, with a smile.

Taillefer returned to stand by them on the deck. "I'll show you." He untied the sack and pulled his catch out of it - a man's overcoat, that was completely water-logged.

"You found this in the river?" the younger man asked.

"I find everything in the river, captain. Food, drink, clothing, friendship, hope - and despair - it's all in the river. I found this last night just a boat length beyond the Pont-au-Change." The coat had been doubled over to fit in the sack; Taillefer held the collar and let it fall open full-length. The front was slashed in several places. "Whoever was wearing this seems to have snagged it on a thorn-bush."

"Those cuts weren't made by a thorn-bush. What else did you find? Did you take this off a body?"

"Calm yourself, captain. Whoever owned this coat was separated from it long before I fished it out of the river. I never rob the dead - Dédé knows me better than that. All these pockets are already empty, so the only value to be got out of this coat is at the Temple market - unless you'd like to buy it, Dédé. It looks better than what you're wearing!" Delourcq spat over the side of the barge. "But come now, I can show you more hospitality than this." Leaving the coat on the deck, he took a key from one of his pockets and unlocked the shack door. "Come inside and warm yourselves at the stove".

As flimsy as Taillefer's lodgings looked from the outside, Lucien and Delourcq realised as they stepped into the warm and dim interior that the outer structure of planks was reinforced by an inner wall of sturdy panels. An iron stove stood in the middle of the enclosed space; Taillefer swung open the grille and threw on to the glowing coals inside two or three off-cuts of wood from a pile in the corner. There were no windows; he lit the wick of an oil-lamp that hung from the ceiling, and its glow pushed back the darkness in the room. There was a simple table and two chairs. Otherwise the place was bare, except that at intervals round the wooden walls hung some half a dozen leather pouches; there was a loaf of bread in one; a bottle of wine in a second; and a third held a tin of tobacco, which Taillefer now took to fill the pipe which he put in his mouth.

"Sit down, gentlemen." He gestured to the two chairs. "I've had enough sitting for the moment. I'll stand, and smoke my pipe, while you tell me what's brought you here." The room filled up with fumes from stove and pipe. "But if you've got your flask inside your coat, Dédé, it would be a kindness if you'd share it with me."

Lucien had been taking in the surroundings. "You say you find everything in the river - but there is next to nothing here. Have you had no success of late?"

Taillefer smiled. "Look over there, captain --" and he used his pipe to point to the far corner of the room. "Can you make out the trapdoor in the floor? That's the way down to the hatch below - and that's where I keep my findings. But I've nothing to hide, not from you and Dédé at least. I'm happy to show you down there.".

Delourcq passed his flask to Taillefer. "There's another name we wanted to ask you about - Estève, or maybe Stevane. The captain has found out that he was an associate of Connassier and Jattée ten years ago, when they were all in the Army in Algeria. Does the name mean anything to you?"

"Never heard it before. Does he live in Paris now?"

"It's possible, but we can't be sure. He was last heard of living near Rouen, a couple of years ago. Since then he seems to have disappeared."

Taillefer drew on his pipe. "I'm sorry to disappoint the captain and yourself, Dédé, but the name means nothing to me. Do you want me to ask around?"

"If you find anything out, let me know as soon as possible."

The scavenger looked at them knowingly. "Is the *Préfet* leaning on you to tie this case up? I've heard there's a shake-up going on."

Lucien bristled. "That's none of your concern," he said sharply, then caught himself. "What I mean is that I am very anxious to find out who is responsible for these killings, for my own sake - and I believe that Monsieur Delourcq is no less keen. We are not simply following the orders of our superiors."

Delourcq hid a wry smile, reflecting that they were not even doing that.

"I respect your conscience, captain. If I hear anything, it will reach your ears as well." He opened the door for them. In the short time that they had been inside Taillefer's home, there seemed to have been a cold boiling of the river, so that a dense fog lay everywhere. From the deck of the barge they could not even see the wall of the embankment above them. "Take care as you climb back up," Taillefer said.

Lucien pulled his gloves tight against his hands, took a firm grip on the hanging rope, and moved slowly upwards, from one ledge to the next. Delourcq stood on the barge, watching as the younger man climbed higher and was enveloped by the fog, and waiting for his call when he reached the top.

It happened before Lucien could gather his wits.

As he swung himself over the embankment wall, he was seized from behind by an unseen attacker, and his arms were pinned back. He saw his second assailant, a short man in a rough jacket, with a cloth tied round his face so that only the eyes were visible. He saw the cudgel as the attacker lifted it up and struck him on the head. He struggled in vain to free himself from the arm-lock. Pushing backwards, he brought his legs up to ward off the assault, and landed a kick in his attacker's stomach. "You'll pay for that, you bastard!" the man growled, and brought the cudgel down with all his force; it dealt a cruel blow to Lucien's shoulder. "Delourcq!" he shouted. "Quickly!" But it was already too late. The third blow was to his head again; it left him slumped and unconscious. Seeing his success, the cudgel-wielder hissed: "Over the wall!"

And, even as Delourcq scrambled desperately up to the last three or four peg-steps, he saw the limp form of the young captain being manhandled over the embankment wall - saw two indistinct figures give it a final push - and saw it tip over the edge and plummet down past him. "Jesus Christ" he breathed. He tried to peer through the fog after the form; he heard a splash, and realised with relief that the captain had fallen straight into the river, missing the deck of the barge. "Taillefer!" he bellowed.

"I heard it!" came the answering call from below.

"It's the captain! Fetch him out!"

He heard a second splash. He had not moved from his perch some four feet below the edge of the quay. There was no sense in pursuing the assailants. He had to see what state the young agent was in. Almost before he knew it, he found himself back on the deck of the barge; his hands burned from the speed with which he had descended, but it was of no consequence. "Taillefer! Where are you?"

He heard a threshing sound from the water. "Throw me a rope!"

Delourcq found a cable on the deck. "But where are you?"

"Forward of the barge - towards the bridge! Hurry, man!"

Delourcq picked his way to the prow; he glimpsed Taillefer's head and shoulders, twenty feet away in the river; he saw that Taillefer was using his right arm to keep the young captain above the surface of the water, and his left to fight against the current. He threw the rope; it was caught; and, with a strength that Delourcq thought had left him many years before, he hauled the rope in. Then he helped Taillefer and his burden on to the barge.

Water was not Delourcq's element, and now it was everywhere. The fog had already drenched his hair and clothes; water streamed off Taillefer like a spring breaking out of a hillside; and a pool formed around the figure of Boizillac that lay on the deck, where they had placed him. There was blood as well; the blows to his head had cut his scalp; and the ooze from his hair was tinged with red.

"Is he dead?" asked Delourcq.

"Not yet," said Taillefer, breathing deeply to recover from his exertions. "But we have no time to lose. We must take him inside. Give me thirty seconds." Taillefer threw down his sodden coat and went into the shack. He returned to Delourcq's side almost at once. Together they carried Lucien along the deck and through the door. Taillefer had moved the table to one side and placed some rough blankets on the floor in front of the stove. They laid the young man on these. "Take off his outer garments," Taillefer commanded. Delourcq did so, while the other man opened the stove grille and raked the coals and wood so that a blaze of heat burst forth. They saw the wounded flesh of his shoulder, as well as the blows to his head. Taillefer brought a bucket of fresh water from a barrel that he kept on deck; they bathed and bandaged he wounds. Then they covered Lucien with a fleece - another of Taillefer's findings - and sat on the chairs, at either side of him. Without being asked, Delourcq shared his flask with the river scavenger.

"Who did this?" Taillefer asked.

"I saw no more than you," Delourcq said, bitterly. "But this is your area. Who do you think did it?"

"It must have been outsiders. None of the locals would dare to shit on my doorstep. And they were lying in wait, weren't they? They knew your captain was coming up the rope. You must have made some enemies."

"You mean like Baudoin?"

"Could be. Maybe he followed the two of you here, and took his chance." Taillefer was standing next to the stove; his sodden clothes were steaming. "Or maybe it was someone else you've offended. I don't suppose the *Sûreté* has many friends."

Delourcq thought of Canler's dismissal. "Fewer and fewer," he said. He looked at the figure stretched out on the floor. "What are we going to do about the captain?"

Taillefer paused. "I don't think those villains broke anything. But we can't move him now, not until we can be sure he's over it. So he'll have to stay here."

"Can you watch over him?"

"Till nightfall, aye. But then I have my living to earn, out on the river. You know the way it is, Delourcq - the fruits fall into the water at night."

"Right. I'll be back here this evening, and take over the night watch. I need to ask around about this attack - and I need to decide what to do about Stevane, now that the captain can't take any decisions."

He made for the door. "Take care, Delourcq," Taillefer called after him. "I don't want to have to dive into the river after you as well."

Delourcq spat his answer over the side of the barge. He expected to find no-one left on the Quai Morland, and he was right. He bowed into the muffling fog and headed back towards the streets of the Ile de la Cité.

Chapter Eleven

Monday 17 November - evening

Rue St. Honoré

"Alexandre? What happened?" There was a note of alarm in Marguerite de Trégonnec's voice. She had heard the two men arrive back in their carriage and climb the stairs to her husband's study. As she rose from her desk to greet them, she heard a great cry, and a glass smashing against a wall. She hurried into the adjoining room and saw her husband standing by the hearth, where shattered fragments lay in the fire. He was like a wild dog, with bristling whiskers and blazing eyes. Godefroi de Lieusaint sat in a chair at the other side of the room, his head in his hands.

"Defeat," Trégonnec hissed. "We have suffered defeat at the hands of that cretinous by-blow at the Elysée Palace!"

"But how is that possible?" she asked.

"Cowardice, and treachery. Godefroi was right. France has been betrayed. Dear God, I would never have believed it!"

"Calm yourself, Alexandre. You are overheating your blood. Come, sit down and drink something." She guided him to a chair, and poured a glass of wine from a decanter. "Save your words for a moment. Godefroi, tell me what happened tonight in the Assembly."

Lieusaint breathed deeply and sat upright. "Forgive me for my lack of courtesy, Marguerite. You see how both your husband and I have been struck down by this reverse." He closed his eyes momentarily and pinched the bridge of his nose. "You know that tonight's vote was on the questors' proposition, to re-affirm the Assembly's right to call on the armed forces for protection? It has been defeated - and not by seven votes, but by a hundred! I expected Bonaparte's followers to rally to his cause, but their victory was secured by the republicans, who also voted against the Assembly's rights."

"The republicans in league with the Bonapartists? Did they explain themselves?"

"That idiot Michel who speaks for them had some empty phrase, about the people of France being the invisible sentinel guarding the Assembly against danger. Invisible sentinel! Much good it will do him when Saint Arnaud's soldiers break down his doors!"

"Hah!" snorted Trégonnec. "I expect no better of Michel and his mob. They come from the gutter, and they see no higher than the kerbstone. But d'Amboise, and his like. There's treachery, there's villainy, there's infamy...!" His face flushed still more deeply.

"Alexandre is right, Marguerite. D'Amboise, who has sat at your table, eaten your food, and drunk to the return of the King -- tonight, d'Amboise voted for

Bonaparte and against the Assembly."

Madame de Trégonnec paused for a few seconds. "D'Amboise is a weathervane, isn't he? If he has turned, then he must have sensed a fierce wind."

"Or taken a fat purse!" Trégonnec exclaimed.

"You may both be right," said Lieusaint. "At all events, d'Amboise sees us as a lost cause."

"And you, Godefroi?" Trégonnec's question, shorn of courtesy, was barked like a command. His wife looked at him with concern.

There was weariness in the reply. "I am sorry to say that I believe d'Amboise to be right. A storm is coming, and the King's house may not survive it."

Trégonnec shot him a challenging glance. He stood up from his chair. "It is time for us to go, Marguerite."

His wife placed her hand on his arm. "Go, Alexandre?"

"Yes, my dear. This city has become a nest of vipers. Tomorrow we shall leave for Finistère. I shall not return - not, at least, until this treachery has spent itself, and our country has recognised that its true interests lie with its King. Godefroi --."

The two men stood facing each other and shook

hands. "This is a sad moment, Alexandre - sad for what is happening to France, and sad for the loss of our friendship."

"But Monsieur de Lieusaint," Marguerite protested, "even if we are no longer in Paris, I hope that we can still count on you as our friend."

"Quiet, my dear." Trégonnec spoke to his wife, but his eyes remained on the other man. "You stay in Paris, Godefroi?" The other man nodded. "Then either you imperil your safety or -- you compromise your principles."

Lieusaint tried and failed to respond with a smile. "A Frenchman must have the right to live in Paris no matter what the colour of the Government, Alexandre."

"I understand." The conversation was at an end. "Forgive us, Monsieur de Lieusaint, we must retire now in order to make an early start in the morning." He turned away and studied the fire.

Lieusaint kissed Marguerite's hand and, without another word, made his way down to the street and departed. The Trégonnecs stood unspeaking; tears glittered in the old general's eyes.

***

Monday 17 November - evening

The Elysée Palace

As soon as the word reached him, Persigny bustled up the stairs and turned into the corridor that led to the study of the President of the Second Republic. His eyes burned brightly; his arms waved like a swimmer trying to carve his way more rapidly through the air around him. The guards stood aside as he burst through the door. "Thrown out by a hundred votes!" he cried. "We have won!"

"I have already informed the Prince-President of the result." Now Persigny saw the two half-brothers standing side-by-side in front of the fire. The look which Morny sent towards the intruder conveyed the disdain which had been drained out of his matter-of-fact remark. Persigny cursed the man. "It was as I predicted."

The President himself seemed unusually animated by the news. "Have you smelt the air, Persigny?" Annoyance gave way to incomprehension in the third man's mind. "Come with me." He put his arm around Persigny's shoulder and walked to the open window with him. The night flowed in, dank and heavy. "Do you smell it, Persigny? It's the *parfum d'Empire*. At last, after so many years of waiting, I can sense that my moment of destiny is at hand."

Excitement struggled in Persigny's breast with lingering distrust for the other man in the room. "And the Comte de Morny?" he asked in a loud voice. "What do his powers of prophecy say about the future of France?"

Morny gave the briefest of smiles. "I need no powers of prophecy to recognise an unstoppable force." He bowed his head towards his half-brother. "All that remains is to plan how that force can best be applied."

Louis-Napoléon stood for a few seconds more in front of the open window, towards his imperial future. Then he turned and announced: "Get Maupas and Saint-Arnaud here. We must prepare to cross the Rubicon."

***

Tuesday 18 November - morning

Quai Morland

Delourcq had learnt the trick of light sleeping when he was a fifteen-year-old volunteer in Napoléon's army, dipping out of consciousness but staying sufficiently alert that any unusual sound woke him instantly. Returning to Taillefer's barge in the evening, he shared a glass of wine and some bread and meat with his host, before the latter rowed off upstream. The young captain still lay on his bed on the floor, pale as death and with his eyes shut, but breathing quietly. Other than moistening his lips from time to time from a jug of water, there was nothing that Delourcq could do but watch and, as the night wore on, listen even as he dozed.

He had spent all the daylight hours on Monday visiting his regular informants, and trying a few irregular ones as well. No-one knew anything about the attack on Boizillac and its perpetrators; or, at least, no-one was prepared to own up to any knowledge. He sensed a nervousness among his contacts, and a lack of confidence in their dealings with him. When he spoke to Pigeon on the Ile de la Cité, the tramp had leered at him and mumbled something about a new broom coming and sweeping all the "filth of the *Sûreté*" into the Seine; and he guessed that the same thought was in the mind of the others to whom he spoke, even if they did not give voice to it. He chose not to enter the Prefecture of Police.

As dusk approached, he made two last calls. He went to the lodgings that he knew Boizillac kept in the Rue du Bac, and told the concierge what had happened to the young captain and where he was. Then he made his way eastwards to his own rooms in the Rue de Reuilly. Françoise was more surprised by the depth of Delourcq's concern for Boizillac than by the news of the attack; but, after so many years together, she knew that, when he took something seriously, he was right to do so. She helped him pack some food and drink, kissed him briefly, and sent him back to the Quai Morland, making him promise to send for her if he needed another pair of hands.

He shivered in spite of the heat from Taillefer's stove. He would have liked to hold his woman now, to feel enveloped by her warmth as the night drained away. Most of their days started like that, and the memory of their embrace was usually in his mind as he sipped his first glass of wine at Ma Friche's. But today was different. He was not in the Rue de Reuilly, but in a barge on the Seine. If Pigeon had known, he would have been proud that his prediction seemed to have come true so quickly.

There was the splash of oars from outside. Delourcq opened the door, glanced back at the young captain, and stepped on to deck. Already Taillefer had tied his rowboat fast and was approaching.

"How is he?"

"No better, no worse."

"And you? You look like something I fished out of the river and then threw back!"

Delourcq spat. "I'll live." He took a deeper breath of the sodden air to clear his thoughts. "How was your haul?" Taillefer still had his bag slung over his shoulder.

"Slim pickings." He reached inside and retrieved a bundle which opened out into a long rectangle of river-smeared and faded cream material.

"What is it?"

"An infant's shawl." Taillefer saw the

interrogatory look in Delourcq's eyes. "It was floating under the Pont au Change. I didn't find the child. The eels got to it first."

Delourcq felt a nausea in his belly. "Why do you do this work, Taillefer? The rest of Paris throws its rubbish into the drains and turns away. But every night you row along the biggest drain of all and cast your nets as if you were catching a prize fish. And all you haul in is this - the cast-offs and leavings from suicides and child-killers."

"You're talking like a *bourgeois* now, Dédé. There's money to be made from the flotsam of the Seine. And I'm the man who makes it."

As they spoke, they heard the noise of a horse and carriage approaching on the quay above them. It stopped for a moment; the carriage door slammed; and the horse and its vehicle moved off again. Their eyes had already turned to look up from where they stood when the figure appeared above them.

"Monsieur Taillefer?"

"The same." The scavenger and his companion on the barge recognised it as a woman's voice before they could make out her features, concealed by the hood that she wore. "And your name is --?"

She put the hood back. Her black hair hung loosely, and showed up the pallor of her face. "Laure Carreleur. Is Lucien de Boizillac here?"

Taillefer glanced sideways. Delourcq's face was impassive, but he was thinking very quickly. Carreleur - the name the captain had mentioned to him the previous morning; the source of the captain's information about Estève; and the brother of "a young woman that he knew". Here she was. "I am Daniel Delourcq, Captain de Boizillac's assistant. Did you speak to the concierge in the Rue du Bac, Mademoiselle Carreleur?" Now he could see her face clearly. God, but she was young, and pretty, and sick with worry. If the captain was not captivated by her, there was no sense left in the world.

"No - I was sent a message by Monsieur de Montholon, who shares the same lodgings. I got it only half an hour ago. Is Lucien here? Can I see him? How do I get down?"

"She loves him." It was said in an undertone by Taillefer, even as he moved to scale the wall. Climbing with the speed of a twenty-year-old, he persuaded Laure to be supported in his left arm and returned to the level of the river grasping the rope in his right. Her only concern was to get to Lucien; she paid no heed to the manner of her descent.

She hurried into the shack on the barge. As the two men followed, they saw her drop to her knees alongside the unmoving form of the young captain. For several moments, she held her face against his. Then she turned round to look at them. "Was he badly beaten? Why did he not protect himself? Why did no-one stop his attackers?"

Her young face had lost all its vitality; and there was no theatricality about her anguish. Her eyes were wild, and brimming with tears. Seeing her sorrow, and sensing the accusation in her words, Delourcq was momentarily at a loss to reply.

"Young lady," Taillefer said, "you have seen how visitors to my barge have to get down here from the quay. The captain climbed back up the same way. His attackers were hidden from sight at the top. They needed no more than a few seconds to seize the captain, knock him about and throw him back into the river. Dédé tried to get up to the quay before it was too late, but there was nothing he could do."

"If I could have taken the blows, I would have done," Delourcq said quietly. "But the captain went up first."

Laure stood up, and wiped her eyes. "Forgive me, Monsieur Delourcq. I didn't mean to blame you. But why would anyone do this to Lucien?"

"The villains may not have known him. There are enough brutes in this city who just need to drink a bottle of wine to turn into cut-throats and murderers. Or, more likely, they did know he was a police agent, and took their chance to settle a few scores. You don't make many friends when you work for the *Préfecture de Police*." He thought again about Pigeon's scornful comments.

"But is he safe here then?"

"Don't worry about that, young lady," Taillefer reassured her. "No-one comes on to my barge without my permission."

"And has a doctor come to look at him? I can pay for one."

"No need for that either," said Taillefer. "Dédé and I have seen enough wounded men in our time to know what to do. The young captain may dress like an aristo, with his fine coat and riding-boots, but he's a lot stronger than he looks. He'll pull through."

"Are you sure?" She looked imploringly at this old man of the river; and he, despite being three times her age, knew that the defences of his maturity had been breached.

"If he can just lie here near the warmth from the stove, with someone to give him a drop of water from time to time, he'll be back on his feet in a week." The glow of relief in Laure's eyes was so intense that the old man had to look away; but he had spoken true.

"Then I shall stay here, to watch over him, and to slake his thirst when he needs it." And she knelt down again and stroked Lucien's hand gently.

"But Mademoiselle Carreleur," Delourcq broke in, "you must have your own home, or family, to look after. Taillefer and I can take care of the captain."

"Has Lucien told you about me, Monsieur Delourcq?"

"He has mentioned your name, nothing else."

"I am an actress." She anticipated their reaction. "Unlike some of the women who give themselves that title, I am part of an acting company, at the *Théâtre Drolatique*. But I have no family, and no home other than a garret in the Rue du Saumon - and, if I don't appear at the theatre for a week, Monsieur Verdant will re-arrange his plays for a smaller company. I must send him a note. Monsieur Taillefer, do you have a pen and some paper I could use?"

Taillefer had already moved to one of the pouches hanging on the wall to fetch what she had asked for, but Delourcq intervened. "Surely you don't mean to stay here for a week? This barge is no place for a young woman, or for a woman of any age. Look at it. You must be the first woman ever to visit it - am I right, Taillefer?"

"It's none of your business, Dédé - but you're wrong." He passed the paper and pen to Laure, who sat at the table. "And if the young lady has made up her mind to look after the captain, you're wasting your breath to try and object." He stepped closer to Delourcq, and spoke almost in a whisper. "Besides, if she's watching over him, you won't have to."

Delourcq thought of being able to return to the

bed he shared with Françoise; he remembered as well his conversation with Lucien the day before, when the younger man had talked about travelling to Rouen. If the captain couldn't go, perhaps he should. He needed to think about it. "I'll come back this evening to see how the captain is, and to see if Mademoiselle Carreleur has changed her mind. It's time for me to leave now."

Laure came over with the folded paper. "Could you send this to Victor Verdant, at the *Théâtre Drolatique*, Monsieur Delourcq?" He nodded and took it from her. "Thank you for being such a good friend." She smiled at him.

Cursing himself for being foolish enough to warm to a young woman's pleasantries, Delourcq hurried out of the shack, tucked the letter into his jacket, and struggled back up to the quay.

***

Tuesday 18 November - dusk

Rue de Chaillot

The lanterns flickered on either side of Gianni. They served as a warning for other carriages, not to help him see in the gathering darkness. The master always claimed that Gianni had the eyes of an owl; years of night-time driving had trained him to watch for patterns of shadow which were missed by passengers who rarely ventured out of doors after nightfall. But now there was still a last dull streak of light in the sky, more than enough for him to scan the road and the adjoining houses for signs of activity.

The carriage was empty. After returning late the night before, the master had spent all that day in his office, writing letters and receiving callers. Gianni had been left in the courtyard; and, conscientious though he was, after eight hours of waiting even he could find little more to polish and groom on the carriage and pair. But at last he had been called to the study. The master was at his desk, alone. He handed Gianni a folded sheet of paper, closed with his own wax seal, and gave him his instructions. "Return by way of the Rue du Rempart. You remember where Monsieur d'Amboise lives. He comes to visit me tonight - you are to collect him around six."

He drove the length of the Rue de Chaillot, cut down to the river, and doubled back. The horses trotted tentatively, seeming to sense Gianni's anticipation. For the second time he passed the gateway on the landward side of the road, and the rutted mud drive that ran back fifty metres to a sandstone mansion with lights burning in the windows.

He saw the shadow move. But more keenly than that he felt a sudden chill in the air that swirled around him, as the shadow caught up with the carriage. The horses whinnied nervously. Suddenly the other man slid on to the bench alongside the driver.

There was a coldness around Gianni's heart.

Without looking away from the road, he took the letter from inside his cape and passed it sideways. At once the other man slipped from the carriage and disappeared into the darkness. Not even Gianni could see where he went. He crossed himself. He never questioned the master's associates, but that one belonged to the Devil. Even the horses sensed it. He whipped them up to give them courage, and drove towards the Avenue de Neuilly.

***

Thursday 20 November - late afternoon

Rouen

"They reek of vomit and scent." He had tried to isolate himself by closing his eyes and humming a tune to drown the conversation; but there was nothing he could do to ward off the sickly smell inside the carriage, which Vauzuron's scornful words had captured well. It was nine hours since Delourcq boarded the coach in Paris. Moments after he had settled in, he was followed by a married couple of a certain age. Installing themselves next to him, their combined bulk forced him into the corner; and, while the woman was drenched in a perfume which called to mind roses blooming in a midden, the man, despite his stern black clothes, blazed with the heat of a farm labourer. After an initial nod of the head, the two of them took no notice of the other travellers; the wife talked incessantly about her sister whom they had just visited in Paris (and the seven nephews and nieces under the same roof), allowing the husband to do no more than offer the repeated comment: "They would all be *much* happier if they moved to Rouen."

On the opposite bench in the carriage sat a family of three: mother, father and daughter, aged about thirteen, Delourcq guessed. The man remained silent throughout; the mother and daughter occasionally spoke to one another in a whisper; their diffidence, gaunt expressions and threadbare clothes were in sharp contrast to the affluent complacency of the couple dressed in black. Delourcq noticed that they looked sideways in his direction; his jacket and trousers were even more well-worn than their clothes, and he sensed that they were only too pleased that he made no attempt to speak to them.

After Laure Carreleur came to the Quai Morland, he had spent the following two days making his rounds through the underworld of the city to no effect, other than worsening his temper. He discovered nothing about the men who had attacked Lucien; and the investigation of the killings of Connassier and Jattée ground to a halt. He spent a second night at Taillefer's barge. Laure was still there; his presence during the night-hours meant that she could sleep, while he watched. He intended to complete a third night's watch as well, but there was better news about the young captain when he returned on Wednesday evening. Laure told him that Lucien had opened his eyes for the first time since the attack and managed to speak a few words, before falling asleep again cradled in her arms. Taillefer agreed that it was a sign that the captain was on the road to recovery. He sent Delourcq back to the Rue de Reuilly, assuring him that he could leave the young man in his care if he wanted to pursue his inquiries in Rouen.

Rouen. It was the best part of twenty years since he had been there, driving through the town (or round it) on a cart which had concealed among the hay-bales three or four packages brought ashore on the Normandy coast at dead of night. He had no regrets for those days, but his companions back then had been more to his taste than the good citizens he was travelling with now.

Darkness had fallen as they jolted into the town. The road ran alongside the Seine again, that was visible as no more than a black band in which points of light were reflected. The buildings clustered round them, as solid and self-satisfied as the corpulent husband and wife returning from Paris. "*Much* happier" intoned the man for the umpteenth time. The carriage wheels scraped over the cobbles as they turned into the courtyard of the *Auberge des Postes*. The door was opened, and they stepped down. Delourcq was last.

He took a room at the inn, and then settled down in the bar with a glass and bottle of thin red wine. There was a log-fire that blazed with the strength that was lacking from the wine. Nine hours of bumping over the ruts and ditches of the road from Paris had done little for his appetite, but out of consideration for the innkeeper he ordered an *assiette normande* of blood sausages and potatoes.

The food was brought to him by an ample, red-faced woman who looked as if she could stun an ox with her bare hands. "There you are, then - that's real cooking, none of your Parisian rubbish." She smiled. "You look as if you need feeding up - turn sideways and you disappear!"

"That can be useful in my line of business," he responded.

"And what that might be?" The inn-keeper who was at the other side of the bar coughed significantly. "If the gentleman doesn't want to say, he'll keep it to himself, won't he?" she called to him, then turned back to Delourcq. "But I think you're quite happy to tell me, even if you do look like a dog that's been left out in the rain all day!"

"Marie!" shouted the inn-keeper. "You watch your tongue!"

Delourcq had been called worse, and the wine and the warmth of the fire took any sting out of her words. "I'm a police agent in Paris."

"You poor man!" Marie exclaimed. It was too much for Delourcq, who gave a great snort of laughter.

"Please excuse her," said the inn-keeper. "She means no offence."

"None taken," said Delourcq. "I like to hear people speak their mind, although I'm not used to being pitied for my work!"

"What were you thinking of, Marie?"

She twisted her hands in her apron. "I just meant, being a police agent and all, it must be terrible having to deal with criminals and bad people all the time. Is that why you're here?"

Delourcq saw the anxiety on the faces of both the inn-keeper and the serving-woman. "Not here, in this inn, no. I'm sure everyone here is quite law-abiding. But tomorrow I shall have to travel further, to pursue an investigation from Paris. That's all I can tell you."

"Well, you be careful. Bad people are like bad meals - they make you sick and cost you too much money! Not like our food. Eat it up and get your strength back." She bustled away into the kitchen.

The inn-keeper came to Delourcq's table with a second bottle of wine. "This one's on the house, monsieur," he said. He looked as though he had been cast from the same mould as his customer - careworn, aged by half a century of turmoil, and with not an ounce of spare flesh on his bones. "She's a good worker, Marie - just a bit soft in the head."

"Obliged, I'm sure," said the Parisian, draining the first bottle. "Will you have a glass yourself?"

The inn-keeper looked round. Business was

slack. He fetched another glass, and sat down at the table. Delourcq filled his glass. "You must be glad of a chance to get out of Paris."

Without even thinking about it, Delourcq knew that the opposite was true. The air of Paris might be rank with the odours of a million people; the streets might run with mud, water and other liquids; the bars might teem with drunkards and villains. But he had the measure of the city and of its inhabitants, and it was what he knew. Now that he had turned his mind to it, he felt even slightly homesick. "No," he said simply, raising his glass to his host. "I shall be happy to be back there."

"But there always seems to be one uprising or another, with barricades in the streets and the army sent to restore order. It can't be long until there's another clash, and the Jacobins try to overthrow the Government and start chopping people's heads off again."

"It's a long time since they've done that," Delourcq laughed.

"Maybe," said the inn-keeper. He shook his glass, and some of the wine splashed on to his hand like a wound. "But blood will flow, unless the Government takes action soon."

"The signs are that the Government is going to do just that," Delourcq commented, in a more sombre tone of voice. "And the blood will flow anyway. It always does."

"Have you always lived in Paris?"

"Always, except when I was in the army, or when I had a travelling trade. But this is the first time I've spent a night outside the city in twenty years."

"Then," said the inn-keeper, "I drink to your loyalty to your native city, though I cannot understand it!"

The two men shared a third bottle of wine before the inn-keeper felt compelled to return to his duties in the kitchen and elsewhere, and Delourcq decided that he should get to his room before his eyes shut and he slumped at the table. He fell on his bed fully clothed, and was asleep at once.

***

Friday 21 November

Lyons-la-Forêt

A fine rain was falling, and had been since Delourcq left the *Auberge des Postes* at first light. It had not changed his decision to walk the twenty or so miles to Lyons-la-Forêt. He felt happier travelling with his feet on the ground, even if it took longer; and his hide was so weather-beaten by now that a little more wind and rain would make no difference. It was to oblige Marie that he accepted the misshapen farmer's hat that she forced upon him when he left, together with some bread and meat wrapped in a piece of cloth. Several hours of steady drizzle had washed the dirt out of the hat, on to his jacket, and then on to the ground; but, while his body was as wet as it often was on his journeys through the streets of Paris, his head was unusually dry, and warm. Several times he took the hat off, and let the rain cool his scalp, before donning the headgear again out of respect for Marie.

This might be a wild goose chase. He remembered the young captain's account of his conversation in the church of Saint-Jean-des-Champs: Estève had last been heard of in Lyons-la-Forêt eighteen months ago. Anything could have happened since then. But Lucien had been determined to try and find him before he was attacked at the Quai Morland, and Delourcq felt that it was his duty to carry on the investigation while the young captain was unable to.

The rain eased in the afternoon. A breeze picked up; the worst of the dampness was blown out of Delourcq's clothes. He reached the village as the light began to fail. But the little that there was to see reminded him again of why Paris was the only place where he could live. Market-day in Lyons-la-Forêt was Wednesday. On any other day of the week, there was no more to the village than the church, half-a-dozen homesteads where cattle, chicken and dogs outnumbered human beings, and an inn with a rusted sign announcing *La Forêt*. Delourcq spat into one of the puddles in the road. "Let's see what sort of village idiots we have here!"

He stepped into the inn. Its poverty made the *Chien Fou* seem like a temple of luxury. It consisted of a single rectangular room. The door occupied half of one wall; two rough wooden benches stood against two of the other walls, and were the only seating; and the bar - a table, supporting a single barrel - filled the fourth wall. It was a good deal smaller than the room on Taillefer's barge where Delourcq had kept watch over Lucien.

There was no fire, but the room was filled with tobacco smoke. Side by side on the benches sat an array of village elders, ruddy-complexioned, bearded, and with eyes glazed by drink and watering from age and pipe smoke. Delourcq was reminded of a bizarre display he had once marvelled at, when he and Françoise had gone to the outskirts of Paris to see a travelling show - a collection of apes, stuffed, dressed in human clothes, and exhibited in a glass case. As he entered, the drinkers in *La Forêt* fell silent and stared at him with the same fixity that he had seen on the faces of the mummified apes.

"Good day to you all," Delourcq said to the assembled company. None of them replied; one by one they looked away and muttered among themselves. He turned to the table with the barrel. Behind it stood a slightly less aged replica of the drinkers, a short man dressed in rough peasant clothes, with hair and beard so long that he brought to mind images of hermits and holy men. Unlike them, however, his beard was discoloured by streaks of wine. "Good day, sir,"

Delourcq spoke. "Could I have some wine?"

The "hermit" stood motionless for a second or two. Then, with a cough that sounded like a death-rattle, he voided his sputum at Delourcq's feet. "Your money," he growled.

Delourcq placed a couple of coins on the table, worth twice as much as he could reasonably expect to pay. The peasant snatched them up immediately, bit both of them, and dropped them into a pocket. He took an earthenware jug from the table, filled it from the barrel, and passed it to the new arrival, with a drinking beaker. "You must stand." His tone softened slightly.

"I'm well used to that," Delourcq replied. He poured himself some wine and raised the beaker. "Your good health." It was not like the wine that he drank at the *Chien Fou*. In fact, it was not much like wine at all; if anything, it was like a young vinegar; but he persevered with it. "Do you serve food here?"

"No." Though the rest of the drinkers had turned their backs on him, the "hermit" was watching him like a hawk. "No food. Just the *vin du pays*."

Delourcq toasted him again. "I compliment you on it."

"We don't get many visitors here." He spat again.

"No. Well, it is a day's march from Rouen."

"That's how we like it." He drank from a beaker that he had by him on the table. "But you're the second today."

Delourcq choked, then recovered. "There's been another stranger here today already?"

"Not an hour ago. Two in the same day."

"And he spoke to you? What did he say?"

"Didn't like him. Didn't buy any wine. Didn't show any money. Just asked about Stevane." I've arrived too late, thought Delourcq. "Are you looking for Stevane?"

"I've come to warn him that he's in danger. Do you know him?"

"Old Michel does." He nodded towards one of the other drinkers. "But he didn't say anything." The "hermit" drank again. "But I did. Never liked Stevane. Stranger. Kept himself to himself." He wiped his mouth with his sleeve. "Danger? What danger?"

"From the man who was here an hour ago. What was he like?"

"Hard to say. Just stood at the door, without coming in. Tall. Fancy way of talking."

"What did you tell him?"

"Told him Stevane used to live in the old gamekeeper's house beyond the church."

"Used to live? Where is he now?"

"Didn't tell him that. Let him waste his time at the old house."

Delourcq dug in his pocket and brought out a franc coin. He set it down on the table. "Tell me where Stevane is now, so that I can warn him."

The coin was tested in the "hermit's" mouth and disappeared instantly. "The track that runs past the church. There's a fork. Go right, you get to the gamekeeper's house. Go left, you climb the hill to the forest. After five minutes you pass a big oak-tree. There's a path, leaves the track on the left. Climb up there for fifteen minutes, you'll find a stone shelter. Stevane's been living there for a year and more."

Delourcq drained his beaker. Then, pausing only to spit amicably on the floor, he hurried out.

He cursed his luck, and his judgement. If he had taken a horse from Rouen rather than walking, he would have arrived before the tall stranger. As it was, he was hurrying in his footsteps, and in the dark - he reckoned that night would have descended completely in not much more than a quarter of an hour. No time to lose.

He passed a gate-post, where a pitchfork had been propped. He took it. He had no other weapon, and he remembered the wounds that had been inflicted on Connassier and Jattée. A long fork to meet with a devil.

He passed the church and bore right. Through a tangle of trees he could make out a low building, set in a small clearing. There was no light, no sign of movement, and the only sound was of his own feet scrabbling over the stony track. At other times he would have trodden silently; now, the urgency and the darkness made that impossible.

He followed the track to the left, and upwards. He was looking for a tree in a forest at night. It was like searching for a pebble in the cobblestones of the mud-splattered Rue aux Fèves. But he found it - an oak, four or five times wider than the slender birch trunks around it. And then, on his left, a gap where there was only blackness, empty of the shadowy outlines of trees. He veered on to the smaller path.

Up and up it went. Now his legs reminded him of the twenty miles he had walked that day. He was almost blind. The way through the wood was no wider than a man, and unseen twigs hit him across the face or tangled round his ankles. He stumbled once, and swore loudly as his left hand came down against one of the prongs of the pitchfork that he was still carrying. It was only a shallow cut; and he had no time to attend to it.

Then he found it. The ground levelled out suddenly, and he was no longer so hemmed in by trees.

The night sky was visible overhead. In the feeble moonlight he saw Stevane's retreat. It was larger than he had expected - not just a cabin where a man could shelter during a rain-storm, but a solid rectangle of stone-built walls, capped by a roof with a chimney. Smoke drifted up from the chimney. Smoke, from a hearth inside.

The shelter had its back to the issue of the path. Delourcq moved round it, slowly.

A gust of wind played on his face. It blew the door to the shelter slightly open. There was a line of red light, a glow from the fire. As Delourcq stood there, he heard a crashing noise from inside the building. "Stevane!" he called. It was involuntary, the call forced out of him by his shock. And he knew that he could delay no longer.

He pushed the door wide open and stood at the threshold. There was a single room inside. Logs burnt low in the hearth, and threw a dull redness over the stone walls. There was little enough in there - a chair, a table, a simple bed over which a crucifix glinted - and a body slumped on the floor. Delourcq dropped the pitchfork and knelt down. The man lay on his face, in a pool of blood that was still warm. But the man was dead, from a stab wound in the back.

He heard the rustle of clothes behind him. He turned. The side of his face was struck by a length of wood; and as he fell over, losing consciousness, there was an explosion of noise and light and the sound of glass shattering. Then the night outside entered his head, and he knew no more.

***

He had ridden all day from Paris. He avoided the inns along the way. He had food and water with him, and consumed it when he stopped to let his horse rest. He reached the village in mid-afternoon. He tethered his horse to a tree, and found *La Forêt*. He stood in the doorway. The smoke in the room made his head spin; he did not enter. He had no time for small talk. He asked his question, got his answer, and went.

He left his horse in the village and strode quickly along the track. There seemed to be no sign of life at the gamekeeper's house. The clearing in which it stood was being reclaimed by the forest; leaves had been blown into heaps against the doors and walls; cobwebs covered the windows.

He tried the front door; it was locked. He walked round the side and looked in through a window. The place was deserted. He rattled the casement, and the pane opened. He climbed inside. Even if Estève was no longer here, he might have left some clue as to where he had gone. He began a search.

After half an hour he had scoured every inch of the building, even checking for loose floor-boards and trap-doors into the roof space. He found nothing. He stood in the deepening darkness in the house, and tried to think of some other approach.

Then he heard footsteps along the track. They came rapidly nearer, then moved away. Was this his quarry? Who else would be hurrying through these woods at this time of day?

He could find no key for the locked front door. It took only a few seconds to squeeze back out of the window and rejoin the track, but the sounds told him that the other man was already well ahead. He took up the chase, moving as swiftly as his quarry but stepping quietly so as not to betray his pursuit.

He missed the side-path at the oak, had to backtrack, and found the gap more by luck than by judgement. But he could hear the other man scrabbling up above him, and he forced himself to quicken his pace even as the slope grew steeper. After ten minutes his chest was heaving with the effort, and it was all he could do to suppress the sound of his panting.

He paused for a moment, wiped the sweat from his brow, and glimpsed the figure that he was pursuing step from the path into a clearing above him. He followed with all speed; saw the shelter; and heard the other man shout out and hurry into the building.

Fools rush in, he thought. With a burst of energy that defied his aching legs, he ran along one side of the shelter to where a rectangle of red light showed a window. He looked in. He saw the body, saw Delourcq kneeling next to it - and saw the dark figure move out of the shadow behind the door, seize the pitchfork and smash it down over Delourcq.

Now, he must act now, before there was another death. He had his pistol ready primed. The shot he fired through the window blinded him momentarily...

***

Delourcq heard his name being repeated insistently. He opened his eyes and seemed to recognise the man looking down at him. "Captain?" Raising himself on his right arm, he rubbed his eyes with his other hand. He felt blood on his face. "Is it really you, Captain? How are you here? And what happened?" He rubbed his face again. "Am I badly hurt?"

Boizillac smiled. "No. You'll have a headache from the blow you took to your temples. But the only cut is to your hand. It might be better if you stopped smearing it across your face." He turned away for a few moments, and came back with a handkerchief that he had soaked in a bucket of water. "Let me help you."

Delourcq protested. "I can do that, captain." He took the cloth, wiped his face and then tied it round his bloodied hand. "But when I left you at Taillefer's two days ago, you were still sick. How did you get here?" He got to his feet, and realised that he had been lying only a pace or two away from the body of Estève. "What happened here? Where were you?" The younger man guided him to sit on the chair.

"Have you got your flask, Delourcq? Then take

a mouthful or two. It will revive you." Delourcq obeyed. "As for me, I felt much stronger yesterday, the day you left Paris. I would have left Taillefer's barge then, but the old man - and Laure - talked me out of it. But this morning I knew that I was fully recovered. And I knew that it was my duty to join you, in case of danger. I set off at first light and rode here." He told Delourcq about asking at the inn in the village, searching in the game-keeper's house, and following his footsteps through the wood to the shelter.

"So the explosion I saw was you firing through the window. But - you didn't wound the assassin?"

"Not badly enough to prevent his escape. He fled into the trees before I could stop him - and then I wanted to see if you were badly wounded." He smiled again. "It seems that both the assassin and I are poor workmen."

"Here's to poor workmanship," said Delourcq raising his flask. "But he did what he came here to do." He nodded towards the body on the floor.

"I examined the body while you were unconscious. He did that job well enough. A single stab wound, from behind, but straight through the heart. There are no signs of a struggle. The assassin must have lain in wait, inside this shelter, while Stevane was outside. Then the moment he came back in, the knife struck. And the next moment you arrived." Boizillac sat down, at the edge of the table. "First Connassier, then Jattée, and now Estève, or Stevane. All the *trois sodomites* killed, and by the same hand, I'm sure. But who is doing this? How did he know where to find them"

"What did you see of him, captain?"

"Little enough in the shadows. A tall man, certainly. He stood as tall as the door-frame. And I fancied that his skin was dark, but I could see only his hands on the pitch-fork that he used to strike you. His face was hidden in a great hood. He wore a cape that was buttoned the full length. And that was all. I fired my pistol, then he had run off."

Delourcq stood up. "Well, captain, what do we do now?"

"Are you recovered from the attack?"

"My head is sore, but I'll live."

"Then we must see whether we can find anything here that will help the investigation. There's nothing on Stevane himself. But perhaps he had something hidden away."

The shelter was only a quarter the size of the game-keeper's house. Boizillac had spent thirty minutes searching there, and found nothing. But it took him and Delourcq only five minutes to scour the shelter and make two discoveries. Below the bed they found a leather pouch that held half a dozen letters. And next to the hearth, partly covered by logs, they spotted a loose floor-stone that could be lifted up to reveal a small copper box, filled with *louis d'or* coins. They took both.

The crime would have to be notified to the rural guardian of law and order, the *garde champêtre*. Stevane had kept a pen, ink and paper under his bed; now it served Boizillac to write an account of his murder, which he left on the table, weighted with a small stone.

They made their final discovery as they left the shelter. There were dark streaks over some of the stones at their feet. It was blood - not the trickle from Delourcq's hand, but great gouts that had spread widely.

"The shot I fired seems to have found its mark."

Delourcq nodded. "I reckon it was a leg wound - otherwise the blood would have been soaked up by his clothes." He spat.

The trail continued down the path, but only for some twenty paces. Then there were no more marks on the ground. Wounded as he was, the assassin had escaped. The two police agents made their way back to the village and found Boizillac's horse where he had left it. They agreed to make for Rouen for the night; Boizillac commandeered a second horse from one of the villagers; and by half past seven Delourcq found himself back at the homely *auberge* which he had left twelve hours earlier.

Chapter Twelve

Saturday 22 November - early morning

Rue de Chaillot

It was several hours after the last carriage had rumbled along the Rue de Chaillot, bringing a banker and his wife back from a dinner in the Place de Rivoli. Lights might still be burning in the heart of the city; out here, at its western edge, there were none.

Unseen, unheard, a horse and rider moved slowly along the road. Both were exhausted. Their journey had taken ten hours.

At the start the man spurred his mount on, away from the place where he had knifed one man, clubbed a second and been shot by a third. But neither of them could maintain the pace. After fifteen minutes he slid to the ground again, tethered the horse to a tree, and dealt with his leg.

The wound was a bad one. Although the bullet did not lodge in his right leg, it ripped open the flesh two or three inches above the ankle. He had not been able to staunch the bleeding as he ran down the track from the shelter. Now he tore a strip from his cloak and tied it tight, so that it covered the gash and stopped the flow. He was weak from losing so much blood. But he could not rest. He took a mouthful of water from the flask that hung from the saddle, and poured some more into a cupped hand to allow his horse to drink. Then it was on into the night, and towards Paris.

As the hours slipped past, their progress slowed. The horse was strong, but this was the second time in a day that it had made this journey. And he felt the weakness in his own body, a sickness that started in his stomach and grew in his head. He drank more water and rubbed his face with it; but the damp and cold held the sickness back only briefly. He realised that he was slipping in and out of sleep, and that they were moving forward only because the horse chose to.

In the end it took him several minutes to realise that the animal had stopped, and was whinnying gently. He heard the answering sounds of another horse. He forced himself to wake, to dismount and open the door to the stables, and shut it again once the horse had entered. Then his strength failed him.

There was one other who had been watching through the night, listening for any sign of his return. He heard the horses. He hurried from the house to the stables. The rider lay on the straw, the hem of his cloak drenched in blood. His eyes were closed; and, though he was breathing, he was unconscious. His discoverer murmured a prayer as he raised the rider up on his shoulders and bore him back into the house.

***

Sunday 23 November - evening

The Church of Saint-Jean-des-Champs

Lucien had lost the habit of regular church attendance in his twentieth year, when the Army had posted him to Algeria. Now he was in the confessional box for the second Sunday in succession. He would have taken comfort from the knowledge that there was a priest on the other side of the screen. But there was no-one. It was over half an hour since he had entered the glutinous darkness of the church and taken his place inside the wooden kiosk. He might wait all night and still be on his own.

He and Delourcq had returned to Paris the day before. The older man wanted no more horseback travel; he made the journey by coach. Lucien rode his horse and was in the capital by mid-afternoon. He had promised to let Laure know when he was back, and what happened at Lyons-la-Forêt. They met late at night in the Rue du Saumon. After the first fever of reunion, Lucien told all, and asked Laure to try and persuade her brother to meet him again. He needed help in making sense of one of Estève's papers.

And now he was waiting to see whether Carreleur had been won over by his sister. "We shall not meet again", he had said a week before. But they must meet - Lucien had no other recourse.

The tolling of the church-bell told him that a full hour had passed. Despite all his experience in the Army and the police, he never found waiting easy - not able to read or to talk to a companion, remaining alert for the moment when there was a noise or some other sign, wondering whether he had missed a signal and should move to another location. And perhaps Carreleur would refuse to come.

It was when he had all but given up hope that the door to the confessional box suddenly flew open. He started to his feet. No-one appeared. "Carreleur?" he asked. No answer. He stepped out. There were two men, both with hoods over their heads. The one on his right seized his arms and twisted them behind his back. The one on the left clamped a foul-smelling cloth over his nose and mouth. He struggled furiously, but in vain. His head fell back; he saw the brilliant haze around the head of the Virgin Mary, hovering above him; then he fell into a deep sleep.

When he opened his eyes again, there was no light at all. He was lying flat, on what his hands told him was a brick floor, running with water. "Where am I?" he groaned.

"In a safe place," came the reply. He recognised the voice.

"Carreleur! Where have you taken me?"

"Somewhere of my choosing, not yours."

"Have you poisoned me?" His head felt heavy.

"No. You inhaled a compound that the British have developed for inducing sleep. The effects wear off quickly."

Lucien raised himself off the ground. A pair of hands held his shoulders. A second voice spoke: "Do not attempt to get up!"

"How many of you are there?" Lucien asked irritably.

"That is no concern of yours, de Boizillac. What did you want to tell me?"

"I found Estève, near the village you mentioned. But I arrived too late - he had already been struck down, by the same assassin who killed Jattée and Connassier. I took some papers from Estève's dwelling. Most of them are of no consequence. But there was one letter among them --"

"I found it in your pocket," Carreleur interrupted. There was the sound of a light being struck, and Lucien was at last able to see his surroundings. He was in a low-vaulted crypt. Carreleur stood above him, still hooded, holding a spluttering torch in one hand and the letter in the other:

"*I thank you for the information which you sent about J and C. I salute your resolution in rejecting their proposals to seek my money for their silence. Be assured that I shall not overlook you, and that I shall also attend to the interests of* le colonel sérieux. *You will hear from me again.*"

He dropped the letter on to Lucien. "Dated a month ago, but unsigned. What of it?"

"You spoke of other accomplices last week. Whoever wrote this letter must have been one of them. Jattée and Connassier wanted Estève to join them in blackmailing him, but Estève refused. Now all three of them have been murdered."

"Thank you for your report, *Capitaine* de Boizillac," the tone was mocking, "but it seems to me that you have made little progress in the last week other than discovering a third corpse. It is impossible to say who wrote that letter."

"But who is *le colonel sérieux*?"

"I have no idea."

"That is why I sought this meeting. You helped me find Estève and, even though I reached him too late, he has left this further pointer which I must follow - if I can. I need you, and your network, to help me track down this colonel. Someone must recognise the title."

Neither man spoke for a few moments. "So be it," said Carreleur. "I shall get word to you if I learn his identity. Now we leave!" At once Lucien's shoulders were freed from their grasp, and his two captors ran swiftly across the crypt. They had reached a set of steps and extinguished the torch before Lucien could get to his feet. He felt his way along the walls and stumbled up the stairs, emerging into a side chapel of Saint-Jean-des-Champs. The others had vanished. He could only hope that Carreleur would contact him again.

***

Monday 24 November - midday

Plaine de Chaillot

Gianni saw that something was wrong. He had been scanning the landscape as he drove towards the clump of willows. The figure emerged well before he brought the carriage to a halt and began to approach them. But this was not the fast-moving shadow of their previous encounters. Now he dragged one leg, like an old dog. Gianni turned his gaze away as the man got into the carriage.

"Give me your report." The passenger held firm to his stick. He gave no signal to drive off again. He had seen everything - the hobbled approach, the awkward genuflection, the shivering.

"Master, it is done."

"But--"

The head sank even further. "But again I was surprised. There were two men. One I struck to the ground. The other fired a gun at me, and I ran away."

He gripped his stick more tightly. "So you were seen?"

"Yes, master."

"Were you followed?"

"No, master. I rode back with all speed, and I have remained in hiding until now. No-one has followed me."

"So, all three are dead now. You have done well. But you are injured?"

The kneeling man's body shook. "The bullet entered my leg. I had a fever. It will pass."

"Let me see your face."

Reluctantly he obeyed. It was the face of a sick man. His natural colour, which had endured despite several weeks spent in the dark chill of Paris, had given way to a sickly pallor; sweat covered his brow and cheeks, though the temperature in the carriage was no different from the autumnal chill of the plain; and his eyes were clouded by pain and fear.

"I salute your courage. Are you strong enough to return to your hiding-place?"

"Yes, master."

"Then remain there. In a few days you will be

released from your duty. Wait for my word. Now go."

With difficulty the kneeling figure stepped out of the carriage. Gianni heard the five knocks and whipped up the horses. Out of the corner of his eye he saw the man slump against one of the trees. May you crawl away and die! he thought, and sped back to the heart of the city.

***

Wednesday 26 November - morning

Ile de la Cité

Boizillac and Delourcq met up again at the start of each day, in the *Chien Fou*, but failed to identify anything more that they could do to drive the investigation forward. They kept out of the Prefecture. From talking to other agents, Delourcq learnt that a sort of paralysis had descended on the *Sûreté* since the departure of Canler. Some spread the rumour that the force was to be disbanded; others had heard that one of Louis-Napoléon's bodyguards was to be appointed as the new chief; and there was even the suggestion that Canler himself was to be brought back. But for the moment the only certainty was that there was universal confusion, and operations were either suspended or cancelled. By force of habit, Delourcq worked his way round the *cabarets* where he had obtained his best information over the years. He was greeted with a mixture of scorn for the immobilisation of the *Sûreté* and nervousness at the prospect that a seizure of power by the Bonapartist camp would mean a crackdown on the law-breakers of Paris. He found it hard to hide the fact that he shared these emotions.

Boizillac fell back on a routine of his own. After spending the first part of the day sharing a bottle of Ma Friche's thin red wine with Delourcq, he climbed on to his horse, trotted slowly southwards from the river, along the Rue Moufetard to the Barrière d'Italie, and then headed out into the open country to spend most of the remaining daylight hours riding. He told himself that fresh air and exercise would help him think more clearly; in truth, his thoughts made no progress, but his spirits rose.

He woke on Wednesday expecting the day to follow the same pattern. But a folded sheet of paper had been slid under the door of his rooms.

"Georges-Robert Alphonse Vauzuron - G R A V Algeria 1832 - 37, as Colonel"

Vauzuron. He had known him only ten years later, as a General; his promotion must have happened soon after his first posting to North Africa. Colonel GRAV - *le colonel sérieux*. What role had he played in the affairs of the *trois sodomites*?

Within half an hour Boizillac reached the *Chien Fou*. For once he was there before his older drinking companion. Delourcq came into the bar rubbing the top of his head with his sleeve. "You're prompt this morning, captain. Sorry I'm late. That fog is worse than ever." He poured himself some wine from the bottle on the table.

"Look at this, Delourcq." The younger man put the note, still folded, on the table.

"Is this from your contact?" Boizillac nodded. Delourcq opened it up and read it quickly. "Do you believe this, captain?" He was more than ready to believe it himself.

"It could be the answer. Or --" he paused, as if searching for words, "it could be a coincidence. I intend to ask Vauzuron myself."

"You mean, go to his house?" Boizillac nodded. "We got a poor enough reception last time."

"We did. And if that note points to the truth, there may have been more to Vauzuron's reaction than the arrogance of an old soldier. At all events, we must go and put the question to him."

Delourcq drained his glass. "I'll come with you to the Rue de Chaillot, captain. But, if you'll allow it, I'll wait on the doorstep. That house is too hot for my comfort."

"So be it," the younger man agreed. "Let's find a cab."

They reached Vauzuron's house in the Rue de Chaillot only a few minutes after nine. Delourcq was even more dubious about the welcome that they would be given so early in the day, but there was no restraining Boizillac. His gloved hand knocked loudly at the door.

It was opened by the Arab servant. His manner had changed since their first visit. Then Delourcq had sensed contempt beneath the surface show of civility. Now the brightness of the young Arab's eyes seemed troubled by a shadow of fear, which deepened when he recognised the visitors.

"Captain Boizillac of the *Sûreté*. I would like to speak to General Vauzuron as a matter of urgency."

"The General will be surprised --"

"That is of no consequence. Show me to him." He stepped into the house.

"And your companion?"

Delourcq looked at Boizillac, then spoke. "I'll stay here. It's better if the captain speaks to the General on his own."

Ben-Ahmed's eyes widened momentarily, then he inclined his head, shut the door, and led Boizillac up the stairs. "Delourcq was right," the young captain thought to himself. "It's like the hot-house at the Jardin des Plantes in here."

The servant opened the door to the drawing

room. "If you would be good enough to wait here, I shall inform the General." Boizillac crossed the room to look out of the windows. He could make out his fellow agent on the drive below. Delourcq was unkempt, and dressed in damp clothes that looked as though they had been bought and sold several times at the Temple flea-market, and had a history of petty crime before he joined the *Sûreté*. But after fifty years of a rough and ready existence he seemed to Boizillac a far better man than his more exalted contemporary whose house this was.

"De Boizillac? Good God, man, you're like a leach. What in hell's name are you doing here again?" An overweight figure in a dressing-gown stood in the doorway to the room. The red silk that enveloped him only emphasised his flushed complexion. "Not still poking your fingers into the filth on the streets of Paris, are you?"

"General Vauzuron, I regret the necessity of disturbing you at this hour of the day."

"Regret it, do you? You damn well should!" He went to sit on the chaise longue by the lighted fire, leaving the other man standing. "Well, what is it this time?"

Boizillac left his position by the windows and walked to the centre of the room. He had no fellow-feeling for Vauzuron, but it was common courtesy to explain to him his investigations of the last fortnight before confronting him with the note that he had found at Estève's shelter. And a slightly extended narrative would also allow him to watch his listener's reactions.

Neither man heard the coach on the driveway. But outside Delourcq saw it swing in from the Rue de Chaillot. The driver halted long enough to gesture to him to approach, then handed him a sealed letter. "For General Vauzuron, at once!" The words were clear enough, though the accent was not entirely French. Then the driver whipped up the horses and the coach raced away.

Even as Delourcq turned back towards the house, the door opened and Ben-Ahmed emerged. "I seem to have been mistaken for you," he said with a grin as he handed the letter over.

The joke was not shared. The Arab servant took the letter nervously, as though it might burn his fingers, and disappeared into the house again. Delourcq spat twice, once on the doorstep, and once in the rut that had been left by the wheels of the coach.

In the drawing-room, Boizillac had spoken the names of the murder victims - Connassier, Jattée and Estève. Vauzuron did not prevent him from telling his story. He asked him some bad-tempered questions about what led him to the third victim and his hideaway in the Normandy countryside, which Boizillac answered with difficulty since he had resolved to conceal his contacts with Carreleur. But Boizillac detected no faltering in the other man's attitude, that the investigation was irrelevant to the most pressing needs of security in general, and to his own concerns in particular.

Boizillac still had the note from Estève's shelter in his hand when the Arab servant knocked and came into the drawing-room. "An urgent message, General." He retreated again.

Vauzuron stood up from his seat when he saw the seal. He broke it open immediately and read the letter, ignoring Boizillac. And now a change came over him. Like a man transfixed, the letter remained in his hand, but his eyes went to the window and stared vacantly through it.

"General Vauzuron --" Boizillac began.

"Who wants me?" It was a mechanical reply. Then the older man recognised the young captain. "De Boizillac? Still here? You must leave at once! I have to attend to a matter of the highest importance." Now his gaze turned on Boizillac with an urgency that was impossible to ignore.

"But I have more to explain, General, and questions to ask."

"Indeed? Well, return this afternoon. Two o'clock - no, three. Better time of day anyway. Is that understood? Good. Now, I *must* ask you to leave."

Boizillac nodded briefly and left the room. The Arab servant was just outside the doors to the drawing-room. Wordlessly he showed the young captain downstairs and opened the main door for him. Then he withdrew.

"That was short and sharp, captain. What did the general have to say about *le colonel sérieux*?"

"He didn't. He received an urgent message while I was talking to him, and that put an end to our interview. We are to return this afternoon, at three."

"I was standing here when it was delivered. It was given to me by the driver of a very fine coach, but that little Arab creature took it from me almost before it was in my hand. So the general hasn't offered us his carriage this time, then?"

"His mind was on other things. We shall have to walk, I'm afraid." They set off. "Was there anything distinctive about the coach that brought the message?"

"I didn't see anything unusual. But I don't think the driver was French. He had an accent, and he looked dark. A Spaniard, maybe."

They had to walk only a quarter of a mile to reach the Seine at the Quai Debilly, where they found a cab that took them back to the Ile de la Cité. Delourcq returned to his table at the *Chien Fou*; Boizillac declined the invitation to share more of the offerings from Ma Friche's wine-cellar. They agreed to meet again in the Rue de Chaillot in mid-afternoon.

Boizillac rode there, after spending most of the intervening hours on horseback. Delourcq chose to walk. They approached the house together. Boizillac dismounted, and tethered his horse to a lime tree that stood to one side of the drive.

He knocked at the door. When a minute or so had elapsed without a response, he knocked again - and again there was no response. "He cannot have gone out, since we agreed that I should return at this time." Delourcq said nothing, but did not share the younger man's confidence in Vauzuron's punctiliousness. "I must ask him about that note!" He seized the heavy iron-ring handle of the door in a fit of impatience. The door was not locked. It opened as he turned the handle. He stepped inside and called "hallo!" Now there was a reply, but it was not the one expected. From somewhere in the depths of the building came the sound of women wailing. The two men glanced at one another and, without another word, hurried in the direction of the crying.

The kitchen was at the back of the house. When Vauzuron had come back from Algeria, he had brought with him Ben-Ahmed and three Arab women from the same family, who cleaned and cooked under the Arab servant's directions. Boizillac and Delourcq found the three women, swathed in their black costume and huddled together in a chorus of lamentation. The sight of the intruders drove them into even louder expressions of despair.

Boizillac took the arm of the oldest of the three

women. "What has happened?" he demanded. "Where is General Vauzuron?"

She bowed her head to avoid his eyes, and kept up her wailing. But, recognising Vauzuron's name in his speech, she pointed with her right arm towards a corner of the kitchen. The two men saw that there was an archway there - and found beneath it a flight of stairs that led to the basement. "Servants' quarters," Delourcq commented. "No place for a general."

The stairs led down to two rows of cellars on either side of a subterranean corridor. Each taking a lighted candle from the kitchen, the two men descended. The line of cellars on the left-hand side which were more centrally beneath the house held bottles of wine, sacks of flour and other provisions. The cellars to the right ended beneath the back wall of the house, and had high narrow windows at the level of the surrounding land. There were four of them side by side. Each had a door on to the corridor. Boizillac guessed that the second, third and fourth were assigned to the Arab women, and that the first was for Ben-Ahmed. But he was not in the cellar. Instead, the candles revealed General Georges-Robert Alphonse Vauzuron, lying in the entrance to the cellar, killed by a long carving-knife that had been plunged into his chest, and clutching his Army pistol - and further back, lying lifeless on the single bed in the cellar, a young Arab man who retained enough of his facial features to be recognisably not Ben-Ahmed, even though his left eye and the surrounding skull had been shattered by a gun-shot.

"No place for a general --" Delourcq repeated the phrase without humour, without expression, in disbelief. "No wonder the women are shrieking."

His words jolted Boizillac out of his shock at the discovery. He knelt down and looked closely at Vauzuron, at his wound and at his pistol. Then, stepping over him, he carried out a similar examination of the second corpse. "The first certainty is that it was Vauzuron's pistol that delivered the *coup de grace* to this man - at point blank range."

"Like an execution," suggested Delourcq. "But if Vauzuron did for him, who did for Vauzuron?"

"Not the dead man. That knife has been driven in to the hilt. Whoever wielded it would be marked with Vauzuron's blood. The dead man's hands are perfectly clean - of this killing at least. But you will notice the bloody bandage round his right ankle. I strongly suspect that I caused that wound, in the woods above Lyons-la-Forêt."

"So Vauzuron shot that fellow, and then someone else killed Vauzuron. Who?"

"Ben-Ahmed?"

"Ben-Ahmed. Where is he now?"

"We must find him, or we shall never get the answers that we need to solve our investigation. We must search the house. He may still be here. At all events, we must also use the opportunity to look for that letter that Vauzuron received this morning, and for any other useful papers."

They went back up the stairs to the kitchen. It was impossible to get any more information from the women, whose hysteria had only increased with the arrival of the two agents. Boizillac agreed with Delourcq that the latter would search the ground floor and the outbuildings at the back of the house, while the younger man looked upstairs.

The drawing-room was still as he had left it earlier in the day. A quick inspection showed that there was nothing of use to the investigation there. But on the other side of the landing was a smaller room which Vauzuron had used as a study. Boizillac glanced rapidly around, taking in the mementoes of military service in North Africa - jewelled daggers, curved swords, silver-chased spears - which covered the walls. There was a cabinet whose doors stood open to show a display of pistols; one was missing. A narrow window at the other side of the room threw a weak light on the General's desk. And there Boizillac saw a letter which had been opened, read and thrown aside. He picked up it, feeling the weight of the wax that had formed the now broken seal.

"*General*

I write to you in a matter of the highest importance.

For several weeks your house has harboured a young Arab, an associate of your man-servant. I have reason to believe that his presence has been concealed from you.

Information provided to me from different sources leaves me in no doubt that he is the man who has carried out a number of recent murders - of the trio of recidivists whom both you and I have good cause to remember from Algeria fifteen years ago.

It is clear that he was acting on the instructions of Estève, the most cunning of the three, who arranged for his two former accomplices to be cut down by the Arab.

I have now received a report that Estève himself has been killed, and by the very assassin whom he had previously engaged. Before he perished, however, he wounded his attacker in the leg.

The assassin is now in your house. He is weakened by his injury, but no less dangerous for that. I fear for your safety. Even more deeply, I fear for your good name. Any connections that might now appear between yourself and Estève and his accomplices could bring even less welcome echoes of former links.

I have judged it better, therefore, not to pass this information any further within official circles - but to urge you to take the resolution of this matter upon yourself.

In the language of the Army which I respect as much as you, this is an immediate call to arms.

M. Paris, November 26."

There was no clue to the author of the message other than the signature "M". Who was this? Who would have such information? Molé, the aristocrat who had been so powerful under Louis-Philippe? Morny, half-brother to the Prince-President? Or Maupas, the Prefect of Police himself? Or was "M" just a code-name? Certainly Vauzuron had known who sent the letter. It was clear to Lucien what must have happened, the moment he and Delourcq had left that morning. Vauzuron had come straight to his study, seized a pistol, and charged down to the cellar, to discover the unknown Arab in Ben-Ahmed's room. All the appearances suggested that he had shot him immediately, in the frenzy of the moment - and had himself been felled by the avenging hand of his own servant. It seemed that "M" was right to suspect that Vauzuron had been ignorant of the Arab's presence: his reactions to Lucien's own questions suggested that as well. And "M" had also correctly divined that Vauzuron was equal to taking the matter into his own hands. But he could not have known that the general would die as a consequence.

Lucien folded up the letter. He looked round the

study carefully, but found no other correspondence or papers that had any bearing on the murders. Delourcq appeared at the door.

"Not much to report, captain, except for one of the stables. I found some blood-stained straw raked up into a corner, but that doesn't tell us very much."

"This tells us more," Lucien replied, and gave him the letter. "This was what Vauzuron received when I was with him this morning."

Delourcq read the letter slowly and considered for a moment. "Signed with an M. It should be signed with a J - for Judas."

"You mean that he betrayed Vauzuron?"

"No," Delourcq breathed in reply. If he had been outside, he would have spat. "He betrayed that Arab. How could M know all these details -- how could he know about the Arab's wound -- unless the Arab was working for him and reporting to him?"

"But why would he want Vauzuron to kill him?"

Delourcq gave the younger man the letter again. "You keep a cat to kill rats. If all the rats are dead, what use is the cat any more?"

They looked at one another without speaking for a few moments. From below the sound of wailing voices could still be heard. Dusk was falling; darkness invaded the house.

"We must find Ben-Ahmed -- " Lucien said finally "-- and then M."

Unless the devil finds us first, Delourcq thought. The two men left the over-heated mortuary and plunged into the evening chill of the city.

Chapter Thirteen

Friday 28 November - afternoon

National Assembly

Henri d'Amboise had waited for his moment. The political credit that he had built up during the last years of Louis-Philippe seemed to have been destroyed in February 1848, when the king had been forced to scuttle away to England by the battles in the streets. But first Cavaignac and then Louis-Napoléon had pulled France back from the cliff's edge, back into a hinterland whose contours d'Amboise knew as well as anyone. He knew which forces were concealed by the folds in the land, and when they were likely to make a move. For so long as the royalists, the moderates and the Bonapartists seemed evenly balanced, he was a friend to all and zealot for none. But now was the moment when that balance would be decisively upset.

Speech was given to man to disguise his thoughts. It was one of finest *aperçus* bequeathed by the man whom d'Amboise admired most - Talleyrand, who had prospered under the Revolution, under the First Empire, and under the Restoration. The moment had come. D'Amboise rose to his feet in the Chamber to give the speech to which his forty years of life had been a careful preparation.

"Three weeks ago I sat at table with some of the finest soldiers who have been entrusted with positions of command in the French Army in recent years. One of them was General Georges-Robert Vauzuron, who served with distinction for many years in Algeria. We discussed how matters stand at present in France. General Vauzuron made clear his particular concern with crime and disorder in Paris, and with the need for rigorous and effective action by the police and the other forces of security.

"Today I learnt that General Vauzuron is dead. Earlier this week he was struck down by an unknown hand. Let me repeat this information. This week, in the heart of Paris, one of our outstanding military commanders has been butchered within the sanctity of his own house.

"I grieve for General Vauzuron, and for those who knew and loved him. But I grieve even more deeply for France. Has it come to this - that even the finest servants of our country are no longer safe against the violence and rapacity of crime? Is this the meaning and purpose of the Republic of 1848? Do we now face a new Reign of Terror, when the victims will be killed not in a public place of execution, but in their own homes?

"I have said that General Vauzuron was struck down by an unknown hand. It is true that the identity of the assassin remains unclear. But can there be any doubt about the forces behind this crime? We know of the secret societies who day by day are plotting the overthrow of the institutions and individuals who act as a shield against anarchy and mayhem. While their puppet colleagues in frock-coats and wing-collars parade in this Chamber and talk of the triumph which they expect in the elections next year, the puppet-masters meet in attics and cellars and draw up plans to gain power without wasting time on democracy.

"This week's victim is Vauzuron. Next week it could be any one of us. I say to you: we must not allow a new Reign of Terror to be inaugurated!

"Some will ask: what is to be done? To them I say: the answer is obvious. Fifty years ago, France rejected the King, installed a Republic, and descended into chaos, to be rescued by one man, who turned dross into gold, cowards into heroes, and despair into glory. Today, once again, there is one man who can bring heroism and glory back to our country, and who bears the same name of golden memory. To those who question, I say: either we shall have a brilliant future with that man, or we shall go into the darkness without him.

"France must choose. Is it to be equality, obscurity and criminality - or security, clarity, and glory?"

His final words were drowned out by the clamour on all sides of the Assembly. The calmer members of the republican faction limited themselves to jeers and hollow laughter; the hotheads were on their feet, waving their fists in fury at him and bellowing abuse. But even their noise was drowned by the cheers of approbation from the Bonapartists and the legitimists, who shook D'Amboise's hand until he felt that it would part from his body, and whose exultant rallying to his summons to action provoked the republicans to still greater expressions of outrage.

In the gallery overlooking the Chamber, partly concealed by the shadows and the plush velvet of the curtains, stood a small group of middle-aged men. They were the Prince-President's closest advisers. Persigny's face glowed and his eyes glittered; he had caught the fanatical infection carried up from below. "This is the clarion call we have been waiting for! France looks to us to secure her future!"

Maupas, the Minister of the Interior, and Mocquard, the President's *chef de cabinet*, kept their own counsel. Persigny might be the oldest adviser to Louis-Napoléon, but he was well-known for allowing his enthusiasm and impatience to get the better of his political judgement. They looked towards the fourth member of the group.

Morny drew on his cigar. He smiled, though the coldness of his eyes was unchanged. D'Amboise had his uses. If D'Amboise was ready to show his hand, he must be confident that no-one would chop it off. For once, the old fool who had been his half-brother's faithful servant for so many years had got it right. "My dear Persigny, I agree with you. Shall we go and report to the Prince-President?" He smiled again to see Persigny hurry away, like a dog rushing to return a stick to its owner. With his other two companions, he followed at a more measured pace. There was no need to hurry. Three days would be long enough to prepare.

***

Saturday 29 November - early evening

Pont de Grainmont

But three days had not been enough for Boizillac and Delourcq. They had exhausted all their contacts in the Paris underworld, and themselves, in their hunt for Ben-Ahmed. For once, the younger man had gone everywhere with Delourcq, to bars and drinking dens that made the *Chien Fou* look like a gentleman's club. It seemed to Boizillac that they had left no stone unturned, and that Delourcq knew every insect that hid from the light of day under them. In one or two places, they were shown Arabs whom fate had abandoned to the worst of existences, as slaves to bar-keepers in the rotten heart of the city. In the face of threats from Delourcq, their owners produced the pale-faced Algerians from the stinking cellars where they were kept. But Ben-Ahmed was not amongst them.

They made a daily call on Taillefer. He found out about most happenings on dry land. He certainly knew about anything or anyone that appeared in the turgid waters of the Seine. He had nothing to tell them.

It was more to raise their morale than in the hope of any news that the two agents went again to the Pont de Grainmont as the feeble light of Saturday was failing. They climbed down on to the barge moored below. The old river scavenger welcomed them on board. Since nursing Boizillac back to health, there was a friendship between them that went unacknowledged in words but was still real enough.

Taillefer was smoking his pipe. "No news, then?" he asked. "I've heard nothing, either. This whole city's as silent as the grave right now. It's almost as if all the little crimes have run away from the big crime that's going to happen."

"What big crime?" Delourcq asked.

"You know - Badinguet is about to steal France from under our noses."

Delourcq laughed, and spat into the river. Boizillac felt the impulse to speak against this mocking description of the head of state, but the words died in his mouth. These men had their own experience of the world which he could not gainsay. "It may be for the best," he offered.

The other two said nothing, but exchanged glances. "Like I said," Taillefer resumed, "I've heard nothing about your Arab. But I did have a thought." Boizillac and Delourcq looked at him. "Have you been back to Vauzuron's house since you found him dead there?"

"No," the young captain said. "We sent a message to the local *commissariat* so that they could take charge of the place. Why do you ask?"

Taillefer drew deeply on his pipe. "You've looked pretty much everywhere else in Paris, without success. What if your Arab went crawling back to his old home after the dust had settled? Maybe it's the only part of Paris that he knows. And as to the local *commissariat*, I doubt if they could find their own arse without looking at a signpost - with all due respect, captain."

Delourcq spat a second time. "Damn me if you're not on to something there. Do you agree, captain?"

But the younger man was already at the foot of the steps up to the quay. "I should have thought of it myself. Come on, Delourcq!"

They found a cab and made yet another trip across Paris to the house in the Rue de Chaillot. Darkness had fallen as they walked up to the front door. Of the local police there was no sign; they had completed their examination of the crime scene on the day after the double murder, moved the corpses to the morgue, and left the house to whatever fate Vauzuron's distant family might decide. If they were trying to find Ben-Ahmed, it was with a good deal less urgency than the two *Sûreté* agents who now rang the bell. Seconds passed. Boizillac rang again, and then a third time.

The door opened a few inches. A face appeared hesitantly; it was the old woman who had been in the kitchen when they discovered the two dead bodies.

Boizillac pushed the door wide open and stepped inside; Delourcq followed. The younger man said : "Ben-Ahmed." The old woman buried her face in her hands and turned away. The agents had expected no more. As they had agreed in the cab, they split up. Delourcq went straight to the kitchen and to the cellars below. Boizillac did a rapid tour of the ground floor and then explored the rooms above. Five minutes later they met up again in the hallway.

"Did you find anything?" Boizillac asked. Delourcq shook his head. "Nor did I."

"But I saw the old woman slip out as I came here just now."

"We must follow her."

Delourcq had seen the cobbled yard at the back of the house on his previous visit. It was closed off at the further side by the stables. Two or three smaller outhouses stood between the house and it. A light flickered in the stables. They ran towards it, their boots striking on the cobbles. As they hurried in past Vauzuron's tethered coach horses, they saw the old woman standing at the far end, holding a lantern; behind her hay-bales were piled up beneath a window, that was open to the night. They heard a thud as, unseen, someone dropped from the window to the ground outside.

Boizillac followed the same escape route, forcing himself through the window. He saw a robed figure running into the darkness, and jumped down to give chase. Immediately he was joined by Delourcq who had doubled back out of the stables and raced round. They ran side by side, Delourcq keeping pace with the younger man. "Ben-Ahmed!" Boizillac shouted breathlessly. "Stop! In the name of the Prefecture of Police, I command you to stop!"

It was to no avail. The effort of calling out had slowed him down; the fugitive was pulling away.

At first the pursuit was across the field behind Vauzuron's house, where his horses had been exercised. The ground was wet and uneven, but it had been cleared of trees and bushes, and they could keep the running figure in view, despite the darkness. Then he scrambled over the enclosing fence and was on a narrow track that flanked the property and threaded between the other houses and villas thrown up on the edge of the Plaine de Chaillot during the past thirty years. The track twisted and curved like a snake. Now the pursuers lost sight of their quarry; still his frantic progress was betrayed by the sound of his feet splashing through the water that had gathered in pits in the track. It was not long before both Boizillac and Delourcq were soaked up to their knees. Neither noticed.

"We must catch him!" Boizillac gasped.

Delourcq gritted his teeth and made an even greater effort. He outstripped the younger man and charged full-pelt round the next bend in the track. But one of his feet came down awkwardly in a pot-hole, throwing him off-balance, and he sprawled across the track. "Damn me for an old fool!" he groaned. Boizillac paused for a moment. "Don't waste time on me!" the older man shouted. "I've only twisted my ankle."

It seemed that the fugitive had also been stopped in his flight by the sound of Delourcq's fall. As Boizillac resumed the pursuit, the robed figure could be seen some twenty yards ahead. "Ben-Ahmed!" The Arab gave the briefest glance backwards over his shoulder, then redoubled his efforts to escape.

The track that they were following ran in an arc from the Rue de Chaillot to the Rue de Longchamps. Now Ben-Ahmed reached the further end and without pausing sped out into the thoroughfare. He may have been momentarily distracted by the sound of his name being shouted by his pursuer. But he failed to see the coach and horses riding into Paris from the Boulevard de Longchamps. The horses reared up as he burst into their path; Ben-Ahmed succeeded in avoiding their hoofs and the coach-wheels, only to collide with the side-panel and be knocked backwards to the edge of the road. He lay, unmoving.

The coach pulled up. The passenger climbed out. It was an elderly man, with a long mane of silver hair, dressed in a double-cape of black worsted. He carried a simple walking-stick, with which he hobbled as quickly as he could to the fallen figure.

Boizillac ran up, breathing heavily; his hair was

dishevelled, his face flushed, and his boots and breeches splattered with mud and ditch-water. Even his yellow gloves had been splashed. "What has happened?"

The passenger from the coach grasped his stick firmly, but spoke in a measured tone. "Who, sir, are you? And who is this unfortunate?" He pointed to the prostrate form.

"Captain Lucien de Boizillac, of the *Sûreté*. And this --" he crouched down to examine his quarry, "is an Algerian servant whom we wish to question."

"And who clearly does not want to give answers. I am sorry to say that he ran into my coach and was sent flying. I regret that my infirmity makes it impossible for me to bend down to see him. How is he?"

"Alive, but unconscious. He must have struck his head."

Delourcq appeared, limping. His appearance had suffered even more than Boizillac's from the chase of the last ten minutes. The coach passenger was again on his guard. "Is this an accomplice?" he asked.

Boizillac stood up. "This is Daniel Delourcq, a senior member of the *Sûreté*, with whom I am working in my investigations."

"Indeed? Well, Captain Boizillac and Monsieur

Delourcq, I should introduce myself. I am Louis, Comte de Bonnevoie. I am sorry to make your acquaintance under such circumstances, although I admire your zeal in discharging your duties at this hour of a Saturday night." He pointed his stick at Ben-Ahmed. "What has this man done?"

"He was employed by General Vauzuron. We think that he can help us with our investigation --"

"Vauzuron, you say? Vauzuron who was murdered in his bed this week?" There was a look of distaste on the face of the Comte. "Was this fellow in bed with him at the time? I'd heard that Vauzuron was turned by his spell in Algeria."

Delourcq had knelt down to examine the fallen man. "Pardon my speaking up, sir, but we need to move him from here quickly. Should we take him to Taillefer's, do you think?"

Boizillac turned to the Comte de Bonnevoie. "Monsieur, would you allow us to transport this man in your coach? If we can get him to a place of safety, we can watch over him and be on hand to question him when he recovers."

The older man leaned heavily on his stick. "It was my coach that was responsible for his condition. I can hardly refuse. Bring him over. I'll tell my driver."

Delourcq had already raised the Arab on his shoulders and followed quickly in the Comte's footsteps. Once again, Boizillac marvelled at the resilience of the older agent who was able to act on thoughts almost before they had been formulated. Ben-Ahmed was laid on the floor of the carriage, with Delourcq's rolled-up jacket under his head. The Comte de Bonnevoie sat against the back of the carriage, Boizillac opposite him. Delourcq climbed up to sit alongside the driver, and the carriage lurched off towards the city centre.

It took little more than a quarter of an hour to reach their destination. At first the passengers inside the carriage were silent. Boizillac kept his eyes on the unconscious figure at his feet; the Comte looked at first through the window at the darkening townscape. He coughed and spoke. "I am sorry about this accident. All the more sorry because this is my last evening in Paris, for some time I think."

Boizillac looked up. "You have an estate outside Paris?"

"At Bonnevoie-sur-Loire, a day's drive to the west. I spend my summers there, and some of the autumn too, when the grapes are picked and pressed. I have been back here for only a few weeks -- and now I am running before the storm!" His face flushed. Boizillac said nothing. "You know what I mean, young man. You've heard what's been said in the Assembly -- in the streets as well, I don't doubt. It's all up with France. By Christmas we shall have our new little Emperor on the throne, and those of us who have spent the last twenty years trying to build the citizenry up can retire with our books of philosophy."

"Forgive me, monsieur," Boizillac ventured, surprised by the older man's remarks, "but with your title and your lands --" He left the sentence hanging, embarrassed by his candour.

"I might be expected to welcome a firm hand at the centre of government?" He smiled. "Thirty years ago -- when I was your age perhaps -- I thought that way. France needed Louis XVIII, to help heal the wounds left by the savagery of the years before. But Louis died too soon, and was succeeded by Charles, who wanted to take France back into the eighteenth century. He failed, but he stoked up the fires of resentment that went on burning under Louis Philippe. As I have grown older, I have become more sensitive to hot and cold. The fires are not extinguished. I sense that they have spread under our feet, along hidden passageways and underground tunnels. They scorched Paris three years ago, and were forced back down. Louis-Napoléon may seize the imperial crown, but he cannot quench the fires. Sooner or later the ardour of the citizens of France will flare up again, and the new Empire will crumble into ashes." He stopped, and passed his hand over his face. "Well, well, these are an old man's nightmares, and I see that you do not share them. But there is no place for me in this city which is about to be annexed by the Bonapartists." He looked out of the window again. "We are stopping. Is this where you wanted to go?"

Boizillac could see dim outline of the Pont de

Grainmont. "Thank you, monsieur, it is." Delourcq was already opening the door. "I hope that you are not too troubled by your nightmares."

"I plan to cultivate my garden, captain. That should divert me."

Delourcq raised Ben-Ahmed on to his shoulders and made for the parapet above the barge. Boizillac gave a salute as the carriage moved off; the Comte de Bonnevoie nodded in acknowledgement, and was gone.

Chapter Fourteen

Monday 1 December - evening

Père Lachaise Cemetery

Georges-Robert Alphonse Vauzuron was buried in Père Lachaise at half past three in the afternoon. Rain had fallen steadily all day. Thin muddy rivulets ran down the embanked earth at the top of his grave, and merged with the puddles that had formed at the base. The Army took charge of his funeral, and was represented by a senior officer and a detachment of guards. Otherwise the mourners consisted of a small number of relatives of his dead wife, and his only surviving brother, who had taken over the estate.

Despite Vauzuron's posthumous celebrity in the Assembly, none of the political factions was present. A week before their thoughts had been with France and the fate of the nation. Now they wanted to save their own skins; the dead could bury themselves. There was one exception. A carriage had driven into the cemetery separately from the main cortege, and stayed to one side. While the mourners followed the priest to the graveside, and bowed their heads as the coffin slid and splashed into the earth, the occupant of the carriage watched from the shadows. He saw the sodden figures embrace, and the soldiers fire off their salute, and the grave-diggers push the soil back into the grave. He waited as they all hurried away under the leaden sky; took a last look at the raw mound of clay that marked the burial; then struck the gold pommel of his stick against the roof. Gianni shook the reins, and they moved off.

An hour later the cemetery was in almost complete darkness. Some of the larger tombs sheltered candles or storm-lanterns which had been lit during the day by visitors; their light struggled ineffectually against the night that covered the necropolis.

Delourcq knew Père Lachaise as well as he knew the Temple market. Both were favoured by the criminal fraternity as hiding-places for contraband, and he was as used to lifting tomb-stones as he was to turning over market-stalls in order to look for stolen plate and ornaments. To be absolutely certain of his ground, he had come to the cemetery in the morning to check on Vauzuron's burial-site. Now he led the way, carrying a dark lantern.

He said nothing; nor did the men behind him. Ben-Ahmed followed obediently, seemingly in a trance. At first when he had regained consciousness on Taillefer's barge on Sunday morning, he had refused to say anything. A day's confinement brought about a change of heart. The young Arab asked to be taken to Vauzuron's burial-place. In return he would tell the agents what he knew. Gusts blew rain into their faces. Delourcq in front and Boizillac at the rear ducked their heads and covered their eyes. Ben-Ahmed faced unflinching into the wind, apparently oblivious to the cold and wet.

"This is it," Delourcq said at last, holding the lantern so that its light fell on the newly turned earth. "This is the grave." The Arab sank to his knees. His head dropped, and his body shook. "Don't leave him too long," Delourcq whispered to Boizillac. "He'll be no good to anyone at this rate."

The young captain put his hand on the Arab's shoulder. "Ben-Ahmed, we have kept our promise, and brought you here. Now you must keep yours."

There was silence for a few moments. Then Ben-Ahmed spoke, still kneeling on the ground, still with his eyes on the grave, but just audible to his two listeners. "I was a boy when I was sent to serve in his household. At the time I did not know whether I would stay for a week, a month or longer. I left my village and travelled for two days to reach Algiers. His household was not as rich then as it later became, but even so I was dazzled by its splendour. He took little notice of me at first, but that changed after the first few months. I could tell that I pleased him.

"When I had been with him for a year, he sent for my father. He said that he wished to arrange that I should remain in his household for so long as he stayed in Algeria. Of course, when the time came for his return to France ten years later, I came here with him. My father made the journey to Algiers, and they agreed on my service. But they discussed other matters too. My father was to pay us another visit in six months' time.

"It was a few weeks afterwards that the patrol

carrying gold and silver coin was ambushed. The captain and the sergeant were killed. Only the three ordinary soldiers returned to Algiers, wounded and empty-handed."

"Jattée, Connassier and Estève," Boizillac said.

"As you say," Ben-Ahmed confirmed. His gaze was fixed on the grave. "The months went by until my father came once more to the house. This time he was accompanied by two of his brothers, and they brought with them bundles of fodder for their horses. But it was not fodder. It was the coin which was stolen from the patrol."

"And you saw the coin?" asked Boizillac.

"Not then," Ben-Ahmed replied. He nodded at the burial mound. "At his command, my father hid the coin in the cellars. But before he returned again to our village, he told me what he had done, and said that he and his brothers had been given one-sixteenth of the coin as their reward. I saw the sacks of money only later, when they were removed."

"When was that?"

"Not long after. A younger officer, who had occasionally visited our household, returned to France a few months after this, and he shipped the coin out hidden in his baggage."

"What officer? What was his name?"

"At the time, I knew him only as M. My own master said that we should never speak his name in full, but that he would act as guardian of the coin and would always be a friend to us. It was more than ten years until we saw him again."

"When General Vauzuron finally left Algeria and came to Paris?"

The Arab's forward gaze faltered. "Those ten years were the happiest of my life, in his household, in my native country. I feared that fate was turning against me when we left, and I think that he did too. Three years ago we came to this Paris of yours --" for a moment his impassive tone of voice gave way to a surge of contempt, "-- this place of darkness, dirt and misery. But he filled the house in the Rue de Chaillot with memories of Algeria, and it came to seem not so vile. Until a few months ago."

"What happened?"

"There was a knock at the door one evening in the summer. I recognised the caller even before he spoke his name. He was much fatter than he had been in Algeria, but there was the same cruel look in his eyes and the same weakness in his flabby lips. *You're a pretty one,* he said, *I wish I'd come across you when I did my service. Run along now, and tell the General that Monsieur Jattée would like a word with him.* He spent an hour upstairs, and I could hear shouting. Then he left, with a grin on his face. Within half an hour, the

General rode out in his carriage. When he came back, late that night, he said only that we would not be troubled by Jattée again. But I knew that he had been to see M."

Delourcq spat with the wind. "Yes, but who is M., for pity's sake?"

Boizillac gestured to him. "There can be little more to tell. We must be patient."

"He had other meetings with M., but chose to tell me nothing about them. And for the last month I kept from him the knowledge that I had of M.'s plans. Four weeks ago, unannounced, my uncle's son Saleem appeared in the Rue de Chaillot. It was the first time that I had seen him since I left Algeria. He told us only that M. had sent a message to our family, to say that after fifteen years the secret of the ambush would be revealed unless the family helped him by wielding an avenging sword. Saleem had been chosen, as the strongest, and had travelled in disguise to stay in hiding with us."

"And the General was not informed?"

Ben-Ahmed's head dropped again. "May I be forgiven for my deceit. Saleem said that M. had commanded that no-one else should be told of his arrival. He hid in the stables, and even the groom knew nothing about him."

"And when we first came to the Rue de Chaillot,

with the scrap of material?"

"I recognised it. It came from our village. It belonged to Saleem. And when I heard your story, I realised what M. had planned to ensure that Jattée and the others could never disclose the secret of the stolen coin. But I said nothing to my master, and he was unaware that the assassin was receiving food and drink from his servants."

"And you had still not told him when he received the letter from M. last week that revealed Saleem's presence in his house?"

"It all happened so suddenly. You called to speak to the General. The letter was delivered. You left. And immediately he came down to our rooms, found Saleem, and emptied his pistol into his head. And suddenly I had nothing in my mind but the words 'an avenging sword', and a knife was in my hand and I --" He paused, breathed deeply, and continued. "And I delivered him into the pit before me." He fell silent.

Delourcq could wait no longer. The figure on the ground was hunched and spent. He took hold of the Arab's shoulder and pulled him round. "But who is M.?" His voice was rough with exasperation.

Ben-Ahmed looked Delourcq up and down in the flickering light, and then turned his gaze towards Boizillac. "Morny." The name hung in the air. "It was Morny who planned the killings of Jattée and the others - and of Saleem." His eyes were still on the young captain. "But it was I who killed the General, and I who must atone!"

In a moment he had leapt to his feet and butted into Boizillac, seizing his pistol and sending him sprawling. Even as Delourcq started to react, Ben-Ahmed knocked the lantern out of his grasp. Delourcq got a hand to the Arab's clothing, and then let go as he was kicked in the stomach. Before either of the agents could recover from the assault, Ben-Ahmed held the pistol to his head and fired. In the blaze of the explosion they saw him fall backwards, onto Vauzuron's grave. Then all was dark again.

Delourcq ran to a tomb nearby and returned with a burning candle inside a glass jar. Boizillac had scrambled across the ground to where the young Arab lay. He looked up at his fellow agent. "He is dead. Another one killed by Morny!"

"Come, captain," said the older man. "You won't bring him back to life by sinking into the earth next to him." He helped him to his feet. "Take this candle. I know where they store the equipment here. I'll fetch what we need to give him a decent burial."

"Bury Ben-Ahmed here and now?"

"What's the point of telling the *commissariat*? They'll only put his body in the morgue, then dump him in a pauper's grave. Better to leave him here, with his master." Delourcq moved off into the night, and returned within five minutes. The two men used the spades that he brought to dig out the grave. Delourcq had found some stout sacks which served as a shroud. They lowered the corpse into the ground and heaped the soil back over. "May he rest in peace," the older man muttered, and spat in valediction.

Boizillac turned from the grave. They were in a higher part of the cemetery, and facing to the south he could see the heart of the city below them. Lights glittered through the haze of falling rain. Down there he knew was the Elysée Palace, the Prince President and his associates - and chief among them the man whose name had been spoken by Ben-Ahmed at the moment of taking his own life. Boizillac was filled with the knowledge of the confrontation that he must seek. "It's between us now," he breathed into the night air.

"You can't arrest Morny." Delourcq's voice cut through the stillness. "He's so far above the law he's invisible!"

"You're right, as usual. But, if I can't arrest him, I can still spell his crimes out to him." He could tell from Delourcq's silence what the older man thought of his plan. "I shall go to his office in the morning. Look for me in the *Chien Fou* at midday."

They left. Rain filled the footprints that they had stamped in the soil of the cemetery.

***

Monday 1 December - towards midnight

Elysée Palace

The guests at the Prince-President's regular Monday evening reception had left. Only a small group of his closest advisers remained with Louis-Napoléon, conferring in the *salon d'argent* under portraits of Napoléon I and Queen Hortense - Mocquard, his private secretary; General Saint-Arnaud; Persigny; and Maupas. Morny was the last to arrive, coming from an evening spent at the Opéra-Comique.

The Prince-President unlocked a drawer in a desk at the side of the room, and took out a folder on which was written the word RUBICON. Slowly and softly, he read out the contents of the documents it contained - a decree dissolving the National Assembly, a message of command to the Army, and a proclamation to the populace at large. Maupas, as Prefect of Police, was to direct the operations of the civil forces; Saint-Arnaud, as War Minister, would deploy the military; Morny was appointed Minister of the Interior, and was to orchestrate everyone's efforts, with accountability only to Louis-Napoléon himself. Persigny had no new role, but his enthusiasm for the long-awaited moment of action overcame his disappointment at being eclipsed by others.

The chimes of midnight marked the end of the meeting; the danger of failure and disgrace seemed to resonate in the conspirators' minds. Looking round the room, Morny said sombrely: "Gentlemen, don't forget that we are risking our skins."

Mocquard, the oldest man there, commented: "My skin is so worn out that I don't have much to lose!" Persigny laughed heartily, and slapped him on the back.

All eyes turned to Louis-Napoléon. He held the folder in front of him and traced with his finger the fateful word on its cover. Then he looked up. "Hope, gentlemen. It has carried me this far. It will carry us through these next few hours." The note of conviction in his voice was at odds with his troubled gaze.

Morny's eyes flashed. "At all events, brother, you can be confident that tomorrow you will still have a guard at your door - for good or ill!" They shook hands, and slipped away into the night.

***

Tuesday 2 December - morning

Rue de Grenelle

Boizillac spent the night in the Rue du Saumon. He had waited until midnight for Laure to return from the theatre. Fortunately, she had been alone, and she let Lucien in behind her. She carried the latest rumours from society. Some said that Louis-Napoléon would move against the Assembly by the weekend; others claimed that the secret societies of Paris and Lyons had agreed to stage an insurrection even sooner. Boizillac did not want to tell her of his plans, but she forced him to explain the state of his clothing, which was still sodden and smeared with mud. When he repeated Ben-Ahmed's story she voiced all the fears for his safety which Delourcq had kept to himself.

It was some time before they fell silent, as sleep overtook Laure. Lucien stayed awake; his thoughts darted between the woman at his side and the task that he faced. As the first thin brightness appeared in the sky and Laure still slept, he got up, dressed, and went out into the street.

Overnight Saint-Arnaud's troops had occupied the printing-presses, to produce posters which now covered walls everywhere. Boizillac read one. The National Assembly was dissolved; universal suffrage was re-introduced; there would be a plebiscite in two weeks' time; a state of siege was in force. There was a signature: Morny, Minister of the Interior.

So they had been right, Taillefer, the Comte de Bonnevoie, and the rumour-mongers Laure had heard - the Republic was being swept away in favour of a Bonapartist regime. Tired as he was, Lucien felt his pulse quicken at the prospect of a return to the glories of fifty years before. The Prince-President might not have the genius of his uncle, but he had the magic of his name. And yet -- he also had Morny as his right-hand man, a smuggler of stolen coin, organiser of a series of murders, betrayer of his own henchmen. Were these the qualities that were needed to seize control of a country?

He walked south towards the centre. As the daylight grew, he saw detachments of soldiers stationed at the intersections of the main thoroughfares. They had been in position for some hours, and already they seemed bored, and were joking among themselves. Even so, their presence on the streets seemed to darken the shadows. Boizillac glanced nervously at them and hastened past.

He knew that the Minister of the Interior had his offices in the Rue de Grenelle, which ran from the Rue Montmartre to the Palais du Louvre. The nearer he came to the Seine, the more troops were in place in the squares and on street corners. For a moment he feared that they would bar his way. But he spoke to the officer in charge of the detachment outside the Ministry and gave his identity as an agent of the *Sûreté*, and entered without further hindrance.

It was now past eight in the morning. The building was already full of activity. Couriers, some in uniform, hurried past him. Clerks walked to and fro with freshly sealed documents. *Grands bourgeois* in top hats and fur coats strolled along the corridors, curious to discover what speculation their good friend Morny was pursuing now. Boizillac found the way to the Minister's outer office and went over to the clerk at the door. "I must speak to the Comte de Morny".

The functionary looked with distaste at Boizillac's coat and boots, still marked by the damp and dirt of Père Lachaise. "The Minister cannot be disturbed at the moment."

"Tell him that it is a matter of extreme urgency. I am Captain Lucien de Boizillac, of the *Sûreté*. I wish to speak to the Comte de Morny in the matter of General Vauzuron's death. Tell him that."

"De Boizillac, you say? Wait here. I shall convey your request." The clerk stepped into the inner office, closing the door smartly behind him. There were others who were waiting to see Morny. They sat in chairs disposed around the outer room; some chatted amongst themselves; others kept their eyes on the door to Morny's sanctum, and now scrutinised this new and slightly bedraggled arrival.

The clerk re-emerged. His attitude had changed. "The Minister has asked me to tell you that he would welcome a conversation with you, Monsieur de Boizillac. He regrets, however, that his immediate pre-occupations make it impossible for him to receive you at this moment. If you would take a seat, he hopes that he will be able to talk to you within an hour." The functionary gestured towards an empty chair, and added in an undertone: "You do realise, Monsieur, that the Minister is currently sending out orders to all Prefectures in order to secure the country against insurrection?"

Lucien said nothing. He sat down. He had no doubt that the mention of Vauzuron's name had struck home. If necessary he was ready to wait all day in order to confront Morny with the truth that he had discovered.

The morning wore on. A constant stream of people flowed past, checked and then released by the clerk at the door. Somewhere in the distance a clock struck nine. The heaviness of immobility settled over Lucien; he felt his eyes close, and his head fell forward. A voice was calling his name. "Monsieur de Boizillac! The Minister can see you now."

He blinked, and rubbed his eyes. "What time is it?" he asked.

"Shortly after ten. Come now, Monsieur, you are keeping the Minister waiting." With a firmness that just stopped short of pushing, he guided Lucien into the inner office and shut the connecting door without following him in.

It was a large room. Smoke hung in the air. To one side three well-padded chairs were clustered round a fireplace; cigar ends had been thrown into the hearth. In the centre were a number of smaller chairs and a couple of slim writing-desks cluttered with papers. Finally, near the windows was a desk as large as a dining-table, with stout legs carved to end in claw-and-ball bases, and holding two matching candelabra which blazed with light. It was obvious that the room had accommodated at least half a dozen people for the last few hours, but now stood empty - except for the figure behind the desk.

"I am sorry to have kept you waiting, captain."

Boizillac strained his eyes against the brilliance of the candles. He realised that two of the points of light were the figure's eyes. They had fixed on him the moment he entered.

"Monsieur de Morny, I am --"

"Lucien de Boizillac. I know. I know that you are a captain in the *Sûreté*, that you have been conducting an investigation over the past month with one Daniel Delourcq, and that you discovered General Vauzuron murdered in his house in the Rue de Chaillot." Boizillac took a step towards the desk. "Please stay where you are, captain. It allows me to see you clearly at last.

"I assume that you have come here with questions about my past. But first of all I want to tell you something about the present, and the future. Today, the Prince-President appointed me Minister of the Interior. Do you know what the Prince-President wants me to do? He wants me to save France from itself.

"Eight out of ten Frenchmen want nothing more than money in their pocket, wine on their table, and a man of character in the Elysée Palace. But for every eight decent citizens, there is one ultra-royalist who wants to turn the others into serfs, and one unreconstructed Jacobin who wants to cut off their heads. And for the last three years the Ultras and the Jacobins have been plotting to take this country back to the last century, by guile if possible, with a bloodbath if necessary. In the name of the Prince-President, I am acting to protect the decent citizens. It was only a matter of weeks until the ghosts of the past tried to drag this country down. Now we shall exorcise them once and for all."

It was a speech that might have been thundered by an orator in the National Assembly. Morny spoke with as little heat and passion as a school-master reading the attendance register. But his determination was unmistakable. "No-one will stop us."

"Monsieur de Morny, I have come here not because of political matters, but because of a series of crimes that have been committed. My investigation has covered the deaths of six people in the last month. The last of these victims, who died only yesterday, named you   with his last words."

"As his killer?"

"No. He committed suicide. It was Ben-Ahmed, General Vauzuron's servant for fifteen years. He explained your connection with Vauzuron and with the three surviving members of an Army patrol that was ambushed in Algeria in 1836. He explained your role in transporting the stolen gold and silver to France. And he explained your involvement in the murders of Jattée, Connassier and Estève, killed by the assassin whom you brought to Paris."

"Did he sign a written attestation of these explanations?"

"No."

"And now he is dead?" Morny let the question hang in the air. He rose from behind the desk and, cigar in hand, walked towards Boizillac. There was a strong facial resemblance between Morny and Louis-Napoléon, accentuated by the cut of moustache and beard, save that, while the Prince-President's expression generally suggested a death-mask, the flash of Morny's eyes and the tautness of his mouth revealed a lively intelligence that was always at work. "You allege that I was an accomplice to the theft of Army treasure fifteen years ago, and that I have now brought about the murders of the main conspirators in that theft, all on the word of an Arab man-servant who has killed himself - no doubt when the balance of his mind was disturbed?" Still there was no emotion in his voice.

Boizillac retrieved something from a pocket of his coat. "I do have one piece of paper. On the day that I found Vauzuron stabbed to death, I discovered this message in his study. *'In the language of the Army which I respect as much as you, this is an immediate call to arms. M.'* Are you not M., Monsieur de Morny?" He offered the letter to the other man, for closer inspection. It was not taken.

"I had two periods of service in Algeria." He drew on the cigar and exhaled the smoke slowly. "My first spell, at the end of 1835, was disastrous. I was caught up in the chaotic retreat from Mascara to Oran, I was ravaged by dysentery, and finally I was invalided back to France. A year later I went back. I took part in the siege of Constantine and saved the life of General Trézel. In January 1837, when I was posted back home, I was given the *légion d'honneur*. Is this the record of a man who would ally himself with a gang of common thieves?" He paused. Lucien offered no response. Morny spoke again, and now there was a more animation in his voice. "But you are right. I did send that message to Vauzuron. It was Vauzuron who persuaded me to join the conspiracy. There may be twenty-five year-olds who could resist the offer of two hundred *louis d'or* and as much again in silver - I was unable to. And it was Vauzuron who came running to me again years later when Jattée started his blackmailing. After fifteen years' living off the wealth that he embezzled, Vauzuron was as weak and soft as an old woman. So I took the matter in hand."

Suddenly there was a knocking at the door. It opened slightly, and the clerk looked round. "Will Monsieur le Ministre see --"

"Not now!" Morny barked. The clerk retreated. "Do you know what sort of man Jattée was?" The question took Boizillac by surprise. "He was filth! No-one, man, woman or child, was so innocent that Jattée would respect them. His only pleasure was in defiling others. And Connassier? A drunken sot, who used his fists to make up for his inability to string a sentence together. And Estève? He had more intelligence and less strength than the other two, so he used them as his instruments, to generate the vice that he was too cowardly to take part in directly. They got their fair share of the coin, and they wasted it in drink and depravity. What further claim did they have, on those who had used the wealth wisely? What further claim did they have on life?"

Boizillac felt his head spinning at this sudden rush of confession. "And Saleem? He carried out your orders - and you incited Vauzuron to kill him."

"When I last saw Saleem, it was clear that he was very ill, probably with blood poisoning caused by the shot which I believe you fired at him. Vauzuron was certain to discover his presence in his house in that condition. I merely precipitated matters -- and arranged what I regard as a mercy killing. I had not expected that Vauzuron would himself be killed. But that too was a mercy - the man had become a mockery of his former self, and an embarrassment to all those who knew him from his time in Algeria." He threw the butt of the cigar into the fire. "But you knew all this before you entered my office." He came up to Boizillac, clamped his hands to the young man's shoulders and looked him straight in the face. "I am proud of you, Lucien. You have fulfilled all my expectations when I had you transferred to the *Sûreté*. Now come, sit down."

He led Boizillac, uncomprehending, to the chairs by the fire. "Listen to me, Lucien. I have confirmed the truth of your suspicions because I know that you will never, can never, repeat what I have said to anyone else."

A surge of anger rose through the confusion in the younger man's mind. "Are you threatening me?"

Morny smiled, reassuringly. "No. You cannot betray my confidence - because we are brothers. You may know that my father is Charles de Flahaut. He is your father too - though our mothers were different women. My mother was Hortense de Beauharnais. Yours was Geneviève de Lassource."

"No! You are wrong! Geneviève de Lassource is my aunt."

"So you have always been told. But Flahaut and Mademoiselle de Lassource had a secret liaison which led to your birth -- and Geneviève's married sister, Madeleine de Boizillac, and her husband agreed to adopt you and raise you as their son."

"I don't believe you."

"Of course you don't. But wait." Morny walked rapidly to the far side of the office and opened a door that Lucien had not noticed before. "*Viens, mon père.*"

Lucien's eyes watched, but his mind struggled to make sense of what they saw. Morny inclined his head as a General of the French Army in full dress uniform stepped into the room. Charles de Flahaut was taller than the Minister, as tall as Lucien himself. His grey hair, furrowed brow and cheeks, and stiffness of movement showed that he was in the winter of his life. But his sixty-five years had not bent his back or clouded his proud gaze, which had seen Austerlitz, Moscow, Leipzig and Waterloo at the side of the

Emperor. Now that gaze was turned on the young man seated by the fire. "Lucien?" he called.

Boizillac stood up and walked slowly towards him. His doubts fell away with each step. The other man was twice his age, but they shared the same gaunt and lengthy build, the same softly curving nose and narrow lips, the same chestnut eyes with long lashes. "I am Lucien de Boizillac, sir."

They met. With a cry of happiness the old man embraced him, then held him again at arm's length. "Forgive me for keeping this secret from you for thirty years. I gave my pledge to your mother and her sister to do so, until they released me from it. They did so a few weeks ago, when I wrote to them in strictest confidence. They are fine, noble women and I owe them an eternal debt."

He turned to Morny and shook his hand. "I thank you, Auguste, for enabling me to meet both my sons on this glorious day!" A clock struck the quarter-hour. "And now I must leave you again. The Emperor -- the Prince-President -- has asked me to be at his side when he rides out into Paris this morning. I must not delay. We shall speak again very soon, Lucien. *Adieu, mes fils!*" He left.

There was silence in the room for some time. Then Morny spoke. "He kept the secret from me as well until this summer. But I see that the meeting has convinced you of our kinship. There are worse families to belong to on the first day of a new Bonapartist regime!"

"And -- does he know why I came here today?"

Morny lit another cigar. "My father knows many of my secrets, but not all of them. When you arrived here this morning, I sent word to him to come here urgently. I told him that it was essential that he should confirm his paternity to you, to provide a sound foundation for a discussion which you and I needed to have today." He sat down by the fire. Lucien was still in the middle of the room. "I needed to say no more at this stage." He looked across at the younger man. "The history that has been revealed in this room this morning is known only to you and me."

"And you ask me never to reveal it."

"Lucien, I shall speak plainly and briefly. I must shortly return to my work on behalf of the Prince-President. I see three pressing reasons for your silence. The first and strongest is your loyalty to your family - to myself, as your father's older son. The second is your duty to the Government, particularly this Government which embodies the ideals that I know you have held dear. And the last reason bears the name Marc Carreleur." Lucien looked at him without understanding. "Marc Carreleur is a member of a secret society which threatens the rule of law and order. Like scores of others, he has been taken into custody overnight, and is in the Conciergerie while the new Government -- the Minister of the Interior -- considers how best to deal with such revolutionary elements. Yes,

Lucien, we know of your friendship with his sister. It is a point in his favour, unless your own behaviour suggests that Marc Carreleur's hostility towards the State has contaminated your views. Your silence would reassure us in that respect. It would also leave us with discretion to treat Monsieur Carreleur more leniently than his fellow conspirators -- at least a dozen of whom have been shot dead today while resisting arrest."

"To save Marc Carreleur's life, I must remain silent?"

"As must Daniel Delourcq. As should any loyal agent of the State."

Their gazes met. It was Morny who looked away first. Lucien walked to where he sat. He took the message to Vauzuron from his pocket again, crumpled it into a ball, and threw it on to the fire. "Goodbye, brother. My silence begins now."

The other man kept his eyes on the flames as Boizillac left the room. The paper fell into ashes. He was smiling.

***

Tuesday 2 December - midday

Ile de la Cité

It was less than thirty minutes' walk from the Rue de Grenelle to the *Chien Fou*. It took Lucien over an hour that morning. His way was blocked by the crowds who had come to the centre out of curiosity, and to watch the triumphant procession of Louis-Napoléon on horseback, accompanied by the old King Jérome, Saint-Arnaud, Fleury, Magnan and Flahaut, and massed outriders of cuirassiers and lancers shouting "Vive Napoléon!". But, even if the streets had been clear, his steps would have been slowed by the turmoil of his thoughts, and his realisation that, although he was headed towards a rendezvous at midday, he had no sense of the direction of his life after that.

Delourcq was in the street, waiting for him. Boizillac had no heart for the bar. "I have a good deal to tell you, but not in there. Let's make for the river."

They walked together to the Pont au Change. Delourcq listened as the younger man told him what had happened at his meeting with Morny, and why the two of them were now bound by a command of silence. They stood watching the sluggish brown water flow beneath them. The morning's parade had gone now, but looking downstream they could see troops and horses occupying the embankments. Delourcq offered Boizillac his flask, emptied the last drops into his own throat, and hid it away again.

"You know that I have always hoped for the return of the great days of the Empire," Lucien said. "Today they have at last come back -- and yet I feel as though my hopes have ended. What am I to do?"

Delourcq spat over the parapet. "When I was in the Army, the old fellows used to say you had a choice between *fer, feu et femmes*. Iron, fire and women. There's the iron --" he nodded towards the soldiers with their guns and swords, "-- too much of it, if you want my opinion. As for the fire in your belly, I'm sorry to say I've just finished off the *eau-de-vie* -- but there's more at Ma Friche's, if you want. And that just leaves women. And, if you'll forgive me, captain, I plan to go back to Françoise now and make sure everything's all right with her."

For the first time, the two men shook hands. Delourcq crossed to the right bank.

Below him the river flowed on. Lucien knew what his choice was.

Historical note

In early 1848, Louis Philippe abdicated; it was the end of monarchical rule in France. The Second Republic was declared, and at the end of 1848 a Presidential election was held, in which **Louis-Napoléon Bonaparte**, nephew of Napoléon I, was voted into office. The constitution provided that the President should enjoy a single, four-year term. This was never likely to satisfy the ambitions of Louis-Napoléon, and on 1-2 December 1851 he staged a *coup d'etat*, dissolving the parliamentary assembly, and paving the way for his nomination as Emperor Napoléon III one year later. He remained in power until France's defeat at the hands of Prussia in 1870, when he stepped down to spend the rest of his life in exile. Born in 1808, he died in 1873.

Louis-Napoléon was the son of Louis Bonaparte, brother to the first Emperor, and Hortense de Beauharnais. As President and then Emperor, Louis-Napoléon's closest associate in power was **Charles, Duc de Morny**. Morny was his half-brother, born in 1811 as the natural son of Hortense de Beauharnais and Charles, Comte de Flahaut. Morny died in 1865, five years before the debacle of the Franco-Prussian war, and after at least a decade of successful financial speculation.

Charles, Comte de Flahaut, was born in 1785, the natural son of Adelaide de Flahaut and Charles Maurice de Talleyrand-Périgord, the supreme diplomat of the Bonapartist era. A hero of Napoléon I's military campaigns against Prussia and Austria, Flahaut formed a close liaison with Hortense de Beauharnais in 1810, which resulted in the birth of Charles de Morny. He rose to the rank of Lieutenant-General by 1815; but the fall of Napoléon I, and estrangement from Hortense, prompted Flahaut to go into exile in England. In the decades that followed, Flahaut and the English family that he acquired had periods of residence on both sides of the Channel. But at the end of 1851 he was in Paris during the *coup d'etat*, and rode in full-dress uniform alongside Louis-Napoléon in the triumphal procession along the Champs Elysées in the morning of 2 December 1851. Flahaut died in 1870.

Jean Gilbert Victor Fialin, **Vicomte de Persigny**, had tied his destiny to Louis-Napoléon many years before the latter became President. Born in the same year of 1808, he died a year before the exiled emperor, in 1872. Persigny was always impatient to push the imperial cause further than others. Louis-Napoléon once said that Persigny was the only true Bonapartist, "and he is mad!"

France's colonisation of **Algeria** began with military invasion in 1830. From the time of the Second Republic onwards, the French Government encouraged migration by its own citizens to Algeria, to take advantage of opportunities for land ownership not available in France. Conflict between European and

Arab communities continued until Algerian independence in 1962.

The **Sûreté** (plain-clothes criminal investigation) division of the Paris Police was set up in 1812, under the leadership of Eugène-François Vidocq, a criminal turned thief-taker. Vidocq brought his insider's knowledge to bear on solving crimes in the French capital; and, though he left the Sûreté in 1827, the division continued to keep one foot in the underworld even as it employed officers from more conventional backgrounds. In March 1849, **Paul-Louis-Alphonse Canler** was appointed head of the Sûreté; a former soldier and long-term member of the Paris police, he brought discipline to a much-expanded organisation. Despite the success which the Sûreté had under his direction, he was dismissed from his post two weeks before the *coup d'etat* of 1851.